AN UNKINDNESS OF MAGICIANS

ALSO BY KAT HOWARD

Roses and Rot

AN UNKINDNESS OF MAGICIANS

KAT HOWARD

SAGA PRESS

LONDON SYDNEY NEW YORK TORONTO NEW DELHI

1230 AVENUE OF THE AMERICAS, NEW YORK, NEW YORK 10020

Cover design by Lizzy Bromeley

Interior design by Hilary Zarycky

The text for this book was set in New Caledonia.

Manufactured in the United States of America

First Saga Press export paperback edition

2 4 6 8 10 9 7 5 3 1

Library of Congress Cataloging-in-Publication Data

Names: Howard, Kat, author.

Title: An unkindness of magicians / Kat Howard.

Description: First edition. | London : Saga Press, [2017]

Identifiers: LCCN 2016053937| ISBN 9781481451192 (hardcover : alk. paper) | | ISBN 9781534415034 (export paperback) | ISBN 9781481451215 (eBook)

Subjects: | BISAC: FICTION / Fairy Tales, Folk Tales, Legends & Mythology. | GSAFD: Fantasy fiction.

Classification: LCC PS3608.O9246 U55 2017 | DDC 813/.6—dc23

LC record available at https://lccn.loc.gov/2016053937

For my parents, who helped me keep body and soul together while writing this book.

But this rough magic I here abjure . . .

—WILLIAM SHAKESPEARE, *The Tempest*

AN UNKINDNESS OF MAGICIANS

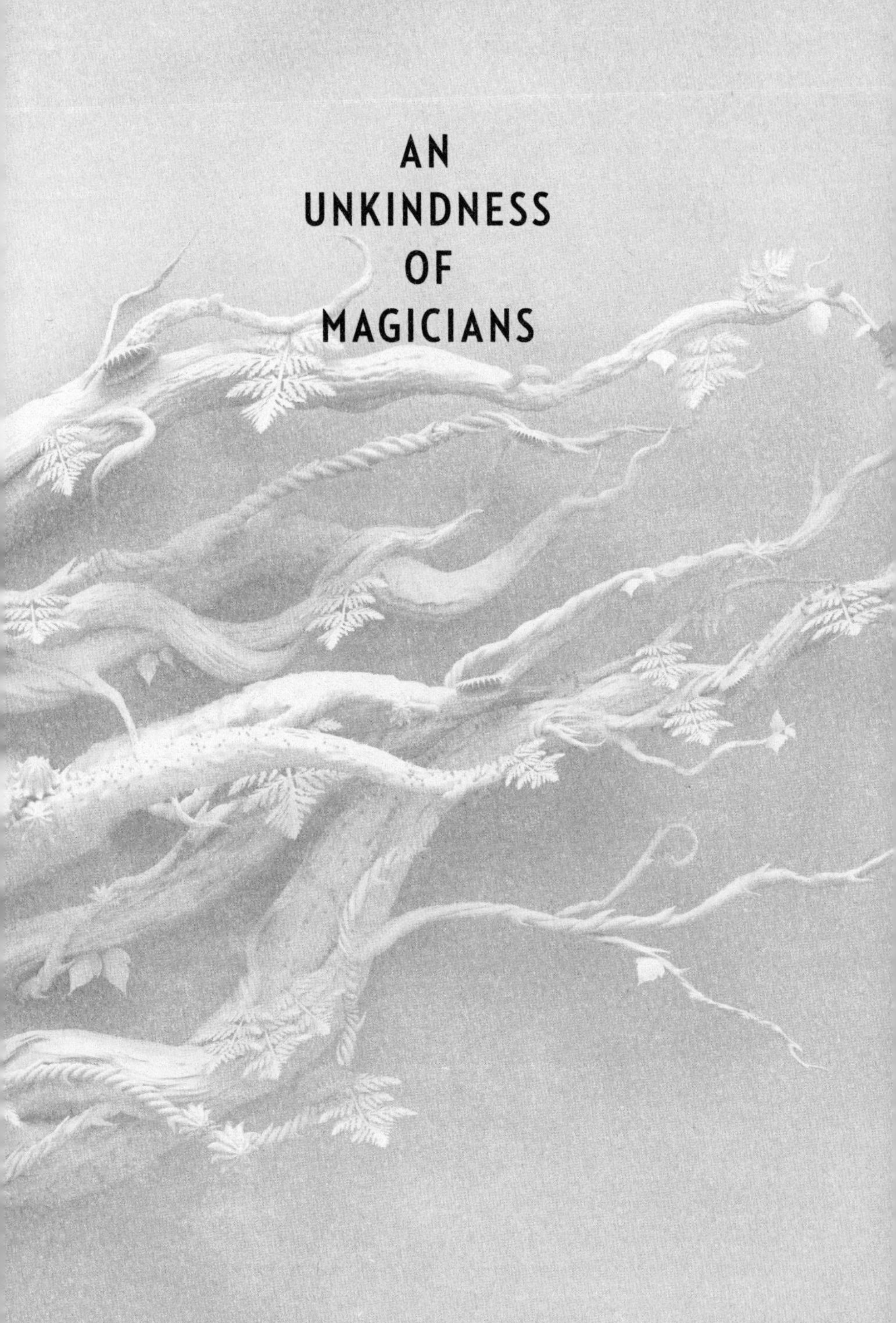

CHAPTER ONE

The young woman cut through the crowded New York sidewalk like a knife. Tall in her red-soled stilettos, black clothing that clung to her like smoke, red-tipped black hair sharp and angular around her face. She looked like the kind of woman people would stop for, stare at, notice.

None of them did.

Stalking down Wall Street, the spire of Trinity Church rising before her, she slid among the suits and tourists like a secret, drawing no eyes, no shouted "hey, babys," not even the casual jar of a shoulder bumped in a crowd. She could have been a ghost. A shadow.

The sun stark, the sky a harsh blue, cloudless and broken only by the glare of reflections. Late-summer heat stewed salt-sweat and heavy cologne together, mingling them with the sizzle rising from sidewalk food carts. The day bright, almost ordinary.

The woman paused at a corner. Her slate-grey eyes flicked up toward some unmarked window in one of the buildings scraping the sky, as if to be sure someone was watching. Her lips, red as blood, quirked up at the corners, and Sydney stepped off the curb and into traffic.

Neither the cars nor their drivers seemed aware of her presence.

Sydney walked to the center of the intersection and raised her arms like a conductor about to begin a symphony. She stood, unmoving, for one breath. Two. Three. If there had been eyes somewhere above that rushing city that were able to watch, they would have seen her lips moving.

And then.

The cars around her, as one, lifted gracefully into the air.

Sydney held them there, rust-stained taxis and sleek black sedans with tinted windows, courier vans and a tour bus blaring the opening number of the latest Broadway hit. Ten feet above the ground, floating through the intersection like some bizarre migration of birds. A smile stretched, bright and wild, across her face. If the people in the cars could have seen it, they might have called it exhilaration. They might have called it joy.

The people in the cars didn't see her. No blaring horns, no cursing drivers. No awe—no reaction—from either the people in the now-flying vehicles, or from any of the passersby. Simply flight, where that shouldn't have been an option.

Sydney directed the cars through the intersection—through the air—with words, with small precise gestures that bent her fingers and hands into severe origami, with no obvious effort.

And then.

Her hands paused. Held like a breath. Two. Three. She lowered her arms to her sides, and as she did, the cars returned to the street as gracefully as they had left it, the flow of traffic uninterrupted. Sydney walked out of the intersection and cut back into the crowd. No heads turned. No one gave her any notice.

She had gone less than half a block when the text alert vibrated through her phone. *The job is yours.*

The message that began everything arrived in a variety of ways. Email. Text. Type-written formalities on plain, business-weight white. Handwritten letters in bordeaux ink, sealed with wax. Though no matter which medium carried it, in each instance, the words were the same:

> *Fortune's Wheel has begun its Turning. When it ceases rotation, all will be made new.*

If somehow you were not a magician, not a member of the Unseen World, and you managed to acquire one of these messages, it would look like nothing. A fortune cookie's paper, a glitch in your email program. Uninteresting and easily discarded.

Miranda Prospero was a magician, and she knew precisely what had just landed on her desk. A surprise, and not a good one.

A precise and elegant woman in her late fifties, Miranda had the sort of face that had been too strong-featured for beauty until she had aged into it. Now, she wore her clothing and makeup like armor, as much of a shield and mask as anything she could have conjured. There to project an image, carefully chosen.

The cool morning light washed over her office where she sat behind an elegantly curved antique rosewood desk. She touched her fingertips to the edge of the paper. She quartered the air above it with her hands, spoke words that smelled harsh and bitter in their echoes. The message looked authentic, and there was magic in place—magic that should be inviolate, locked carefully away from influence—that would prevent such a message from being sent in error. But it was early, very early, for a Turning to be happening again. Normally, there would be at least twenty years between one and the next. Only thirteen years this time, barely more than half a generation.

Well. Thirteen years, five months, one week, and four days. Miranda knew the circumstances of the previous Turning well. They had, in many ways, made her.

A flash of light, and a sigil floated in the air above the paper: the Rota Fortunae. Blindfolded Fortune, turning a wheel.

What was written, then, was true.

The beginning of fear, its tiny barbed threads, lodged themselves in her heart. There were reasons why a Turning might come again so soon. None of them were comfortable.

She was prepared. She had been preparing for every day of those last slightly more than thirteen years. But she had hoped for more time in between. She had done everything she could to make sure that Prospero was a strong House. Well placed. Established and powerful enough that she would have no difficulty finding someone willing to represent it.

She pressed her fingertips to her temples, then rested them on her desk. She knew by now what a Turning involved, the rules and the stakes—she had been through them before—but details were homes for devils, and no more so than here. And so she read:

Any House may contract out their participation. Any such contracted champions will be deemed members of Houses with all attendant rights and responsibilities for the duration of their contract. Once contracted, a champion cannot be substituted. Any House that does not contract out its involvement accepts full consequences to its members, including death and disappearance, and forswears vengeance outside of the sanctioned challenges. The actions of a champion, contracted or otherwise, during the course of a duel are final.

Any House that, by the activity of any member, Blood or Contract, exposes the Unseen World to mundane attention will be unmade. Any House that chooses not to participate will be unmade. Malicious interference in an active challenge may result in magic being stripped from the magician or the interfering House being unmade.

Miranda's mouth twisted. All of that would be taken as seriously as it ever was, with the first major breach of one of the rules committed by the end of the first week, if not the end of the first duel, and then the first time someone shook off that breach with some variant of "Fortune's Wheel does turn" immediately following. The Unseen World liked its rules, but only when they were convenient.

Any House whose champion, either Blood or Contracted, dies in the course of a duel will be exempt from the next required sacrifice to the House of Shadows.

The House ranked highest at the end of the

Turning will become the head of the Unseen World.

And those last few clauses would be followed, convenient or not. Because underneath the pageantry and shine, those last few clauses were the purpose of the Turning.

Everything was as she expected. All the usual terms. No surprises. Those would come during the Turning itself. They always did.

Miranda refolded the letter, precise along its crease, and set it aside. House Prospero would maintain its tradition and contract out to a champion. There were always those willing to trade the risks inherent in a Turning for a large enough amount of money or the promise of membership in a House. She pulled her files, notes she'd kept on skilled younger sons and daughters, on talented cousins with no hope of inheriting a House on their own. She pushed aside the cold lump of fear that had settled itself in the center of her chest, and made her plans.

"Your mother," Laurent said, "is going to lose her Chanel-wearing shit when she finds out you're doing this."

"As far as Miranda is concerned, I'm no longer her son, so I doubt she'll do anything other than make sure that whoever she hires as champion knows I'm one more obstacle to be neutralized in her quest for power." Grey poured whiskey, heavy with smoke and peat, for both of them, then set the bottle back on the bar cart. "Cheers."

They sat at a long butcher-block table in Laurent's apartment. Glass and chrome, granite and pale wood, high enough to make the lights and noise of New York City a scene in a silent movie below them. Laurent was particularly skilled in magic related to luck and chance, and had parlayed that and a more mundane skill set into a very healthy investment portfolio.

"Do you think so?" Laurent asked. "Even when she learns you're representing yourself? I mean, eventually the duels are mortal. I know you two aren't speaking, but do you really think she'd be cool with you winding up dead?"

Five years ago, Laurent had bought his parents a retirement home in the Pacific Northwest, two hours north of Seattle. "Woods and water, that's what I want," his dad had always said. His mom added that she'd like some grandbabies to spoil: "And there's certainly enough room here for you to come visit." He'd told them he'd start with the woods and water, and putting the keys in their hands had been one of his happiest days. Opposite coasts and life happening meant he didn't see his parents more than once or twice a year, but they loved each other. He couldn't imagine either one of them coldly telling someone that all he was was an obstacle.

"If she were to lower herself to speak to me in any way whatsoever about this, she would simply remind me that"—Grey's voice changed, becoming an exaggeration of Miranda's pitch and cadences—"I had an excellent and assured place as the heir to House Prospero, and the fact that I now do not came about solely through my own folly. I agreed that I would accept the consequences of my actions, and these are no more than continuing consequences." He smirked and took another drink.

Laurent laughed. "Your mother is a real piece of work."

"Believe me," Grey said. "I know."

It had been just over three years since she had disinherited him. That particular procedure had been bloodless—swipes of pens on papers messengered from one office to the next.

The rift had begun over a matter of magic. Grey felt comfortable pushing boundaries, looking for access to power in places that Miranda didn't. She was, at her heart, a traditionalist. She felt he had crossed a line, and so she had taken everything from him.

They hadn't spoken since.

"Oh, and speaking of your family," Laurent said.

"Do we have to?" Grey pushed back in his chair.

"I ran into your cousin Madison downtown the other day. She looked good. We grabbed coffee."

"Oh, she looked that kind of good, did she?" Grey leered.

"Not everything is about getting laid, you player." Laurent shook his head in mock disapproval.

"Yeah, but most things are. So, how is she? I haven't seen her since she left school."

"She said she had just made partner at some big law firm—Wellington & Ketchum, maybe?"

"Good firm. Prospero uses it. Actually, that's probably why she's there. Almost all the Houses have people in place to deal with their mundane world interests. It's better when it's family. They understand how important magic is, and they don't complain about the secrecy."

It wasn't one of the things that got talked about, but it happened. Every so often there were members of Houses who weren't strong enough magicians to maintain membership in the Unseen World, or who chose to renounce their magic. They were cast out, but only so far. The Unseen World might keep secrets from the mundane one, but it understood it was still part of it, and someone had to do the busywork.

"She asked about the Turning, didn't seem surprised that you were in it," Laurent said.

"I wouldn't have thought it was the kind of thing she would care about." Grey shrugged the thought away and finished his drink. "Have you found your champion?"

"I think so."

"You *think*?" Grey poured himself more whiskey and held out the bottle to Laurent, who shook his head. "Things start soon. You need to have someone in place. Unless you've changed your mind and decided to represent yourself. It's not like you don't have the talent and balls to do well."

Laurent snorted. "Thanks. No, I still want to watch one of these before I try it, so a champion it is. But she hasn't signed the contract yet."

"Do you honestly think that she won't? Maybe you should invite her up here, impress her with all you can offer." Grey gestured toward the window, the lights of city outside glittering like jewels spread out against velvet.

"Ha ha. It's not that—I think she's happy with the terms I offered, but she's good enough to have her pick. More than good enough." Laurent passed a hand over the tight crop of his black hair. "Her spell was astounding—complex and delicate, and completely hidden from the mundanes. Even the ones caught up in it. I've never seen anyone do magic like that, and she just walked in and out of the spell like this was what she did every Tuesday."

Grey's face tightened. "Where did you say she was from again?"

"I didn't—she's unHoused."

"An outsider with that kind of power? That ought to make things interesting," Grey said. "Give us all something to talk about other than how fast this Turning happened. I figured it would be another ten years, at least."

"It's the only way either of us become Houses," Laurent answered. "Better that it happens now."

"Agreed," Grey said. "I'm tired of waiting." He had been, with decreasing patience, every day of the last three years. It was long past time.

"Besides." Laurent grinned. "An enormous magic fight? This is going to be fun."

High above the city, they toasted each other, their potential, and the turn of Fortune's Wheel.

Not for the first time, Harper Douglas wished she had stronger magic. Wished she had any magic really, beyond the ability to light a candle with a word. Which actually took a lot more effort than using a match did, and gave her a splitting headache after.

She had seen the woman with red and black hair, the one that no one else had seemed to notice. Had watched her walk down the sidewalk and into the street. Tracking her progress made Harper dizzy, then made her feel as if she might vomit, but she had kept the woman in view until she had stepped into the intersection, because she had known what that queasy dizziness meant. It meant she was close.

Then Harper had felt the woman's magic, a dull-bronze

electric-fence feeling in her mouth, but she hadn't been strong enough to see the spell. She'd tried to get closer, but the woman's power had hit her like a tidal wave.

Overwhelmed, Harper had collapsed outside a bodega. She'd opened her eyes to the awareness that her left elbow had landed in something worryingly squishy. She tried to sit up.

"You look very bad. Stay where you are." An elderly Russian woman was squatting down next to her. She fished around in a cloth bag, then handed Harper a plastic bottle of orange juice. "Drink this."

"Did you see her?" Harper asked. She had been so close—her mouth still tasted like electricity.

"See who? Someone did this to you?" The woman looked around sharply.

"No, no. No one did this. I just thought I saw someone. Someone important." Her rescuer wouldn't have seen the woman though, not unless she was in the Unseen World, in which case she'd never tell Harper about the woman.

"Did you hit your head? Is that why you see things? Do you need a doctor?" Eyes narrow, mouth pursed.

"No, this is enough. Thank you," Harper said, in between gulps of the juice. She could feel her blood sugar perking back up, her hands growing steady.

"Are you going to fall down again?" the older woman

asked, in a tone that implied that Harper ought to make better choices than keeling over on a sidewalk.

"No, ma'am. I feel much better. Here, let me get you some money for the juice."

She swatted Harper's hand. "What kind of manners did you learn? You don't pay someone for kindness. You say thank you."

"Thank you. Truly." Harper picked herself up off of the sidewalk, peeled the remains of someone's cream-filled doughnut off of her arm with a shudder, and walked in the direction she had last seen the magician, toward the great bronze doors of Trinity Church.

Nothing. Not even a hint of magic remained, not that she had expected otherwise. If a magician didn't want to be seen by mundane eyes, they wouldn't be. And for all Harper had brute-forced her way into the tiniest bit of magic use, she was definitely mundane. She turned in a circle once more, looking carefully, just in case, then walked down the steps to Wall Street station, into the rattle and roar of the subway.

Close. She had come close. If she could just get a little bit closer, then she'd be able to find her way into the Unseen World. Then she'd be able to keep her promise.

As Sydney crossed the threshold of her building, the veil of magic she had draped herself in sloughed off, and she was again visible to the world around her. "Any messages, Henry?" she asked the doorman.

"Not today, miss."

She smiled her thanks and took the elevator up to the seventh floor. Sydney lived in a mundane building on purpose—no one from the Unseen World would think to look for her there. The snobbery was as useful as it was predictable—she had set up a series of wards when she'd first moved in six months ago, and they'd never even been tested, much less crossed.

She closed her door, locked it behind her, and stepped out of her shoes, rolling the aches from her arches. Pulled her phone from her pocket and texted her acceptance to Laurent.

Done.

Barefoot, Sydney walked to her kitchen island and poured a glass of dark red wine. She had set the wheels turning. Not Fortune's Wheel—she had little enough patience for the trappings of the Unseen World—but her own.

She drank, savoring the curl of the liquid down her throat, enjoying the richness of it. Being able to indulge in pleasures, even ones as small as a glass of wine when she wanted, was still something new. Something she'd worked hard enough for that she still luxuriated in the indulgence of it.

Working with Laurent would be good. She'd wanted a candidate House, hoped for an outsider. Someone unestablished, less likely to have accepted all of the Unseen World's dirty little secrets as gospel. Someone who might come to see things as she did, might even be an ally.

She planned to drag all those dirty little secrets out of the shadows and into the light, and if necessary, the light would be cast by the flames she had lit as she burned the Unseen World to the ground.

She raised her glass, toasting its destruction.

Tremors racked her. The wine sloshed over the rim of the glass, spilling drops as red as blood. A dull knife of pain took up residence in her wrists and shoulders, and she felt herself hollow out, as if she were caught in the grip of a fever. Sweat beaded up on her skin.

This was the price for today's magic.

Sydney set her glass down and breathed into the shaking, the ache, the hollowness in her bones. She centered herself in it until she was steady, the pain not gone but acknowledged. She was used to acknowledging pain. It had become, over time and trial, rather a specialty of hers. She raised her glass again, held it steady, her hand unshaking.

She drank.

CHAPTER TWO

At 12:01 a.m., her celebratory toast nothing more than a glass upended on a drying rack, Sydney stood on the southern shore of the Central Park Reservoir. She lit matches with the flick of her thumbnail. One, two, three.

Before the smoke of the last had faded, a wooden boat rose through the dark water. Old and worn, it seemed as if a touch might scuttle it. The boat bumped gently against the shore, waiting.

Sydney stepped on board. It creaked and swayed beneath her feet as it moved across the water.

She rode standing. The magic that propelled the boat did not extend to drying the seats, and she didn't like using her own here where the House might notice. And the House would notice. The House noticed everything.

The darkness thickened before her and resolved itself into the House of Shadows. Low and secret, it sat on the water like a toad, crouching upon an island made of bones and misery, hulked atop a place that should have never been. That place had been her home from the day she was given to pay someone else's price until the day she had grown powerful enough to open its doors and walk out of them.

Sydney hated it.

The boat fetched up against its steps, and Sydney went inside.

Cold. The kind of cold that seeped up through the soles of her shoes and sank into her bones until they ached. She could use no magic the House didn't permit while she was inside its doors, not without fighting the House for the privilege, and she had learned long ago that it would deny her comfort. It had become a matter of pride not to ask. Back straight, head up, she refused to let herself shiver. No weakness.

She would give the House nothing it did not take, and it had taken enough already.

Dim lights flickered on the walls. Fireflies underwater, luminescence below glass. The only sound the muted echo of her footsteps.

The House could have brought her to Shara directly. Could have arranged itself so that she stepped into a warm, well-lit room. Could have done any number of things to make Sydney's life easier.

Of course, it could also hold her here, behind its doors, rearranging itself like a labyrinth until she dropped dead of exhaustion, could open its floors over an oubliette and seal her in it, could offer any number of other fatal unpleasantries. It could make her walk past the rooms where magic was extracted from the less-lucky residents of the House, the ones who would be used up and cast aside, who would never leave. Could make her listen to the screams, the sounds made by throats torn raw, the pleading. Could bring the scents of blood and fear to her nose. Could force her to stand and watch, to see and feel again what she had been made to endure.

Her earliest memories were of those rooms. Phantom scars ghosted across her skin. Echoes of past screams rose in her throat.

She swallowed hard. A long walk in the cold dark was nothing.

"You're late." Shara's voice appeared before the light did. The light was a watery blue, cold enough to burn, making the shadows knife-edged. The House was in a mood tonight.

Sydney said nothing. No matter that she had lit the matches at precisely the appointed time, no matter that it was the House's mood that had made her late. This was neither the time nor the place for small talk.

"I trust you haven't failed in any other ways today." Shara's face as marble-cold as her voice. Fish-belly pale from having lived her whole life in Shadows, she wore her hair as long and tangled as a medieval sorceress and a dress that might have been woven from the shadows she ruled. Her eyes bright blue, lights in the darkness. Sydney had never once heard her speak kindness. "What do you have to report?"

"As you instructed, I am contracted to a House for the duration of this Turning," Sydney said. There was a plan, and this was its beginning.

"Which House?" Shara walked closer, her shadow elongating behind her. It flickered in the changing light, but it was smooth at its edges. Whole.

"Laurent Beauchamps." Sydney's hands ached, and she could feel frost gathering in her hair. Shara, of course, looked perfectly comfortable.

"A candidate House. Interesting choice."

Sydney held her silence. If Shara wanted a disagreement, to scold Sydney for one thing or another, she would make that clear soon enough. But without a reason, Sydney did not want to say anything she would come to regret. There were secrets that needed to be kept, even here.

Especially here.

"Very well. Continue to proceed as we discussed. There's nothing else at this time."

Sydney turned on her heel.

"Except, of course, the contract." Shara's voice sly and pleased, almost happy for the first time in the conversation.

Except. Of course.

Long before she had contracted herself to Laurent to help him win legitimacy in the eyes of the Unseen World by founding a House, Sydney had been contracted by the House of

Shadows. It made no matter that she had not entered into that contract voluntarily. The House kept careful records of debts. She was a long way from paying hers.

On a table by Shara, a pen, the contract, and a knife, bone-handled. Its blade as dark as shadow, its edge as sharp and fine as truth.

Shara picked up the knife. She gathered Sydney's shadow into her hand. The sensation was the crawling of skin, her flesh rising into goose bumps, but she felt it inside, like needing to shudder and vomit all at once.

Shara sliced, cutting away enough to curl into the barrel of the pen to use as ink. The cut was the flaying of an already raw nerve, salt in a wound, fire on her soul. It was nothing that had not happened before and nothing that would not happen again, and it was that—that ever and ongoing debt—that was the worst of it.

Sydney forced her mind to blankness and, once again, signed her name. As she re-signed her name every time she was summoned here, as she would again and again until she had balanced the weighted scales and was free. Shadows would decide when that was—Sydney couldn't even count the days.

The day that she had first signed that contract, she had thought the ritual would become easier, that the pain would grow less. She had been wrong. At least she had learned to keep her hand steady, she thought, as the tears that had broken through her lashes froze on her skin.

"You will be called for again when you are required, and you will not be late," Shara said. "That will be all."

Sydney did not look back as she left. The House opened immediately to the outside, to the half-flooded boat that had carried her across the water. She stood, hands clenched so hard her nails pierced her skin, focusing only on those bright, sharp cuts, not on the fresh and weeping wound in her shadow, not on anything but the wood and water beneath her feet, the night air against her skin, until she fetched up on the far shore, until the boat faded back into night and shadow.

Then, as she walked, she let her own plans fill her head. The ones that began in the same place as those of Shadows but ended somewhere far different.

Deep inside the belly of the House of Shadows, Grace Valentine lay in the cold, in the dark, and waited for the blood on her hands to dry. She flexed her fingers, wincing as some of the unhealed cuts reopened.

The hands were the worst—the pain lingered there, like the magic. Plus, the cuts were a reminder of how she had come to be in here in the first place, a reminder that set her hands to bleeding again, as her clenched fists reopened the rest of the damage.

Still, the carving of her hands had been the only thing she'd been made to endure today. It had seemed like in the past few . . . weeks? months?—she was never really sure how time passed in here, even when the House wasn't altering her perception of events to make things hurt worse, or for a longer time—she had spent less time having her magic taken, having pain inflicted as a way to increase that power in what was collected, and had spent more time learning the magic that was unique to Shadows.

That still hurt, of course. Everything here did, sometimes even breathing. But it was a better kind of hurt. Because if she could endure that new kind of hurt, the one that had power underneath it, if she could learn what Shadows was teaching her, then she could use that magic to leave.

She had heard of it happening, once, long before she was hidden away in here. She had felt the ripples through the House—seen it bleed—when someone else had managed it. She locked the possibility in her heart, the darkest of secrets.

Hidden away and forgotten, Grace Valentine lay in the darkness of the House of Shadows. As the blood dried on her hands, she counted scars to fall asleep. She dreamed revenge.

Miranda had chosen to interview candidates for House Prospero's champion in person. Flashy magic was all well and good, and she would certainly require a demonstration of ability before she made a decision, but the fact of the matter was the champion would represent the House. She wanted to be sure the House liked them.

She also wanted to be sure that she was able to—if not like—at least respect them. They and their magic would represent Prospero, would be the face of the House. Power, ability—those mattered, but character did as well, particularly as the champions' decisions during a challenge were final. There was always the risk that someone whose goals did not fully match with hers would choose poorly, or in service of their own ends. And once the challenges turned mortal, she was asking someone to potentially die for the House. She wanted to be sure they would.

As her final preparation for the morning's interviews, Miranda gathered defensive magic, spindling the power around her fingers, then releasing it into an empty ink bottle for storage. Knocking the bottle over would trigger the spell. It was unlikely that she'd need to use it at all, but there was always the possibility that someone would move against House Prospero before the duels began. Better to be prepared.

She glanced at her office once more, her eyes measuring the alignment of the items on her desk, the bloom of the flowers—all white, green accents, and none with overly heady fragrances—that stood on a side table, noting the angle of the light that streamed in from the windows behind her. She moved a letter opener a fraction of a centimeter to the right, then nodded.

"All right," she told the House. "Send in the first candidate."

He is an addition to your schedule.

The House didn't actually speak with a voice. Rather, Miranda had made a series of spelled mirrors when she became its Head. They were keyed to her voice and presence, and if the House wanted to say something to her without being addressed first, the words that appeared on the mirror's surface would be accompanied by a faint chime. No one else in the room would see the words or hear the chime ring. The spell also allowed her to respond mentally, thus enabling a completely secret conversation, if necessary.

Miranda raised an eyebrow at the House's boldness. Then Ian Merlin walked into her office, and she moved her left hand to rest on top of her desk, near the magic-filled bottle.

"Madame Prospero." He inclined his head to the exact correct degree. He'd dressed politely as well—a black-on-black suit, well cut and quiet. It wasn't the sort of detail that would have mattered to everyone, but it did to her, and she appreciated the effort.

"Ian. Did we have an appointment?" She allowed a hint of mild curiosity into the question.

He folded like a knife into an antique chair. "I heard your House required a champion. I'd like to convince you it should be me."

She'd seen his magic before. There was no need for her to require a test of his abilities—if the magician existed who was better, Miranda hadn't met them yet. "Forgive me for stating the obvious, but you're the heir to House Merlin." It didn't mean he couldn't represent another House, couldn't strike out and attempt to found a House of his own, but such a choice wasn't usual. "And you haven't been much of a presence in the Unseen World recently. So I am a bit surprised to see you here."

"You still have your gift for understatement," Ian said. "You should know that I'm not the heir to House Merlin. I renounced all claims when I left. My father hasn't named my sister heir because he hopes I'll change my mind, something I have no intention of doing."

"I see." Miranda straightened in her chair as she considered. Hiring him would be a coup, but she still wasn't sure what he had to gain by contracting himself out. "Why House Prospero? Why not take advantage of the Turning and try to establish your own House?"

"I don't like how the Unseen World runs. I'd like to change it, and it will be easier to do that from inside of a powerful, established House.

"Also, my father doesn't like you, and I'm in the mood to aggravate him. Helping you win the Turning—winning the leadership of the Unseen World away from him—would do that nicely." He paused. "Forgive me for being blunt, but it seems better to be honest."

Miranda tapped the fingers of her left hand on her desk. It was a reason she could appreciate. "I don't much like Miles, either, and I like the way he's been running things for the past thirteen years even less. But I like to know what I'm supporting. What, exactly, are you hoping to change?"

"The reliance on the House of Shadows. If you hire me, and if House Prospero then finds itself leading the Unseen World at the end of this Turning, I want your support in ending it. You understand why I want the outside support." It had been House Merlin, Ian's great-grandfather, that had founded the House of Shadows, that had begun the spell that allowed members of the Unseen World to draw on a store of collected power, to use magic at no personal cost, beyond that of a House sacrifice once a generation. Though Fortune's Wheel did turn, House Merlin had been in power ever since.

Miranda kept her voice neutral. "I believe I could be persuaded to do that. Is there anything else you want?"

"No," he said. "Only the support, and only under those conditions."

"Then I accept your terms," she said. "Do you have any questions?"

"I saw Grey's name on the list of candidate Houses. How

do you want me to deal with him in a duel?" His question and tone were both carefully neutral.

Miranda didn't even blink at the confirmation that Grey would be participating in the Turning. It was what she had expected from him. "Should he challenge the House, deal with him as required by the terms of engagement."

A very polite call and response that meant that Ian could kill Grey in a mortal challenge if one was made. Ian waited a beat. When Miranda said nothing else, he continued. "All right. Do you require a demonstration of magic?"

"I've watched you grow up, Ian. I'm quite satisfied with your magical abilities. I'm happy to sign the contract if you are," Miranda said.

"I already have." He smiled then and opened his right hand, spreading the fingers. The top drawer of her desk opened.

She pulled the thick sheet of paper from her drawer. The standard agreement, modified for his terms for payment. His signature at the bottom, the ink still drying. "And if we hadn't reached an agreement?"

"It would have remained blank, and I would have been disappointed."

He had done this spell while sitting across from her. Very elegant—she hadn't even felt it. Miranda smiled as she countersigned, secure in the knowledge that her House would not only survive the Wheel's Turning, but triumph. "Excellent," she said. "House Prospero appreciates your service."

"I believe it will." That slight bow of the head again as he left.

Miranda watched him go, heard the House close its doors after him. "Thank you," she told the House. "This should be interesting."

If the House had an opinion, it did not share it. The mirror remained blank.

Harper pressed send on her latest CV, rolled her head from side to side until her neck cracked, then leaned back in her desk chair. She closed her eyes, balanced on her toes, holding herself in place just on the edge of tipping backward, then heaved a sigh and dropped back down. She'd spent the last few months researching what were usually called Special Projects Divisions at various white-shoe New York law firms. It had taken some time, as that wasn't the sort of practice group that generally got listed on the letterhead. Having a Special Projects Division almost always meant that the firm handled the legal affairs of at least one of the great Houses of the Unseen World. Magicians, as it turned out, needed lawyers, too.

Working for a firm like that, one that would almost certainly have at least one magician attached as counsel, was one possible way into the Unseen World, the one that seemed most likely to work. Two of the firms she had recently sent her CV to had scouted her in law school, before she'd even heard of the Unseen World. Both had expressed happiness on hearing from her now. She had an interview with a third later this week.

Whatever it took, she'd find her way in. She had a promise to keep.

On the wall over her desk was a framed photo of Harper and the woman who had been her best friend, Rose Morgan. They were smiling, arms slung around each other, faces shining with delight. Rose had been the person to teach her to light the candle, the person who had cracked open the doors of the Unseen World and let her look inside.

Two years ago someone had killed her, and Harper had been the one to find her body.

She had gotten there almost in time. In time to see a man—his face obscured by shadows—stand up from Rose's body, his hands covered in blood. In time to see him carve a doorway out of darkness with those same bloody hands, step through it, and disappear. Needless to say, no one believed her. They had been kind about it, blaming it on the stress of finding her murdered best friend, but they hadn't taken her seriously. When it came down to it, she understood. If she'd heard her story from someone else, she wouldn't have believed it either.

The police had no leads. Harper didn't think they'd ever

find any—Rose had said the one thing the Unseen World was best at was keeping secrets. So Harper had decided that she would find her way into that world.

She would find her way into that world, and she would figure out who had killed Rose, and she would finally get justice for her best friend.

Harper touched her fingers to Rose's picture, then turned back to her computer. She entered a password and opened the locked file, the one where she kept information on magic and magicians. She marked her locations from yesterday on the map. Rose had said that they tended to live in the same areas of the city, and so there wound up being enclaves—the magical equivalent of Billionaires' Row. Harper didn't have enough data points to make any guesses, not yet—she had the most near Central Park, but everyone went to Central Park, so she didn't weight those all that heavily—but she could almost, sort of, out of the corner of her eye, see patterns forming.

That done, she checked her automated searches. Most of the results they found were crap, although there was a link to a new Penn and Teller illusion. Not exactly the kind of magic she was looking for, but she bookmarked it for later. They were always fun to watch.

Then a YouTube video. Twenty-seven seconds long and uploaded with the title "Sxxxy Hogwarts." Probably nothing, and almost certainly something she'd regret clicking, but it was only twenty-seven seconds, and it wasn't like she had to watch the entire thing if it really was awful.

She clicked, then sat up straight and hit the expand screen button. There was the Trinity Church steeple, out of focus in the right-hand corner of the frame.

It was the same intersection she'd been at yesterday.

The recording jumped, glitched, and then. Her. The magician, standing in the intersection, cars flying around her.

Cars. Flying.

Even the recorded magic was enough to make Harper's head ache from watching, but she did, again and again. Beneath the headache, adrenaline fizzed through her, lightning in her veins. This, this was what she'd been looking for.

Flying cars. In the air like it was nothing. Unfucking-believable. She barely breathed while watching.

Then the video caught. Hung. Announced that it was rebuffering. Harper's internet signal dropped. She knew. She knew what it meant, knew that once again the secrets of the Unseen World were keeping themselves. She cursed herself for not taking a screencap, at least getting a picture of the woman's face.

When her internet reconnected, the video was gone.

Harper leaned back in her chair and reminded herself to be logical. This was just a video confirming what she already knew: Magic existed, and she'd been close enough to almost make contact with someone who could do it.

Still. She'd been trying for two years, and this was the closest she'd come to anyone. She hadn't really understood what Rose meant about the Unseen World being good at secrets until she'd tried to talk to Rose's parents after the funeral. Never mind that she'd had dinner at their house twice before, she couldn't find the place, not without Rose there. Well, she could find the address, but she'd walked up to an Apple store in a commercial district, not an elegant home in a quiet neighborhood. She'd called the phone numbers in Rose's contacts and had gotten nothing but white noise.

She'd slowly come to realize that the only way to find someone who could help her would be to physically find another magician, to tell them in person what she'd seen that night. This video was proof she almost had.

Harper scrubbed at her eyes and rolled the stress from her shoulders. Then she got up to put a pot of coffee on. She still had contracts to review.

Grey stood on worn carpet in a hallway that stank of mildew and boiled cabbage. He set his hand on his apartment door's lock and made a clicking sound in the back of his throat. The metal went cold to the touch as the wards released. He jiggled his key and opened the door.

Inside, he reset the useless button lock, the slightly less useless chain, and the wards that were technically a violation of his lease. "There's wards on the building, and those'll do you just fine. I gotta be able to get into the place if there's a leak or something," his landlord had said.

Grey had nodded, signed the lease, and installed personal wards anyway. The amount he was paying in rent meant that the landlord's wards could be trusted about as much as that chain lock.

Today he was adding a second layer of personal wards. He placed thumbtacks in the window frames and then stretched thin wire over the glass, anchoring it on the tacks. He stepped into the center of the apartment and clapped his hands together in an off-rhythm pattern. The scent of hot metal rose into the air.

He choked on the smell and reached his hands through the wires to open the windows. "Fuck!" The back of his left hand, scraped raw and bleeding. Too much effort to take the wires down and recast the spell—he'd just let the stench of the magic add itself to all the other smells in the place. After a minute or two, there wouldn't be any difference.

He hated this shitty apartment, with its cracking floors, the toilet that refused to stop running, and the massive roach problem. As soon as the Turning was over and he was named a House, he was out of here. He tapped his hand on a broken piece of mirror on the wall. "Soon."

The mirror was why he'd cast the extra wards, even though

a private residence should be off-limits except in case of an active challenge, and he'd never agree to allowing anyone to see that this was where he lived. Even Laurent had never been here—he sure as hell wasn't going to host a challenge in this rat hole.

But the mirror was proof that not everything went as planned in a Turning, was a reminder of what had been stolen from him. A piece of a spell that had gone wrong—cracked and come apart. One of its larger pieces had flown into his father, killing him instantly. The smaller section, the one he'd kept these thirteen years, had lodged itself in Grey's shoulder. He had been twelve.

His magic had never fully recovered from the injury. Still, he'd learned how to compensate. He opened a cupboard above the oven and took out an almost empty glass jar. One small bone rattled loosely in it. He dumped the bone into a mortar, then said a rough, consonant-filled phrase. The air in the room flashed hot, and the bone crumbled to dust. Grey poured in enough honey to bind the particles of dust, some wine to cover the taste, then thinned it with water to make it drinkable.

The pulverized bones still caught in his throat and tasted more like grit than sweetness. But in the grit was stored power—magic that would aid his own.

Grey set the mortar in the sink with the rest of the dishes.

He'd have to go out, refill his supply soon, but this should get him through his first challenge. And when the Turning was over—when he had his own House, maybe even all of the collected power of the Unseen World to call on—he wouldn't have to resort to this. He'd have what should have been his all along.

CHAPTER THREE

Miles Merlin, leonine and silver-haired, nose like a crag and bright blue eyes that missed nothing, was the current leader of the Unseen World. But like all its members, he, too, was subject to the turn of Fortune's Wheel. The Turning carried the same risks for House Merlin as it did for any other House—loss of position and power balanced with a chance for prestige. It was a great, pleasurable game, and one he relished playing.

Although officially structured as a series of individual duels pitting one House—established or candidate—against the next, the Turning wasn't ever only that. It was strategy—which Houses to challenge early and which it might be safe to save until after an invocation of mortality was required. And once the Turning officially began, those wouldn't be questions to contemplate in solitude. InterHouse alliances would be built, future promises made, unHoused candidates cultivated. But tonight, tonight was for quiet. Tonight was for planning on his own.

Sitting at the head of his white marble kitchen table,

enjoying the steak and potatoes he'd made himself, he passed his hand over the collection of images on his tablet. Everyone participating in the Turning was required to register and officially name their champion. He was looking over the current list for pressure points. It was his favorite part of a Turning, these moments before. They felt like holding a full hand of cards, all possibility.

He had won the last time, securing House Merlin's place at the pinnacle of the Unseen World once again, cementing his position here and his influence over events in the mundane world as well. He hadn't won because he was the best magician—he allowed himself no illusions on that score. He won because he was able to see weak points and exploit them. Because he was smart enough to point dangerous Houses at each other and then stay out of the way until the dust settled.

But the Turning had come again soon—the shortest interval yet. Too soon. Things were unsettled, uncertain, even in his own House. He'd expected Ian to apologize by now, to come back. He'd held off naming his champion in the hope of that return. And here he was, still waiting, only a matter of hours left.

Merlin ate as he read, cutting sliver-thin pieces of rare steak. The Turning wasn't only a time to increase House Merlin's influence directly. It was a time to be subtle. To push the Unseen World—both directly and less so—in his chosen directions. There would be people on the list who would help him do this, some of them even voluntarily. He made notes, highlighted names, shuffled his deck and his strategies.

He paused. Laurent Beauchamps had hired an outsider. Strange, that. Magic coming from outside the Houses was unusual enough, but for there to be two people, for them to both find each other and work together, that was even more so. He took another bite, washed it down with a swallow of an excellent Burgundy. That pair would bear watching if they made it out of the opening round. Any new source of magic was worth keeping track of, perhaps worth cultivating. And if it wasn't possible to cultivate it, new magic was worth keeping out. There were such things as standards, after all.

He clicked to the next page and nearly choked. Merlin spat the piece of half-chewed steak into his napkin. Set down his fork. Looked at the picture again. He twisted his mouth and pushed the plate to the side. After tossing away his inheritance and disappearing for years, to come back like this. Slinking like a dog and lapping for scraps from Miranda Prospero.

Miles pressed a hand to his stomach. The news had given him indigestion.

Still, Ian was a smart boy. Now that his little fit of petulance was over, now that he was back in the Unseen World, he'd come to regret his decision, his foolish reasons for breaking with his family. Once he did, it might be useful to have an ally inside Prospero. Champions' decisions were final during challenges. And if he continued to refuse to see reason, it wouldn't be that hard to manipulate him into Miles' own desired outcome. His son always was too soft-hearted.

Merlin made a note in his tablet to tell his daughter, Lara, that she'd stand as champion for the House in place of her brother when they had breakfast tomorrow. For all his flaws, Ian loved his sister and would never hurt her. And while Lara returned that affection, Ian's soft-heartedness was not a flaw that Lara shared. Which meant that one way or another House Merlin could beat House Prospero in a mortal challenge. That would help his position in the Turning nicely.

There. He felt much better. He would, he thought, have dessert.

Ian's wards slid into place as his door closed and locked behind him. Word would get out soon enough, if it hadn't already, about House Prospero's new champion. His father would be furious, and there were plenty of people willing to court Miles Merlin's favor.

Easy enough for a stray spell to go awry, for a misplaced bit of magic to have unforeseen and oh-so-tragic consequences. It was a Turning; accidents not only happened, but they were expected, and if anyone knew how to help one along, it was his father. Miles probably had a list, rank-ordered and waiting, of people he could call on to assist with the problem of his recalcitrant son.

Ian made himself a caprese sandwich and took his laptop to his rooftop garden, where he could sit high above the city, above the noise and the crowds, surrounded by the fading flowers of late summer, Central Park green and blooming below him. He could see the shadows that clung together on the reservoir. They looked like nothing from here, though that was true for him even when he was standing on the reservoir's edge. The House of Shadows knew how to stay hidden. But he knew it was there, even if he couldn't see it, and its presence was malevolent. It was something that should never have happened, and it had been there for far too long.

He angled his chair away from the view and put Shadows at his back.

After he'd eaten, he pulled up his thin file on the one magician he didn't know: Laurent Beauchamps' champion, Sydney. No last name. The video he had started after the spell began, so he couldn't see her set up. But the ease with which she stood and the command precision with which she worked was incredible.

He froze the screen, enlarged the image. She wasn't even sweating.

Ian knew nothing about her. She hadn't come up through the Houses or gone to any of the usual schools, but she certainly had been trained. Which meant she was probably a Shadow. Which was interesting. He'd heard nothing about one of them getting out recently, not even from Verenice. Maybe Sydney had been hiding, waiting until now to make her presence known. Surprise was as much a weapon as anything else.

Whoever she was, wherever she'd come from, he doubted she'd be any kind of secret much longer. He watched the video again. She was like no one he'd ever seen.

He looked up the list of declared challenges. He wanted to see her cast in person. Wanted to see *her* in person. Anyone who could do magic like that was worth getting to know, preferably before they met on opposite sides of a duel.

Ian closed his laptop and leaned back in his chair. The air felt heavy, electric. There was a storm coming in. He was ready.

"I would prefer," Laurent said, "not to challenge Grey directly."

Sydney looked up at him from her perch in the window seat, the whole of the city spread out below her. Laurent's penthouse apartment stretched much higher into the air than her own seventh-floor rooms, and after the huddled darkness of Shadows, she reveled in high, open places. This much sky below her felt glorious. The sunlight, the empty space, all possibility.

"Any particular reason?" she asked. Shara had given her

files, histories, background on the major players in the Unseen World, everyone she was likely to encounter and their connections to one another. She knew the two men were friends. But there was always more to relationships than facts in files.

"He's my best friend. Maybe that sounds ridiculous, since this whole thing is full of friends and families who are competing against each other, but he's the first person who told me I was a magician. He's been there for me ever since." Laurent shrugged, brushing the words away.

"You didn't grow up here, either?" Again, she knew the answer, but wanted to hear his response.

"Here as in, in the city? Sure. Here as in the Unseen World? Not even a little bit. No, I got all the way through middle school before I clued into the fact that I was luckier than anyone had a right to be, particularly if I said out loud what I wanted to happen. I mean, for a long time, I just figured that 'throw a penny in the fountain and make a wish' stuff was true." His grin lit his entire face.

"So how'd you figure it out?" Genuinely curious. There had never been a time when Sydney had not been at least as aware of her magic as she was of her skin. It had always been who she was.

"I wished to meet a wizard. The next morning I woke up with an intense desire—like an itch in my brain—to go to the Rare Books room at the New York Public Library. Grey was the only one there—he'd warded the room so that no one without magic would be able to get in. When I did, he very kindly explained to me that 'wizard' was the wrong word."

"Very kindly," Sydney repeated, climbing out of the window seat to pour herself more blood orange juice. It had been a breakfast meeting, and Laurent had provided a generous spread. "I'm sure."

"Well, for certain values of kindly. But he was the one who explained things to me, so I didn't feel so weird. And then, when I decided I wanted to jump into all of this—which took me, like, five seconds, because what fourteen-year-old boy doesn't want to be a magician—he was the one who introduced me to people, who made sure I didn't sit by myself at lunch when I started going to school with all of them. He made me feel like I belonged here."

"All right, then. You do know I'm a better magician than he is." She hadn't seen Grey cast yet, but she didn't need to. She knew what she was, what she was capable of. She wasn't worried about someone who'd slid through life with the magical equivalent of a gentleman's C.

"I know. And if it comes down to it, I won't ask you to hesitate or hold back, but—he's like family. So I'd like to avoid it." Laurent shrugged. "I mean, the best that happens is you knock him out of contention, and then I'm the one responsible for taking away something he really wants. And he really wants this—he's been getting ready for a Turning since Miranda disinherited him."

"If a challenge becomes unavoidable?" No Houses were required to challenge each other, and in the early part of the Turning, before the duels became mortal, engagements could be declined, though doing so had dire consequences to the ranking of the House that did. The overall number of Houses generally held steady—there had been thirteen for the past three Turnings, and there were twenty-seven established and candidate Houses competing this Turning, so the rankings would matter in the early rounds.

After that, staying alive would.

Laurent blew out a breath. "Please keep the interaction nonlethal."

She nodded. Again, in the early rounds that would be easy enough. The challenges were staggered—the early ones being showpieces for magical ability, nuance, and finesse. Mortality could be invoked if both parties agreed beforehand, but only the last round required that it be. Sydney was sure Grey would fall out of competition by that point. And if he didn't, well, she'd discuss that with Laurent when she had to. "Of course. As I said, I'm better than he is. Is there anyone else I should be similarly aware of?"

"No. All's fair, right?"

"Something like that," Sydney said. "How are we starting?"

"I challenged House Dee," Laurent said. "It's old and

traditionally powerful enough that defeating them will make a nice splash. Strong enough magically that a victory will serve as a warning to anyone who sees me as an easy target."

It was a good strategy, the suggestion that she would have made herself, and for those precise reasons. "Do you have a preferred method of engagement?"

"I'll leave that to your discretion."

Sydney smiled.

As she walked home in the greying late-fall light, Sydney considered whether there was anyone in her life whose friendship she valued as much as Laurent valued Grey's, anyone she would consider sacrificing her goals for.

In her earliest days there, Shadows had lent itself only to survival. Friendship wasn't even a word she knew, much less a concept she had felt. As she grew older, as it became increasingly clear that Sydney could take all the ways that Shadows tried to break her and transmute them into her own power, she became even more isolated, was kept separate from her fellow sacrifices. They were fodder. She would be a phoenix, made to rise from ashes.

A phoenix was a solitary thing.

A group of girls passed by her on the sidewalk, leaning into one another, as close as secrets. Laughing, smiling. Hands in each other's pockets, arms slung around shoulders, heads tipped back, faces relaxed. No one wary, no one suspicious. The air between them soft and permeable, as if each of them might slip into each other's life and rest there, safe.

They were so beautiful, so happy, it ached to look at them, and so Sydney turned away, walked faster, her shoes loud on the sidewalk as she passed their tight knot.

If that was what friendship meant, then no. She had never had it.

In a dark, quiet part of Central Park, one made darker and quieter through judicious use of magic, Grey stood over a body and curled his lip at the mess of it.

The girl hadn't even been that pretty when she was alive. Not that it had mattered. Grey hadn't chosen her for her looks. He'd chosen her—sitting next to her at the bar, buying her drink after drink, pretending like he was interested in what she said, so that she'd lean close, hold his hand, leave with him—for the faintest hint of magic that ran through her blood. Just enough to keep her in the Unseen World, not enough that she was important to it.

He'd learned the hard way that it was easier if they didn't have a lot of magic. They tended to fight back, once they realized what Grey was doing, and the more magic they had, the harder they were to overpower.

The first girl, the one Miranda had disinherited him over,

she'd had more magic than he'd thought. She had fought back. Had gotten away. Told people. There had been consequences. Consequences that had been unpleasant enough that he'd waited almost a year before trying again.

This one had not fought back. She had leaned against him, buzzed and smiling, as he'd kissed her in the park. Had giggled and pulled at his belt buckle as he'd moved her into the darkness, where they'd be less likely to be interrupted. Had blinked in confusion when his hands had tightened on her throat, when he'd spoken the words that pulled the darkness closer around them and kept them hidden, that kept her alive and immobile until the ritual no longer required that she be breathing. She was much less pretty, now that the ritual was finished.

He knelt by her side and used a knife to slit open the skin of her hands. Then he reached through still warm blood and muscle and pulled out her finger bones, using the knife again when he had to slice through tendons. Magic tended to concentrate in these bones more than anywhere else since the hands were so often used to focus casting. The last thumb bone came loose with an audible pop. The empty flesh splatted to the ground. Blood and dirt spattered across his shoes and cuffs.

"Oh, fuck this." Annoyed, he brushed at his clothes, smearing the stains into the fabric. Whatever. It was dark. No one would see. He could wash them when he got home, throw them out if he had to.

He finished gathering the bones, tucking them in a bag that he stuffed into his jacket pocket, then squeezed the girl's empty fingers to be sure he hadn't left any behind. He was fairly certain this would give him enough of a supply that he'd have power until the challenges turned mortal. He'd see how things went—he didn't like not having some in reserve.

Although—he could always get more. That was another thing he'd learned: There was always another girl no one would miss.

He cut a door into the air and stepped through, leaving the dead girl behind him.

CHAPTER FOUR

The earliest memory Sydney let herself have was of learning magic, and the first spells that she remembered learning were for silence. After that, spells for obfuscation and deflection—things that would counterfeit invisibility, make people look away, not see, ignore, forget. True invisibility came later, but it was a soonish sort of later.

After that, after she had learned the names of nine qualities and thirteen degrees of silence, after she had learned to wrap herself in shadows, or a fold in a wall, or step into a tree and pull its bark closed after her, only then did Sydney learn how to cast other magic. And it was always, always, cast alongside those spells designed to hide her, to render her not just invisible, but utterly disappeared. The Unseen World prided itself on its invisibility; the House of Shadows was the rumor of its secrets. Even after she had left Shadows, Sydney had been a kept secret, a hidden thing, made to wait until the Turning to reveal herself.

Tonight, Sydney planned on being seen.

The Turning always officially opened with a party. An excuse for the Houses and aspirants to mingle in an armed truce. The first duel would be fought there, but tradition held that it would be little more than friendly rivalry. Spectacle rather than spite. A feint to gauge the strength of possible opponents.

Sydney didn't believe in feints.

She walked through the gates of House Dee in a dress the color of fresh blood, her lips painted to match. It wasn't that no heads turned to take in her progress across the marble floor, that no eyes followed the bend of her wrist as she plucked a glass of champagne from a passing tray. It was that those eyes paid her no more attention than they would have given any other beautiful woman. For now that was fine. Proof that she had done her job so far. She'd provide a focus for their attention soon enough.

House Dee in its architectural incarnation was old and elaborate, the kind of space meant to remind people that it, and its inhabitants, had been here a while and were likely to remain. Set-dressed to exude power and wealth, it was warm and baroque. Light glinted off crystal glasses and chandeliers. It shone on wallpaper rich in texture and color; it warmed the beeswax polish on the furniture. Establishment and tradition perfumed the air.

Smile on face, glass in hand, Sydney passed through the crowd, pausing at the edge of a conversation to eavesdrop as the crème of the Unseen World, tuxedoed and begowned, arranged their faces in social masks and gossiped about her.

"Some nobody, and representing an upstart House. Could you imagine if he's hired an outsider? He won't make it past tonight with magic like that."

"Beauchamps came from money, didn't he? And is friends with the Prospero boy. You'd think he could do better."

"Not the Prospero boy any longer, remember. Miranda kicked him out, erased his name from the family tree. He's an upstart this Turning, too."

"Really. What will Miranda do?"

"Kill him, probably. She's hired Ian Merlin."

That name an invocation strong enough to send whispers racing even into the corners of the room. Sydney placed her half-full glass on a passing tray. This would complicate things. The former heir of a House now allied with his father's greatest rival. Ian Merlin had been worth watching even without that because of House Merlin's connections to Shadows—but also because he was one of the few magicians strong enough that Sydney thought he might be an actual challenge. And now he had just gotten a lot more interesting.

Shara would want to know about this turn of events, and Sydney would need to rethink her own strategies, but those were considerations for later, not for now. Now was for personal considerations.

She continued to make her way through the crowd, looking for Miranda Prospero.

There.

Straight-backed and elegant, dark hair with one thick streak of white in it. Legend was that section of her hair had turned white overnight in the previous Turning, the night her husband had been killed, a sign of her grief. Diamonds dripped from her ears and sparkled like ice on her hands. She radiated power.

Sydney stepped back, out of Miranda's eyeline. Later would be soon enough for that particular introduction.

Elizabeth Dee strode to the center of the room to officially open the Turning. "Thank you all for joining us tonight as we host the first duel and celebrate the spinning of Fortune's Wheel."

Sydney let the speech flow over her, tuning out continuous mentions of Fortune's Wheel and the saccharine description of the Turning as an event designed to ensure that the Unseen World was led by the strongest, most capable magicians. The Turning might be about many things—individual duels might even be decided by magical strength and ability—but finding the strongest and most capable magicians was certainly not its purpose.

She refocused when Elizabeth spoke the words that officially began the duel: "House Dee accepts the challenge of the candidate House Beauchamps."

The type of spell had been negotiated as part of the offered and accepted challenge. Tonight's was influence. As the challenged House, Dee had the right to choose whether to cast first or second. Not so critical at this early stage, with everyone expecting things to be simply a warm-up, a collective thrown gauntlet, but as things progressed, it would matter. One could always alter a spell after seeing what the opponent chose, to make it flashier or more beautiful, to fine-tune the response. Sydney had known Dee would choose to cast first, that they would be certain that a hired proxy for a candidate House would be nobody that they would need to concern themselves with.

She wouldn't need to fine-tune her response. She knew precisely what she was here to do.

House Dee took pride in representing itself from within. Not through its heir, of course—there was no need to be reckless—but her younger brother. Bryce Dee stepped out onto the floor, removed his tuxedo jacket and cuff links, and rolled back his sleeves. The edge of Sydney's mouth curled. He shouldn't attempt showmanship if that was the best he could muster.

Bryce raised his hands and squinted, and—as one—all of the waiters raised their silver trays of drinks over their heads. They looked right, left, stomped their feet. Bryce sent them moving through the crowd like a precision dance team.

The challenge had been influence. The spell was adequate.

Competent. It looked flashy enough, all of those sharp moves and percussive steps, and Bryce had been smart to use the waitstaff—the matching uniforms made for an arresting visual—but there was nothing beyond the surface. Plus, Bryce's arms were trembling, and sweat stained the armpits of his shirt. Too much visible effort for such a simple spell.

Sydney could see the other magicians recognizing that as well. Miranda Prospero wasn't even bothering to hide her contempt.

He really should have kept the jacket on.

The applause, when Bryce finished, was polite.

"The Challenger, representing the candidate House Beauchamps."

Sydney did not step forward, but curled the last three fingers on her left hand and rotated her wrist a quarter turn.

An invisible violin began to play a waltz.

Sydney moved her right hand, bending her fingers into sharp angles. She stepped twice on the floor with her left heel and spoke the word that unlocked the spell she had prepared.

All of the assembled members of the Unseen World turned to the person next to them, and once partnered, began to dance.

Everyone except Sydney, who smiled to watch the magicians move through her chosen patterns, and the man who walked through the crowd to her side. Dark-haired and sharp-featured, magic coiled beneath his skin. Ian Merlin. Interesting, that he had been unaffected by the spell's influence. She had tailored it very specifically.

"You seem," he said, "in need of a partner."

Sydney looked at him. "I seem to be doing just fine on my own."

"They'll hate you less, when the spell is over, if you're dancing too."

"And why," she asked, "would you care if they hate me?"

"Because you seem interesting." He held out his hands.

"I suppose that's a good enough reason." Sydney stepped close and allowed Ian to lead her in the dance, an exact mimic of the enchanted magicians. He was a good dancer, graceful and confident. She could feel the warmth of him through his tuxedo, in his hand on the skin of her bare back.

"They'll be furious," Ian said, looking around at the dancing magicians.

"Most of them," Sydney agreed. "They'll also realize that I'm no one to be trifled with. They'll pay attention to me—they'll see me, and my magic."

"And why does that matter?" Ian asked. "You look like the sort of woman who gets noticed on a regular basis."

"Noticed," she said, "is very different from seen." The fingers of Sydney's left hand fluttered against Ian's back as she ended the spell.

She ignored the fade of the music, the stunned hush of the room that turned into whispers that turned into noise. "Do you want to get out of here?"

Ian took her offered hand. "Your magic was the only thing I came to see."

"I hope it was worth it."

"Very much."

She paused as they got to the street. "Just to be clear, I asked you to leave with me because I want take you to bed. How do you feel about that?"

Ian swallowed hard. "Good. I feel good."

She smiled, and flagged down a cab.

Sydney slipped from Ian's bed and into a bathroom down the hall, closing the door behind her. She pressed her back against the cold tile of the wall. The aftereffects of magic could only be delayed so long, and her spell had been big. The cost must be paid.

Hot and cold flashed through her, shaking her until her joints ached. Blood dripped from her nose and trickled down the back of her throat. She reached over and turned on the faucet so that no sound of weakness might leak from the walls.

She breathed in. Let the pain expand to fill her skin, let it become one with breath and bone, until it was nothing more than an ache—until the throb of magic was the same as the bruised pain in her feet from her shoes, as the blister coming up on one heel, as the much more pleasant ache in her thighs from the sex. One pain among others. It was nothing more. She wouldn't let it be.

She thought of Bryce Dee, sweating from the effort of casting, even with a waiting pool of magic to access. Imagined that he slept peacefully, his cost already paid.

She had been one of the ones to pay it, and now she paid her own.

"Sydney?" Ian's voice, sleepy and warm from the bedroom. She turned off the faucet. There were more pleasant ways to distract herself.

Later, Sydney walked home, thirty-seven blocks, in her heels. She had refused Ian's offer of a cab: "I like the night."

The air was cool on her flushed cheeks, and the distance long enough for her to finally feel grounded again after a spell of that size and its aftershocks. The pain now no more than background noise, but remnants of magic still burned through her blood as she walked past the warmth and light of restaurants and bars, past beautifully decorated store windows. She slowed a bit passing those, looking at their jewel-box designs, color and pattern like a fairy tale on acid, dressed up in this season's fashion. She craved beauty like that, showy and strange. Like what magic should have been.

Six months and thirteen days. That was how long she had been out of Shadows. Not free, not yet. But out. It was getting easier to believe—last week she had gone an entire day without wondering if that would be the day Shara changed her mind and forced her to return forever, the doors sealed shut behind her. That was impossible, yes—her magic had broken those doors open before and could again. But there was a type of terror that didn't care about reality, a fear that lived in secret places, and it clawed at her soft insides. It clawed harder at night, which was another thing she hated. But she'd been out long enough to almost sleep through the night now, most nights. There were nightmares still, of course, but things were getting easier.

Easier, but not safe. Not free.

Not yet.

The first night she'd spent outside of Shadows, she hadn't slept at all. She hadn't even tried. Instead, she had spent the entire night—her shadow still weeping pieces of darkness from that first deep cut necessary to sign her name on her contract, to indicate the measure of her debt to the House—standing outside, watching the stars and imagining what she would do when she truly earned her freedom.

She had imagined scrawling "fuck you" after her name on that heavy grey paper, imagined breaking the bottle where her shadow was converted to ink, imagined snapping the pen in her hand. Imagined driving that pen through Shara's heart, or her throat, or some other soft and vulnerable place. She had imagined a thousand ways that freedom would feel. She had begun to plan, then, a way to get to it faster.

Now, at night, when she couldn't sleep, she didn't count sheep. She imagined a match and a contract burning. She fell asleep to the image of smoke rising through the air.

A cab slowed next to her, but she waved the driver on.

"Are you sure, lady? Those shoes look like killers."

"So am I," she called back. The window shut as the car sped away.

Her heartbeat was close to normal now, her muscles languid and warm. The remaining fizz of magic was only an ache in her hands. She was pleased with the spell, pleased with the night as a whole. Fortune's Wheel was turning, and she would make certain that the Unseen World changed with it. Tonight had been a good beginning.

Home. Sydney walked across her building's empty lobby to the elevator. She kept her killer heels on until she was inside her door. No weakness, even here. Once inside, she slipped out of the shoes and dress and into black leggings and an oversize T-shirt. Paused for a moment to ground herself: There were blankets piled at the foot of the bed, topped with a quilt embroidered in stars. There were glasses in every richness of blue in the cupboard, because even glasses could be beautiful, and so why shouldn't they be? There was a sofa, dark red velvet, and a sculpture of leaves—brass and bronze and copper—on the wall above it. Her own tiny jewel box of beauty, a longing made real.

Settled, she made herself coffee. She had no desire to have nightmares, and there was work still to do.

The results came to Laurent the following morning, just before they went to the rest of the Unseen World. Winner's privilege. Sydney thought it might more realistically be called the last moments of calm before she became a walking target, but that took a bit longer to say. Not that she was complaining—it was exactly what she wanted.

The email appeared on his screen, using the same techno-magic protocols the notification of the Turning had done. The spell was a masterwork of collective magic. Fully anonymous voting by the magicians in attendance, scores tabulated by the spell itself, a spell also designed to flag anomalies in magic use. It was the same magic that regulated all aspects of the Turning, impossible for any one House to override. The screen shimmered, almost iridescent.

"We won!" Laurent said, turning around in his chair to smile at her, his delight so obvious Sydney grinned back.

"Good," she said. "I would have been astounded if you hadn't."

“I wish I had been able to see it in person. I heard you did gorgeous work.”

He hadn’t even been invited to House Dee’s party, where his challenge was fought, House Dee being somewhat particular about those it considered suitable members of the Unseen World. They had been careful to make sure it got back to Laurent that outsiders who hadn’t even been born in the Unseen World and who had the arrogance to think they deserved to found a House were not on their list.

“They’re snobs.” Sydney shrugged, dismissing the entirety of the Unseen World with the movement of her shoulders. “But they’re snobs who recognize power. You’ll be invited to everything from now on, I’m guessing.”

“You’ve strengthened your wards, taken whatever precautions you should?” Laurent asked. “I’ve heard that accidents can happen on purpose during these things—I don’t want you to be one.”

She smiled. “Even you don’t know where I live. I’ll be fine.”

“I’m serious. I don’t mean to sound like a dick, but I have money. A lot of it. If the choice is between paying your rent or making sure you’re safe, know that I consider your safety a business expense. Buy whatever you need and I’ll reimburse you, or let me know what it is, and I’ll make sure you have it.”

“I know what you’re paying me to represent you, Laurent. And we’re sitting in your five-bedroom apartment on the

Upper East Side. The fact that you have money is not a secret."

"Sydney."

Laurent looked concerned enough that Sydney decided he actually meant what he said. "If cost becomes an object to my personal safety, I will let you know. But trust me—I want to get through to the end of this. I have no intention of dying—either in an accident or during a duel. The goal is to make sure that you're the founder of a House when this is over, and for that to happen, I need to stay alive. I've taken precautions, and I'm good at what I do."

He kept his eyes on hers, then nodded. "All right."

"So, what's the next move?" she asked.

"I've been thinking about that. And my first thought was there's something to be said for going after the powerful Houses now," Laurent said. "Get them out of the way before things shift and all the duels are mortal."

"And your second thought?" Sydney asked.

"That there's a more subtle strategy to play—just because a House is powerful doesn't mean their champion is. A lot of the old Houses are too insular to hire a champion, and their magic suffers for it. So I want to work my way through this differently."

"I think that's a smart call," Sydney said. "House Dee is one of the oldest and most established Houses, but Bryce's spell was nothing. If you want my advice?"

Laurent nodded. “Of course.”

“You have some time. Watch what happens this round before you decide who to challenge in the next. Watch the results, the type of spells cast, who falls out of contention. Alliances among the Houses will shift, too. All those pings on your phone while we've been talking? I'm guessing that a good percentage of them are Heads of Houses, or other candidates, inviting you to drinks, to dinners, to events where they can learn more about who you are and whether your way of thinking about magic lines up with theirs.”

Laurent glanced at the screen of his phone, scrolled, nodded. “And there's the expected subtlety, sure, but isn't it a little early for any of them to care what I think about magic?”

“It's really not. After last night, they aren't just wondering whether you'll be made a House. They're wondering what might happen to magic if you win.”

“Like, what, I'm going to make people pay dues in order to use it or something?” He laughed the idea off.

“The thing is, you could. The winner of the Turning leads the Unseen World. If that's you, you'll have a lot of say in how magic is used and who gets to use it. You came from outside—maybe you'd be interested in opening things up. Some Houses will think that's great. Others will hate that idea so much they'll wish you were representing yourself so they could kill you when this turns mortal.”

He winced.

"But if people discover that you think the same way they do, and that you can do the hard work for them during the challenges—removing the people who don't think the same from contention—then maybe they decide it's better to support you than to challenge you." Not every House met in challenges. The Turning wasn't ever meant to scorch the earth of the Unseen World, only to shake it up a bit. Some alliances needed to remain alliances. From what she'd seen of him so far, Laurent had a head for strategy. And if he was focused on that, that would give her some time to think about what to do with Ian Merlin being at House Prospero and how much of all of that Shara needed to know. She now had plans of her own she needed to rethink.

Laurent leaned against the counter. "Miles Merlin's been in control for as long as I've been here. The way he runs things is all I know about the Unseen World, and magic, any of it. Which, I guess might make some people think I'd be happy to go along with the status quo and, honestly, right now I'm happy to have them think that."

"But?" Sydney asked.

"They call me an outsider. Like it's a title, except a bad one. Because I wasn't born in a House. House Dee wouldn't even let me in the door last night, and no one said a word against that. I am the only person with skin darker than pale who is competing in the Turning, and I'd bet every dollar in my bank accounts that I'd be the first black man to be named a House.

"I want power. I won't pretend that I don't. But the other reason I'm in this is that there are kids like I was, and they belong here, too. Even if I can't open up the entire Unseen World to them, I can open up my House and give them a place.

"So, sure. I'll wait and see for now, and once things become clearer, I'll decide who to challenge next."

"All right, then," she said. "One other thing I want to ask you to think about—what to do about Grey."

"I said—"

She cut him off. "I know what you said. That he's off-limits. I'm not saying to change that, but you need to keep in mind that at some point the challenges become mortal. You can only duel a House or candidate once."

"So it might be better to do it early and risk knocking him out than to do it later and risk killing him." Laurent looked unhappy. "I don't like it, but I get it. I'll think about it. I'm not promising anything else, but I'll think about it."

"That's all I wanted," Sydney said, though it wasn't, not really. She wanted him to consider that his own success meant the challenge might come from Grey, and what he might do about that, but this clearly wasn't the time to have that conversation. "Send me the next challenge when you decide who it is."

• • •

There were a number of spells put in place when the House of Shadows was established. One of those spells looked like an angel.

The Angel of the Waters, on top of the Bethesda Fountain, set in the red brick of Central Park's Bethesda Terrace. Striding forward, her wings open, arms outstretched, a lily in one hand. Sydney stood, facing the cooing pigeons perched in a line atop the statue's wings.

The statue wasn't magic in and of itself. It had been there before Shadows was created—made as a celebration of clean water, a symbol of freshness, of purity, a fact that had rendered Sydney incandescent when she learned it. After its appropriation by the spell that created Shadows, that governed the magic that came from that place, it was neither of those things.

If it had been associated with anything other than Shadows, Sydney would have found the statue beautiful. But knowing what it was, even with the setting sun making a watercolor of the sky and clouds behind it, she could barely stand to look at it.

But to break a spell you needed to know how it worked in the first place. That required that she do more than look at the statue.

Sydney walked around the fountain, keeping it in the periphery of her gaze. Shadows clung more deeply to it than they did to the other things in the park. But the effect was a subtle one. A photographer or painter, someone who worked with light, might notice it, but it seemed unlikely that most mundanes would. It was a well-hidden piece of magic.

She spoke a word to draw the air around her like a cloak. Its syllables broke and fell like soft rain. She extended her hands, a mirror reverse of the statue, and she *reached* into the magic that was anchored in it.

Dark copper and rot, the feel of clotting blood between her fingers, and that was exactly what she expected to find. Shadows' magic. This, she knew. This, she could unmake.

She breathed in, she breathed out, and sank deeper.

Magic whipped around her like ropes, like barbed wire, holding, pulling, sinking in claws. Hungry. Some other spell, knitted into the magic from Shadows. Some other spell, trying to pull magic out of her. Fingers clutching at her heart, searching.

Sydney gritted a word out through clenched teeth, singeing the air, breaking her connection to the magic running through the Angel. She spat a curse, the aftermath of that second, searching spell lingering in her mouth like bile. An ache, dull and hollow, crouched just behind her ribs.

She narrowed her eyes and resumed her walk around the fountain, this time in the opposite direction. It was possible that Shara knew about this other, second spell. That this was another test: Could Sydney discover it? Would she tell when she did? But none of the instructions Shara had given her, none of Shadows' plans, involved the statue.

It was also possible Shara didn't know about this other spell, and that was something worth thinking on.

There were rumors—Sydney had heard them; she had spent her first month out of Shadows learning how to function in the mundane world and her second month learning everything she could about the Unseen World—that there was something wrong with magic. Tiny spells that went awry, or that had to be recast, or that weren't quite what was expected. Small rumors, but enough of them that she was sure there was truth lurking in the whispers.

Shara had said nothing about any of that.

Which made sense, if the problem was with the spell that was anchored in the Angel. The magic would be fine coming out of Shadows, and then here—Sydney braced and reached into it again, more cautiously this time, stopping just before that hungry, lurking presence. Just close enough to feel the emptiness underneath.

Whatever it was, this was where things were going wrong.

Laurent met Grey three times a week, early in the morning, to run around the Central Park Reservoir. Grey had gone on a fitness kick about three years back—he'd said being in better physical condition would help make their magic stronger, a healthy mind in a healthy body and all that. Grey was always getting ideas about what he could do to improve his magic, make it stronger, some of which were a little out there, but running was pretty benign, even if early mornings weren't, so Laurent showed up and he ran.

They set a pace that was comfortable enough to let them talk. "How'd your first challenge go?" Laurent asked.

"Fine. Another candidate, some second cousin or stepchild from the Morgan family looking to establish their own House. Pissed at Miranda about something and looking to take it out on me. This whole thing will be much less of a pain in my ass once people realize that she won't care if I lose, by the way. But I had choice of magic, and I chose locations and did an unfolding map spell, so I won."

"Nice. What will you do next?"

"Trying to steal my strategy?" Grey laughed. "I'm going after one of the big Houses. Make a point. Beating them will show I can't be fucked with. You?"

"Strategy first. Meetings. Drinks. All the background shuffling before I decide. You know how it is."

"Not really," Grey said. The remnants of yellow crime scene tape fluttered in the wind as they ran by. "No one's asked me for any of that."

Laurent tried to minimize his mistake. Grey was always

happiest when he felt connected. "Well, people probably think they already know you well enough to be direct. You were born here—I'm an outsider, remember?"

"Right," Grey said, looking over his shoulder to the dark gap in the trees. "I'm sure that's it."

"What happened over there?" Laurent asked, nodding back at the dark space in the trees.

"I can't see enough to tell," Grey said, turning and running backward for a few steps to better see the crime scene. But all that was visible was the bedraggled police tape.

"Did you hear about that woman who was murdered and had all her finger bones removed? Maybe that was where she was found."

"Huh," Grey said. "Maybe."

"So creepy, right? Like, who steals someone's finger bones? That is, like, Brothers Grimm shit."

"Seems like," Grey said, turning back around.

"Anyway, back to strategy, do you have any advice?" Laurent asked. "Who I should trust, that sort of thing?" He could tell from Grey's face that had been the right question to ask.

"Hard to go wrong following a winner," Grey said.

"Merlin, you mean?"

"It's the oldest House. That kind of history, that's power and standing. Plus, Miles knows all the secrets, everything that goes on."

"I thought your family hated him."

"*Miranda* hates him. Point in his favor, as far as I'm concerned."

Laurent laughed.

They finished the loop and slowed to a walk. "One other thing," Laurent said. "I've been thinking it might be smart to challenge each other now, while things are still low-key."

Grey coughed, spitting water on the ground. "What the fuck! Low-key? If you have too many losses, you don't advance. One of us could knock the other out. Forget it."

"It's forgotten." Laurent drank from his own water bottle. "This whole thing is so weird."

"Weird or not, you better figure it out fast, and stop coming up with crazy shit like that." Grey slapped his friend on the back and headed for his subway stop. "Fortune's Wheel keeps turning!"

Laurent stood in the cooling air, the wind drying his sweat against his skin. Fortune's Wheel did turn, and it didn't always leave people on top. Sometimes it rolled right over them. Shaking the stiffness from his limbs, he started for home.

"Anything for me today, Henry?" Sydney asked as she crossed the lobby of her apartment building.

"Yes, miss."

She stopped, raised a brow. She didn't generally order

things for delivery. The pool of people who knew her actual address was two, and she didn't think Shara would ever use the postal system, so the question was more a habit than something she expected an affirmative answer to.

"Well, not a thing, miss, so much a person. She said you weren't expecting her, and so she'd just sit right down and wait."

Sydney shifted her weight back on her heels. She was definitely not expecting a visitor. Nothing had triggered her wards, but not every unpleasantry had to be caused by magic. It would be easier to protect Henry if she was closer to him. "She?"

"That's right, miss. Right over there."

The white-haired woman wore all black, perfectly tailored for her straight-backed frame. Her lipstick was as red as Sydney's, and while the passage of time had marked itself on her skin, power and beauty went bone-deep beneath it. She rose from the chair, as poised as a queen. "Hello, Sydney. I'm Verenice Tenebrae."

Sydney knew the name. And that was why her wards—keyed to magicians who used the magic that came from Shadows—hadn't gone off.

"Thanks, Henry. It's fine." He nodded his acknowledgment, and Sydney walked closer to the waiting woman. She shaped a minor silence with her left hand as she did, making sure no one would be able to overhear their conversation. "Tenebrae. You're the other Shadow who got out."

"Indeed." She inclined her head. "It's a pleasure to meet you. I was hoping we could talk."

Now that she was closer, the signs of Verenice's origins were unmistakable. Sydney saw them herself in every mirror: the way Verenice held herself, the lines of her spine and the awareness in her eyes. The magic that ran closer to the surface than it did in those who'd never had to be a channel for others. The ragged edges of her shadow. "There's a very good bakery, about a block and a half away, if you don't mind the walk."

"I do love *pain au chocolat*. And you don't want me in your apartment and you're too diplomatic to say. I quite understand."

Sydney said nothing because it was true. She didn't want Verenice in her apartment. Shara had told her, when she left, to look for Verenice, had mentioned that the other woman could help her navigate the Unseen World. Sydney trusted few people to begin with, and trusted anyone Shara recommended even less. So she had not gone looking for Verenice, and while she wasn't surprised to have been sought out, she wasn't pleased, either.

She watched Verenice as they walked, but the older woman gave away nothing. It would have been a shock if she had. Shadows was nothing if not thorough in its training.

After they were seated, Verenice with hot chocolate to accompany her pastry and Sydney with rose and violet macarons, Verenice said, "My debt is paid. Fully. Shadows has no hold on me, and I have no loyalty to that place." The last word bitter as salt. "I'm here for myself, because I was curious about you, not because Shara asked me to spy."

"I'm hardly anyone worth being curious about," Sydney said.

"Forty years," Verenice said, stirring her hot chocolate.

"I'm sorry?"

"I left Shadows forty years ago. Before you were born, even. No one before me and no one in between walked out of those doors. You and I both know to a nicety what the other endured to be here. False modesty does not become us." She looked up then, directly at Sydney.

"Fine. Then tell me how I can satisfy your curiosity."

Verenice smiled. "I do like you. So precise. So careful. So much like I was. Though you want more, I think. No, don't interrupt. I know it makes you uncomfortable that I know what you are, and you'd really rather not be here. You want to deny, to deflect, to try to draw one more layer of 'don't see me' around yourself. I'd be willing to bet that the only reason you haven't warded this conversation is that you don't want it to be important.

"But I have practice in seeing, and I'll tell you what I think.

I think that you're out of Shadows and working with that handsome young man because Shadows has told you to—to be contracted to someone, if not him specifically—and because Shara and the House will cut little pieces of you away, slowly if you do what you're told and much faster if you don't.

"I also think that you're doing something else, and not just because you'd be a lot less careful in what you said to me if you had nothing to hide from Shara. Who probably told you to seek me out because she knew it would be the last thing you would do if she did, and she wanted to deny you an ally."

A brow raised as question. Sydney kept her face clear of an answer, but it was precisely the sort of thing Shara would do.

Verenice continued. "I'll tell you again that I'm not here on her behalf, that I haven't spoken to her since I paid off my contract, but I don't expect you to believe me—I wouldn't, in your position. But I know how you filtered your influence spell during the first challenge—you set it up so that it would affect only the magicians who use the magic from Shadows to pay their cost. I think, perhaps, you were looking for allies."

And that was close, very close. Sydney had set up the spell that way, though with the intent of counting enemies rather than of finding allies. She had wanted to see how deep Shadows' influence was, to have some idea what the size of the fire would be when she lit the match. Apparently, a conflagration was in order. "Any other speculations?"

"I think you're using the Turning as a way to move against Shadows, and I want to help you." Verenice's hands were flat on the table where Sydney could see them. Not that a magician had to use her hands to cast, but keeping them so obviously visible and unmoving was a sign that no magic was being done.

And then Sydney did ward the conversation, dipping a finger in her tea and drawing a quick symbol on the surface of the table.

"Assuming any of what you said is true, why would you want to get involved? Going up against Shadows would be risky. Dangerous even. If you're out, you're safe," Sydney said, stepping hard on the last word. She might not trust Verenice, but she wouldn't send anyone back into Shara's clutches.

The lines of Verenice's face changed then, and Sydney could see all the time, all the pain that had made them. "I opened the doors of the House when I was thirty-three. It held me under contract for ten years after. And for those ten years, and the thirty beyond them, I have lived in the Unseen World and known what went on in Shadows. Known I couldn't stop or change it. Not on my own. That's why."

Sydney looked around the elegant patisserie, at the cream-and-gilt walls, the staff in the black-and-white uniforms, aprons edged with lace. She breathed in the scents of sugar and butter, cinnamon and chocolate, and thought how very far away they both were from where they had started.

She looked at Verenice's shadow again. The rips, the torn places, the ragged edges. So much worse than her own, and the pain of her own, when she allowed herself to acknowledge it, was the constant shriek of skin flayed away, of open wounds. The balm to the pain, to the rage that lay underneath it, was the idea that she could change things. Could end them. Could make sure that no one else was broken and cut into pieces for the ease of other people's magic.

She could almost have understood the existence of Shadows if it had been more than that. If using the magic that came out of it had been somehow a boost—if it let people be more powerful magicians. People were greedy and for power in particular. But the magic that came from Shadows didn't give extra power. It made no one stronger. All it did was make things easier, because the pool of magic was always there, and ensure that those who used it faced no consequences for their magic use because someone else had paid them already.

Sydney had been one of those someone elses, for the first twenty-five years of her life, and Verenice had, too, for eight years of her life beyond that. She felt herself shake inside. She owed Verenice this choice, even if it made the other woman less safe. There were times when safety didn't matter. And she didn't have to trust Verenice to be able to use her.

"Okay," Sydney said. "Okay."

Verenice nodded. "You let me know when you've decided how I can be of use."

"There is one thing," Sydney said. She could start by asking the question Shara had wanted her to. That way there'd be nothing lost if it turned out Verenice wasn't trustworthy after all. "Who do I most need to worry about?"

"Miles Merlin." Verenice didn't even have to consider her answer. "He's furious already, because his son won't use Shadows magic. He hates me because I'm the one who taught Ian that he didn't have to. And once he learns what you are, where you're from, he'll come at you. He'll be subtle, at the beginning, but don't mistake that for him being anything less than dangerous. He'll see any threat to Shadows as a threat to his power, and he won't like it."

"You're the one who taught Ian?" Sydney said. A flicker of surprise before the realization that it made sense. Someone had to, and the choices were extremely limited. "Is he good?"

"Very."

"One more thing, then," Sydney said. "Have you heard about any failures of magic?"

"A little," Verenice said. "Nothing concrete."

"Please let me know if you do. It would, possibly, be a helpful thing to know, if I were actually planning any of the things you wondered about." Her phrasing was vague enough that she could explain her way out of things if the request did get back to Shara.

Verenice collected her things, then paused. "Sydney. Thank you."

"You may not want to thank me by the end of this," Sydney said.

"If the end of this means an end to Shadows, I will."

The next day, Sydney sent Verenice flowers. A kind gesture, nothing more.

Except for what it signaled, something she knew Verenice would understand: that Verenice, too, was findable. And there was the small matter of the spell, woven into the flowers, that would have wilted them on the instant had there been traces of any magic that came from Shadows in Verenice's house, had she actually been in communication with Shara. And the secondary spell, set so if that magic wasn't found, they opened exuberantly, in bright profusion, offering unmistakable signs of suspicion.

Verenice smiled and sent flowers in return. The card read, *May our friendship, like these flowers, never wilt.* Woven into the writing, a spell of her own. A binding to loyalty, making her unable to cast direct magic against Sydney.

Sydney held the card in her hand. There were ways—there were always ways—to get around such a binding. Verenice could very easily move against Sydney indirectly, or hurt someone else for leverage. But this, unasked for, was a strong sign that she had meant what she said—that she wasn't bound to Shara or to Shadows any longer, and that she would work to help Sydney if that help was needed.

It was a good start.

CHAPTER FIVE

The bar was casual, out of the way of the financial crowd and not trendy enough for the hipsters. Welcoming, with caramel wood and warm brass and old red brick. The blond woman sitting at the end of the bar in her severely tailored sheath dress looked more polished than the place, but she laughed with the bartender and asked the hostess about her sister's art exhibit.

"This really is your regular spot." Sydney slid onto the stool next to Madison and ordered a dirty martini.

"I've been coming here since law school. Will used to tend bar to help pay for tuition. Then he decided he preferred this kind of bar to the legal kind. He wound up buying this place, what, two years ago?"

Will nodded as he set down their drinks. "Thinking about expanding the kitchen so we can do more than just bar snacks, too. My husband wants to have fancy sandwiches and some desserts."

"It's a great place. And you make a fantastic martini," Sydney said.

"Thanks. Let me know if you get hungry. I've got some of that pickled asparagus you like, Mads."

"Just send it out now. Maybe in a vat," Madison said. "You know I can't resist that stuff."

After Will left, she turned back to Sydney. "It's started. The Turning."

"It has. Thanks for passing on your impression of Laurent, by the way. You're right—he's a good guy, if a bit naive about the world he lives in." Rather than following Shara's directive and going to Verenice for assistance, Sydney had done her own research into members of the Unseen World who might help her make her way through it. Madison had been a Prospero, and had left over the existence of Shadows, both of which factors made her perfect. The fact that Sydney had grown to genuinely like her had been an unexpected bonus.

"No problem." Madison smiled her thanks as Will slid a platter with pickled asparagus and a variety of other small snacks over to them. "You should try the stuffed peppers, by the way. I didn't know Laurent well growing up—he showed up just before I left—but he always struck me as one of the good ones. How's working together?"

Sydney sipped her drink. "Fine so far. He's good at strategy, which I appreciate."

"You do love a plan."

"The more the merrier." She had a number of them. "We were the opening challenge."

"I heard. House lawyers don't count as 'exposure to the mundane world' for purposes of gossip, and you and your magic are good gossip right now. Did you really make them all dance? Please tell me it was something like the zombie dance from 'Thriller.'" Madison raised her glass in a mock toast.

Sydney laughed. "Sadly, it was a waltz, as a zombie dance didn't occur to me when I was planning the spell. I wish it had. Any other good gossip?"

"Prospero hiring Ian is the other big one. No one can quite believe that he gave up his place in House Merlin, and everyone's waiting for Miles' head to explode over Ian working for Prospero rather than trying to establish a House of his own."

"Does anyone have any ideas about what's actually going on there?" Sydney asked.

"I haven't heard anything that's worth taking seriously," Madison said. "Most of it's conspiracy theory stuff, about how this is just Merlin outsmarting everyone and making a move to gain control of Prospero. Which, no. If she thought for a second Ian wasn't loyal, Miranda would eviscerate him. With a spoon.

"Why—do you know anything?"

"Maybe. Ian's not using the magic from Shadows, and I'd put money on that being the reason he's left his House."

"Just for that?" Madison held up a hand. "Don't get me wrong. I'm sitting here with you because I fucking hate that system and won't be part of it. But we all do have a choice."

"Except that House Merlin founded Shadows back in the day and created the spell that makes the transfer of consequences possible. So I imagine Ian's choice was a bit less of one."

Madison nodded her head slowly. "That's right. And I've heard that Merlin still handles their obligation in blood. One of the few older Houses to do so."

"Obligation?" Sydney said.

Madison looked at her empty glass like she could will it to refill. "It's what the official term for the sacrifices is. Blood obligation means they keep it in the family, rather than procuring an infant by other means."

"Don't look so uncomfortable. I honestly don't give a fuck what they call it to make themselves feel better, or less culpable. There is no name that makes any of this worse than it is. But I do wonder if Ian knows who his House sent, and that's why he has a conscience about it. Although even that doesn't explain the alliance with Miranda, of all people."

"There were rumors that it was his mom, actually. That something happened when Lara Merlin was born, something bad, and so instead of giving the baby up, Miles paid his debt with his wife," Madison said.

"I would have been too young to notice someone like that being brought in, but that might explain it. Especially if Ian was old enough to remember her but not to understand."

"Right. So, changing the subject to something less utterly horrific, gossip also says the two of you left the opening challenge together, quick, fast, and in a hurry." Madison wriggled her eyebrows. "Are there good details? Please tell me if there are good details."

Sydney smiled over the rim of her glass.

"There are good details, and you're just not going to tell me. Got it. Anything else?" Madison ate the last piece of pickled asparagus. "I should just buy stock in this stuff."

"See if you can find out if there's anything I should know about Verenice Tenebrae." Sydney wanted to trust her, but she also didn't want any nasty surprises. Lawyers always knew where to find the nasty surprises.

"Did you meet her?" Madison asked. "She's like something out of a myth, escaping Shadows."

Sydney looked at her over the rim of her glass.

"Okay, fair enough. I guess you are too. But what is she like?"

"Strong. Maybe even mythic. But check her out for me anyway." Sydney tucked money under her coaster and got up. "Breakfast next week?"

"I'll let you know if I can't. And, Sydney, take care."

• • •

In the early part of the Turning, things progressed in about the fashion Sydney had expected: Houses fought challenges meant to settle thirteen years' worth of grudges, of slights over dinner and bad breakups. Informal alliances of Houses—both candidate and established—formed and broke apart and re-formed as the first hints of where power might shift to when the Turning was ended appeared. The Unseen World was full of secret meetings, shadowed negotiations, veiled threats, and contingent promises. It was an exercise in intrigue as blood sport, with remarkably little actual blood.

And then, things didn't go as expected.

It might have been ignored, except one of the magicians involved was Ian. He was, as Madison had said, good gossip. Some foolish candidate House that under normal circumstances would have passed in and out of the Turning like fallen leaves challenged House Prospero. The duel was expected to be so unimportant that Miranda wasn't even in attendance. Ian was casting first.

"What's the choice of magic?" Sydney asked. This evening's challenge had far fewer formal trappings than most of the previous ones, even with House Prospero being involved. No champagne and canapés, no uniformed staff. Just a large open room in an apartment so devoid of personality it seemed staged.

"Time," Ian said.

It was a complicated, ambitious choice. Sydney glanced at the candidate magician, who waited, blank-faced and collected. "I think I'm impressed. His choice or yours?"

"His, actually. But I hope you won't be too disappointed by what I do with it."

"Please," Sydney said, "feel free to fully impress me."

Ian grinned.

The challenge began.

Ian reached into his pocket and removed a small brown kernel. A seed, it looked like. He set it on the table and began counting backward from midnight, naming the hours and all their fractions. As he spoke, the seed sprouted green, the green stretched into shoots, and then into canes. He continued to count. The canes burst into thorn and leaf and then into bud and bloom. The scent of roses filled the room.

Ian stopped counting. He said another word, and the ticking of clocks rattled the air. The rose unbloomed. Faster and faster it happened, neither petal nor leaf falling, just the plant pulling back in on itself.

The clocks stopped. Only the seed remained.

As the watching magicians applauded, Ian handed the seed to Sydney. "It will grow if you plant it."

"I'll buy a container."

The other magician, Hawkins, began his casting.

Perhaps thirty seconds had passed when Ian's attention sharpened. He walked over to Hawkins. Stopped. Walked one full circle around him, staring at his hands, watching them jerk and reshape themselves. One of Hawkins' fingers dislocated with an audible *pop*.

"Are you able to halt the progression of the spell?" Ian asked.

Hawkins shook his head wildly, his hands still moving, the words of the spell still pouring from his mouth. Blood dripped like sweat from his temples, leaked from his eyes and ears. Another finger dislocated.

Ian spoke clearly, addressing the waiting crowd. "There has been an error of magic. House Prospero forfeits this challenge until such time as it can be proved that the error was in the magic, and not in the magician, and a null result declared.

"The rest of you, unless you want to watch this man bleed out, go home."

Had it been anyone other than Ian, the assembled crowd probably would have ignored him and stayed to watch, as Hawkins, caught in the grip of a horrifically misfiring spell, died. But it was Ian, and it was House Prospero that had just forfeited, and if the error in magic wasn't proved, that would count against their rankings, and there was such gossip to be had. And so they left.

Sydney stayed. "With your permission, I'd like to see if I can help."

Hawkins nodded frantically. He was no longer able to speak. His teeth were clenched so hard Sydney could hear them breaking. She raised her hands on either side of Hawkins' face, and the shadows in the room drew closer. She hummed a low note. Cut it off. "This is . . . What is happening to you, it's not because of magic. It's an absence." And beneath that absence, the same clawing hunger she'd felt in the magic in the Angel of the Waters. It settled on her like dread. "It's an absence that is acting like a . . . I don't know, a black hole. It's pulling your magic through. It will . . . it will pull until there is nothing left. Until it uses you up. I am so sorry."

Ian swore and looked away.

"I can ease your passing," she told Hawkins, her voice kind.

Hawkins nodded.

Sydney's words were soft and low, a lullaby.

Hawkins' eyes closed, his body still fracturing itself, but his face was at peace. He shuddered out a breath, then coughed up a gout of blood. His flesh dissolved, rising up in a hissing, foul-smelling smoke, leaving only his bones behind, a fallen heap on the floor.

Ian punched the wall hard enough to split the skin on his knuckles. Pain flared through his hand and into his wrist. "What a fucking waste."

"Is there any part of this that isn't?" Sydney asked. "Never mind. Rhetorical."

"If he had cast first—" Ian began.

Sydney shrugged. "Probably still the same result. You don't use the same magic. Which, if I hadn't known before, I'd be sure of now."

Ian's face went blank.

"Your nose is bleeding."

Ian dug into his pocket for a handkerchief. When he looked up, cloth pressed to his nose to stanch the bleeding, Sydney was gone.

Sydney sank down into the bath, the water—as hot as she could bear it—flushing her skin. It hadn't been a shock that the Turning involved death. There would be a time when death was the entire point. But the sensation of Hawkins just *stopping* beneath her hand . . . There was a wrongness there that was offensive. It was, as Ian had said, a waste.

Water sluiced from her fingers, down her arm, as she reached for the glass of wine she'd left on the edge of the tub.

She hadn't known Hawkins. Wouldn't in other circumstances have cared about his death. Had she faced him on the opposite side of a mortal challenge, she would have killed him without thinking twice. But she couldn't rinse the bitterness of what had happened to him from her mouth.

The spell that had killed him was a horror, one that went

beyond the horror already woven into the magic that came from Shadows. It wasn't a failure of magic, not really, though surely that's what it would be ruled for purposes of the Turning. It was a gorging on it.

Whatever she had felt was hungry, and she was certain it was not done feeding.

CHAPTER SIX

Madison looked at the résumé on her tablet and then again at the woman sitting across from her. Late twenties, maybe thirty, she thought. Neat, professional dress. Shoes that were interesting enough to suggest personal style, but not so much as to give the senior partners the vapors. Dark hair worn fashionably short, just on the office-appropriate side of punk.

All of which mattered much less than a strong résumé to go with the person, which there was—NYU Law with honors, a Seventh Circuit clerkship, currently employed at a solid mundane firm. But still. Sometimes her department attracted unusual candidates. The last guy she'd interviewed had no red flags in his CV, and yet had shown up in "wizard's robes." Said robes had resembled nothing so much a purple satin quilted bathrobe. True wizards, he had explained into the silence of her shock, only wore robes, and also wore nothing but their robes. He offered her proof.

He had not gotten a callback.

Today's interviewee, thankfully, appeared much more

promising. "Ms. Douglas. Madison Prospero—nice to meet you. This says you're applying for our Special Projects Division."

"I've been in Trusts and Estates at Alexander, Harad, and Hill for a little over two years now. It was time to let the wheel turn," Harper said. The cadence of her voice changed as she spoke, overemphasizing the last four words.

"There really needs to be a better identifying phrase," Madison said, and laughed. "I always feel like I'm in the parody of a spy movie instead of interviewing someone. But since you knew it, I assume you're also able to demonstrate some ability."

There were three basic spells used for testing. Lighting a candle, levitating a small object—usually a pen in an interview setting—or casting a blooming flower illusion. Most mundanes who were willing to work very, very hard could learn to cast one of them adequately—something to do with will and focus rather than true magical ability. But the tests weren't there to screen out non-magical people—they were there for the same reason the awkward pass phrase was: to know it, you had to have been taught by a member of the Unseen World. It was proof you knew enough to belong, at least on the periphery.

"I can light a candle," Harper said, sitting straighter in her chair.

Madison placed a white votive on her desk and moved a stack of papers to the floor. "Nothing personal. But I had a candidate miss the candle and send an entire file up in flames once."

"Did they get the job?" Harper asked.

"We never finished the interview—it scared him so badly that he left. He does securities work for a fully mundane firm now. Nice guy.

"Are you ready?" Madison asked.

Harper nodded and stared at the candle. Drew breath in and out of her lungs. Placed her hands on the desk and carefully spoke the words of the spell.

The flame sparked once, twice, then caught. Harper reached up and pinched the bridge of her nose, pressing against the headache that was already beginning to bloom. "I promise, I'm a much better lawyer than I am magician."

"The test is just to confirm that you really do know what you're getting into and that I can be confident letting you get into it. Trust me, if I need magic, I'll call a magician. Normally, I'd ask you to come back for a second interview, but it's a Turning—basically a mandatory and sometimes fatal magical status competition—and so nothing is normal right now. Everyone is redoing wills and switching their financials, and there have been three divorce filings just this week, and I'm pretty sure two are going to stick. We're absolutely swamped with extra work. Your résumé is stellar, and you seem like someone I could work with, so the job is yours if you want it."

Harper clenched her fists in her lap. "I do. Very much."

"Great," Madison said. "It'll be boring at first—basically, the first thing I need is someone who can deal with all of the mundane stuff I've had to push to the side."

"I understand," Harper said. "I have to close out a couple of files, but I can be here on Monday."

"You're a lifesaver." Madison stood up from her desk and held out her hand. "Welcome to the Unseen World, Wellington & Ketchum branch."

"Thanks," Harper said, and shook.

It was still early, not yet noon, so instead of going home, Harper made two stops. The first, at a florist's, for a bunch of sunflowers. Then she took the train far past her usual stop, out to Woodlawn Cemetery, to Rose's grave. She laid the flowers against the headstone. "I wanted to tell you that I miss you and that I got one step closer today. A real step. I'll find him, Rose. I promise."

Laurent pushed open the heavy door of the Art Deco building on the Upper East Side. A white-gloved attendant waited inside. "Are you a member, sir?"

"I'm not, but I'm the guest of one. Laurent Beauchamps to see Miles Merlin." The atrium's ceiling was three stories high, an embossed pattern of geometric shapes decorating it. The walls were dark green, and all the fixtures were rubbed brass. Everything designed to imply prosperity and power by a decorator with no imagination. Or a decorator who realized their clients had no imagination.

The attendant scanned the screen of a tablet, then gave a short nod. "Very good, sir. Mr. Merlin has already arrived. Please follow me."

Laurent was mildly disappointed as he was led over the black-and-white marble chessboard floor of the Mages' Club. He'd thought a private club for magicians would be more interesting than a private club for Fortune 500 types. So far, the two seemed indistinguishable.

"Mr. Beauchamps. So pleased you were able to join me." Here, again, the impression was of a prosperous businessman, albeit one in a suit that showed more style than the surroundings. Merlin's tie and pocket square were almost the same shade of silver as the lion's mane of his hair.

"Thank you for the invitation. And please, call me Laurent." Laurent offered a smile and a polite handshake. He hadn't been surprised by the invitation. Sydney had said this was what would happen, this open door into the back halls of the Unseen World, and he owed it to Grey—and to himself—to take it. If Miles was the person who held the most power, it was important to take his measure in person.

"Then you must call me Miles. A drink?" Merlin settled back into the rich leather of his wing chair and signaled a discreetly waiting attendant.

"Bourbon, neat."

"We do allow smoking here as well, if you're a cigar man," Merlin said.

"I'm not, but don't let me stop you from indulging. This seems like an excellent establishment." This room, too, was high-ceilinged, dark wood and brass. Thick patterned carpets placed at precise intervals on the polished wood floor and leather-bound books shelved in the walls. Laurent wondered if they were actually read, or if they had been bought by the yard because the bindings matched the décor. He murmured a quick spell that would let him read the titles from this distance: *Springtime for Poets*; *Boll-Weevil Eradication: Best Practices*; *The Proceedings of the Congress of Vienna*. Definitely unread.

Only a few other men sat in the club, mostly at their own tables, everyone maintaining a respectful enough distance to allow the illusion of privacy. There were no women to be seen, not even as staff. Hard to tell if it was an officially segregated establishment, or if the lack was because—even now—so few women held Houses. The Unseen World could be as small-minded in its conception of what power looked like as the mundane one it shadowed, and Houses still almost always passed from father to son.

Those sons also seemed largely absent today. This was a room where "young" meant anyone under forty-five, and where the bulk of the men were sixty or older. Laurent saw only one other person he recognized from school. All of the besuited men were white.

He'd asked Grey once: "So if this is the Unseen *World*, why is it so small?"

"What?" Grey looked blank.

"I mean, it's just a bunch of people from the city. All of you live in the same few blocks, pretty much, and I'm the only new guy since I don't know how long. Aren't there other magicians anywhere?"

"Sure. But this is how we do things here, and since we're here, this is what matters."

It had been an unsatisfying answer at fifteen and had grown even more so in the years since.

"My home away from home," Merlin said. "I'd be delighted to put you up for membership at the end of the Turning."

"If I'm ranked high enough to be able to establish a House," Laurent said. "There's still a lot that could happen."

"Even this early, it seems an outcome worth betting on. That girl you hired is quite something. I'll bet she's fun to work with."

"Sydney is an extremely gifted magician, yes."

"Of course, of course. I didn't mean to imply anything untoward," Merlin said, in a voice that suggested that was precisely what he had meant to imply and that he was a bit surprised Laurent had caught on. "Obviously, you're to be commended for finding her. That's the kind of strategic thinking I like to see, knowing who to hire to get things done. We could use more of that sort of thinking among the Houses. Too many traditionalists who think there's only one way to go about things."

"I hadn't realized hiring a champion was so novel. House Prospero does the same. Other Houses as well," Laurent said.

"Well, yes, but no one knows where your girl came from." Merlin leaned forward just the slightest bit, in anticipation of being offered a secret. "There are so many rumors."

"No one knew where I came from either. It's worked out okay for me so far," Laurent said.

Merlin smiled and nodded, a politician performing approval. "That's certainly true. Though, really, where did you find her? Is she also an outsider? Did you know her in your mundane life?"

"She answered an online posting."

Merlin barked out a laugh. "No. Really?"

"As you pointed out, I'm new here. Not a traditionalist. I issued an open call, and I liked her response."

"Really. And you hired her just like that?" Merlin asked. "Without knowing anything else?"

"I didn't need to know anything else. What I did know is she did the most powerful piece of magic I've ever seen for her audition spell and didn't even break a sweat doing it."

"Well, I'm just sorry I didn't find her first. Another drink?"

Laurent looked deliberately at his still-full glass and stood up. "I'm afraid I have a social engagement this evening. But thank you again. I do feel this was a very useful meeting."

"Likewise. We should do this again—maybe even with Sydney next time. If she's going to be part of this world, I ought to get to know her." Merlin's practiced smile didn't quite reach his eyes.

"I'll be sure to pass that along." He didn't bother with the smile. Whatever this meeting had been, it hadn't been about making an alliance.

As he left the room, Laurent texted Sydney, to let her know of Merlin's interest.

His phone lit with her response: *Good.*

They met in a park, both in peacoats, scarves wrapped around their necks against the oncoming winter. Ian arrived first, then Lara joined him on the opposite side of the chessboard. "I'm glad you finally decided to say hello," she said. "I'd begun to think you'd turned your back on your entire family."

"You still live at the House. It's not like I was going to stop by for dinner."

"Yes, but as you see, it's quite possible for us to meet other places. I am your sister, Ian. I'm your family."

"Family," he said, "is precisely why I left."

"And it's why I stayed. Fine. Let's not have that fight again. Lovely to see you. So glad you're back. Now, are we going to play or just talk?"

"To play." Ian moved a white pawn to open the game, then hit the timer.

"Dad's convinced you'll be sorry. That you'll apologize and come back and be a Merlin again," Lara said. She was bird-boned and sharp-eyed, a raptor with short, Ziggy Stardust–red hair. She made her move and hit the timer. "Or, better still, that you'll feel bad enough about your—how did he put it? Oh, yes—your gross betrayal of House and family, that you'll make up for it by sabotaging Prospero from the inside, preferably during a challenge."

"I'm not sorry for leaving, and I don't plan to do any of that. I made a choice. One our House should have made a long time ago." Ian's hand hesitated over a pawn, then moved to a knight.

"He named me champion. Heir for now as well, though I suspect if you do as you're told he'll bump me right out of that. He told me all this over omelets. Ham and Gruyère. Quite good, really. Dad has his issues, but he can cook. I am, of course, honored by the opportunity to represent the House. Which is good, as I wasn't given a choice in the matter. Also, if you do that, I'll have you in check in three moves."

"I haven't beaten you at chess since you were nine, Lara. It's not like I think today's going to be my lucky day." He knocked over a rook. It shattered into words on the board.

Magic is failing.

Lara's hand paused, but only for a moment, before tipping a pawn.

Dad's fault?

And that was the crux of it: Because of their family's connection to the House of Shadows, because of Miles' connection in particular, it could be. It was House Merlin that maintained the spell. A knight cracked and dissolved.

Not sure. Ideas?

She moved her bishop. Another pawn disappeared from the board.

No. Will watch.

"Our House—" Ian began. "If this is Dad's fault, if that gets out, House Merlin will be unmade. Your magic could be stripped, Lara."

"I'm aware." No change in her expression.

"I'm just saying, maybe you ought to consider whether he's worth your loyalty." A castle melted into words.

Be careful.

"He's going to ask me to kill you, you know." Lara looked straight at Ian. "During a challenge. And I may well be better at chess, but I also know which one of us is better at magic. So maybe you ought to consider your loyalties, too."

Ian's glance flicked down to the chessboard, but no secret letters spelled out an alternate message.

"Because that is what he'll make it come down to, Ian: Betray your principles or murder your sister. You forget—Dad's even better at chess than I am." Lara reached out and tipped over his king.

The Unseen World watched Sydney this time. The hall where the challenge was taking place was packed with people, most of them not even bothering to pretend that they weren't staring at her or that it wasn't her name that fell in whispers and speculation from their lips. Sydney kept her head up, her eyes bright and fierce, as she walked past them.

They had begun to whisper the word "Shadow" when they saw her. Just whispers, just on the edge of things. As if there were something shameful—as if she were the one who ought to be ashamed. She had nothing to lose over what gossip claimed about her, particularly when it was so unimaginative as to think the truth was the worst possible thing, and she didn't care if people stared.

It was a nonmortal challenge, another magician from the fringes of Grey's and Laurent's crowd, Colin Blackwood, who had not been named heir of his House and who wanted the power that would have come with founding one on his own. Laurent recognized him from the Mages' Club and leaned over to tell Sydney. "Plus, he was the youngest guy there, outside of me, by, like, a generation."

Her eyes, already alert, sharpened. "That's interesting. Did Merlin talk to him while you were there?"

"No, but he was only a couple of tables over. Easy enough to overhear. Do you think they're allied somehow?" Laurent kept his voice low, close.

"Is Merlin here?" she asked.

Laurent, taller than Sydney, scanned the crowd. "Yes—in the corner on that side of the room, talking to Colin."

"Then yes, I do." Possibly nothing more than just the normal alliances of a Turning, but it was too coincidental to ignore.

The call for silence came, and the room was cleared. Sydney had chosen to cast second. She stood in the first row of the crowd so she could watch as Colin began his casting.

It had been listed as a duel of shadows spell—the casting magician would create a simulacrum of their own shadow, and then duel it. Magicians were allowed any choice of weapon, but swords were popular—fencing was dramatic to watch. The idea was that in a well-executed version of the spell the shadow would have its own agency, its own actions, and not simply act as a mirror to the magician, and it was easier to see that when the weapons required skill on both sides. So there was no reaction from the watching crowd when Colin conjured up a foil, or when he gave one to his shadow. No one showed concern when the action of the duel carried Colin and his shadow closer and closer.

Nothing appeared to be out of the expected until the shadow turned from Colin and stabbed his blade through Sydney's shoulder.

She reacted quickly—casting spells to destroy the simulacrum, wards to shield herself and those standing around her from Colin, who seemed determined to finish what his shadow had started.

Through the pain in her shoulder, she heard a few voices calling out, declaring the challenge forfeit, due to the aggression of the other magician, calls for him to be disqualified from the rest of the Turning. She did not hear anyone casting spells to help her, to ward her, to bind Colin, who was still lunging at her, weapon in hand. Most of the people in the crowd stood silent, waiting. Watching.

She spoke a word that sounded like glass shattering, and his sword snapped into pieces. Blood running down her arm from the blade still stuck in it, Sydney twisted shadows into ropes and tied Colin's hands and feet. Only then did she pull the blade from her shoulder. She held it in her hand, in the opening line of engagement, as if she, too, would duel.

Then Sydney cast her own version of the dueling shadows spell. The shadows of each of the magicians in the room separated from their originators and drew swords. "*En garde!*" she called. Then: "*Prêt. Allez!*"

Sydney saluted, and the fencing shadows ranged around the room—in between people, around chairs, blades flashing darkness, the sound of their engagement like slashing scissors. As they fell, the watching members of the Unseen World felt their shadows' wounds pass through them like phantoms. An ache in a shoulder, a tear in their chest. Some even looked down, pressed hands to their bodies to check, to be sure they weren't really hurt, weren't bleeding for someone else's magic.

The room grew quieter and quieter until Sydney stood at its center, alone and bloody. All of the dueling shadows but one had fallen. Her own. Then she raised the blade in her hand and stepped into a lunge, stabbing the remaining shadow through the heart, ending the spell. She snapped her blade, the one she had pulled from her shoulder, in two, dropped the pieces to the floor next to Colin, and left without looking back.

Sydney pressed the heel of her hand against the hole in her shoulder. She'd tried twice already to stop the bleeding, but her spells had proven only stopgaps. There was—she could feel it, grinding against bone—still a broken shred of shadow trapped inside. But she couldn't get a grip on it, and the consequences of her own magic use were manifesting. Shudders racked her like fever spasms, and there was far more blood soaking her shirt than she felt comfortable with. Laurent had texted to see how she was, if she needed anything. She had lied and told him she was fine. It was only a small lie. Probably.

She watched the numbers tick up in the elevator and hoped she hadn't misjudged.

Ian was waiting as the doors opened. He looked startled and then, carefully, blank.

"I triggered your wards on purpose," she said.

"I never would have thought otherwise." Ian slipped an arm around her, taking most of her weight as he helped her into his apartment. "You do know your blood should generally stay on the inside, yes?"

"Normally I keep it there, but there's a broken bit of magic that has other ideas. How's your healing?"

His hands tightened around her, then relaxed. "Good enough to help."

She eased herself down onto his bathroom tiles, closing her eyes in relief at their coolness. Ian's hands paused on the hem of her ruined shirt. "This will be easier if I can see the injury."

"Can you cut it away?" she asked. "I don't think I can move well enough to help you take it off."

He used the scissors from his medicine cabinet. Hissed out a breath when he saw her shoulder. Black mixed with red and wept from the wound like ichor. The surrounding skin was puffy and inflamed, the edges of the wound ragged. "This is likely to hurt."

"It hurts now." She spoke through gritted teeth.

"It's going to hurt worse." Ian set his fingertips in a star pattern against her shoulder by placing one hand on her chest and the other on her back, the wound at the center. Heat traced in outlines between them, constellations of magic blooming on her skin.

He pressed hard. Spoke words sharp as knives, and the inside of her shoulder went white, pain in starbursts at the edges of her vision. She pulled in a breath, blew it out.

A hiss and fizz, and shadows poured out of the wound, an infection clearing. The heat changed to warmth, star patterns knitting together pierced veins, torn skin.

"You might have a scar," Ian said, hands tender now, soothing.

"I've lots already. Another won't matter," Sydney said. She sat straighter, rolled her shoulder to check the range of motion. "Much better. Thank you."

"So was that the result of magic gone wrong, or was it on purpose?" Ian began cleaning up.

"Very much on purpose. He would have killed me if he could." She closed her eyes against the shaking that still rattled through her. She had more control over the aftereffects now, but the blowback from her own spells had settled into her bones, made her joints hot and hollow. "Still, nothing

I couldn't handle. Can I borrow a shirt to go home in?"

"Of course. You don't have to leave though, if things like a shower or rest seem like a better idea. I know they'd seem good to me, after an injury like that," Ian said.

There was a piece of her that wanted to say yes. That wanted the animal comfort of a hot shower, clean skin, and a warm body in a bed. There were things that mattered more than what she wanted, however. "Just the shirt, thanks. And thanks again for patching me up."

"I'd say anytime, but I'd rather not have to do that again." He handed her a shirt, soft and clean, from his laundry basket. "Take care of yourself, Sydney."

"Blood on the inside, got it." She pulled the T-shirt over her head and left.

The House of Shadows breathed, and Shara lived at the center of inhale and exhale. She felt its breath like her own. When its heart beat, its pulse beat in time with hers. She knew its thoughts as she knew her own, and she felt its pain. She was its avatar, and it was the seat of her power.

The House of Shadows was invisible, it was locked away, it was as forgotten as such a place could be.

She walked the halls, footsteps punctuating her thoughts. Only her footsteps. The other residents of the House of Shadows were shut away, and there were no visitors here.

There were never what might be called "visitors" here. Only those who came to pay their tolls, blank-faced and silent, or weeping and judgmental. As if it were Shara who benefited from their sacrifice, as if she had made their decisions for them. As if she were the one who benefited from what they—in the end—gave away willingly.

The House sighed, rearranged itself. The hallway shifted beneath her feet, turning away from the rooms where the sacrifices waited, dreaming nightmares, and toward the great doors. To the outside world. The night was very cool, the lake quiet.

The outside world. The Unseen World. They kept her hidden here, like a secret, like a shame. A thing unbearable to look at, when all she did was work to ease their pain.

She walked closer to the waves, stepping forward until her feet almost touched them. Until the spell that bound her there, to the House, hooked into her, holding her in place. Her lips curled back from her teeth, and she backed away from the shore.

Hidden away. Prevented from leaving. Made powerless. But she held the key to their power, and she intended to use it to claim power for herself. It was why she had sent Sydney out into the Unseen World. Shara had strategized and planned in the hopes that the end of the Turning would see Sydney in a position of influence in the Unseen World—perhaps even as the Head of a House. There were circumstances that would allow it, and she was pushing things as hard in the direction of those circumstances as she could. Magic would be stronger then, because of her. Shadows could grow healthy again.

And when Shadows was healthy enough, strong enough, Shara would order Sydney to break the spell that bound her to this island. Then she would take her rightful place in the Unseen World, a Head of House like all the others, her presence there a constant reminder of where their power came from, of what they all owed Shadows, owed her.

Shara walked back inside the doors.

The House, the magic, wasn't healthy now. Shadows was weak, and growing weaker. The balance was off; the spell had somehow gone wrong. It was unraveling. She couldn't tell why or how.

She couldn't stop it.

That was the pit in her stomach, the tremble in her step. There should be no magic here she couldn't control, not in this place that she wore like a skin.

Sometimes bargains needed to be remade, a name signed again and again on a contract.

The sacrifice might not have been hers to pay, but she knew—oh, she knew—what it took to pay it. She also knew, knew in her bones, what the Unseen World did not. That magic was only truly yours if it came from your own pain, your own sacrifice.

This magic was hers.

In a room at the heart of the House of Shadows, Shara took a knife. She cut into her hand. She cut until she reached that bone, and she inscribed her spell, letter after letter, word after word.

She cut and she cut and she offered her blood and pain as sacrifice—not to the Unseen World, but to Shadows. She cut, and she bled, and each was a prayer.

When Shadows' doors had opened, Grace had been close enough to smell the cold of the air outside, the flat mineral quality of it, almost buried beneath the watery scent of the reservoir. Not quite close enough to see the waves that lapped against the shore, not quite certain enough to push her way through the doors and into the outside. Into freedom.

She stepped back, sinking herself further into the shadows, and watched.

Each cut Shara had made into her own skin and bone had drawn itself across Grace's arms, an echo of her own scars. An echo of wounds that she had seen made on limbs so small it seemed impossible that there was enough space for the glyphs to be carved, on bodies that had not lived long enough for the bleeding to stop and for scars to form.

Grace fisted her hands, then opened them, stretching her fingers as far as she could, releasing the ache of the magic pooled there.

She had tried, once, in her early days in Shadows, to offer comfort to the other sacrifices. A child with a soft fluff of white hair, like a dandelion, that she had picked up, held, crooned to through her own pain and terror. Everything that had been done to her would have been easier to endure, if she just could have helped someone else.

She had felt the House's glee as Shara took the child from her arms.

Memories were merciful sometimes, and so she remembered that white hair and the red of her blood smeared on the baby's skin from where her hands had held it, and not the next part. Not that. Not while she was awake, at least.

Grace had never offered comfort again.

But she bore witness: Someone should watch what it was the House did. And the House let her, because watching hurt. And she bore witness now, because Shara's actions meant the House was hurt, and because Grace had, for just a moment, smelled the night beyond the doors. There was winter in the air.

Frost silvered over Central Park, and Laurent's and Grey's breath puffed into the air as they ran. "Is it just me, or is it getting cold earlier this year?" Laurent asked.

"We'll have to start meeting at the gym soon." Grey sounded excited. Laurent was . . . not. Running on a grey piece of plastic that went nowhere while facing an infinite number of wall-screen televisions that all showed the same cable news channel was his idea of a level of hell in a modern take on the *Inferno*.

They passed another quarter mile in silence. Then Grey said, “So how was your meeting with Merlin?”

“Fine. Sort of anticlimactic. Like, I was expecting the Mages’ Club to feel, more, I don’t know, magical. Instead, it was just boring and out of touch. The whole thing felt like a college interview.”

“So no big offer of alliance or anything like that?”

“Not even close. I’m glad—I’d rather make my own choices. Like you always say, if tradition holds us back, we need to think outside of it.” They came to a stop, and Laurent bent down to fix a loose shoelace.

“We should talk about that sometime,” Grey said. “There’s all sorts of things that could be done, ways to strengthen magic, to make the Unseen World more powerful, that people aren’t even thinking of yet.”

“We’re the future, right?” Laurent said. “That’s the point of the Turning. Clean out what isn’t working, bring in what could. Speaking of, when’s your next duel?”

“Two days from now,” Grey said.

“Why don’t you stop by after? We should discuss our own strategy. We don’t need Merlin in order to make an alliance.”

“Exactly,” Grey said. “I’ll text you later, set it up.”

Laurent waved goodbye, and Grey headed for the subway.

After the debacle with Miranda, he hadn't told anyone how he supplemented his power. Maybe it was time. It wasn't like Laurent had any great attachment to Unseen World traditions, and he might be able to see the potential in what Grey was doing. He'd decide after the next challenge.

Outside the Mages' Club, Miles waved off his car and driver and walked home in the wind-tossed night. The air smelled like the promise of snow, and the damp soaked into his joints.

They ached.

It had been that sensation years ago—waking up with pain in his joints, the reminder of his own mortality sitting on him like a smog—that had made him realize what was happening. The small spells that he'd come to think of as background noise, the ones he used constantly, that should have kept him from feeling the minor aches and pains of age, were failing. And there was only one reason for such basic spells to fail: He was losing his magic.

Unacceptable, of course. No one could hold a House if they didn't have magic.

Once he had realized what was happening, he had taken steps, made changes. So much magic came out of Shadows, and the Angel of the Waters was the perfect conduit. It hadn't taken that much to set some aside. To collect the magic and store it against need. His need.

But lately he could feel the signs again in his body, in his magic. He knew them. The slowness, the aches, the tremors, all returning. It seemed that what he had thought of as a permanent solution was merely a stopgap.

There had been a failure of magic today. Not in a duel. And so it was impossible to comfort himself with the idea that magic had halted in its path because of the words of a spell spoken out of order, or a magician's failure of nerve in a moment of pressure. It had been a dishwashing spell, at the Mages' Club. The kind of spell that had been cast thousands of times, a spell that barely even required thinking about. Instead of clean glassware, there was a shattered heap of useless fragments, still stained.

Magic was breaking.

The wind picked up, tossing plastic bags and fallen leaves with abandon. The temperature dropped, and rain—hard, angry rain, just on this side of ice—spat from the sky.

Here, where no one could see, where no one would know, Miles gestured, his hand hidden in his coat pocket. He spoke a word under his breath, the will mattering more than the sound.

The rain parted, and fell around him.

He exhaled. He had enough magic. Today, he still had enough.

But.

His joints ached.

CHAPTER SEVEN

Grey leaned against the rough brick wall of the building and pulled his illusions closer to his body. The thing that mattered right now, more than the jagged press of brick into his side, more than the rot rising from the uncollected trash bags on the corner, more than the thousand potential distractions and annoyances sharing the sidewalk with him, was that no one notice how badly he was hurt, especially not here in the mundane world. Someone actually seeing his wounds would mean things like doctors and hospitals and explanations that wouldn't be believed anyway. Better to stay hidden, even if being hidden made things like walking more difficult.

The duel had gone poorly. No. The duel had been a fucking mess. It was the heir to House Morgan. Violet, her name was. Or Daisy. Something like that. All the girls in that House were named after flowers. He hadn't thought anyone there knew anything about his relationship with Rose, but someone must have suspected because what should have been a fairly easy challenge had turned bloody. Marigold or Peony or whatever had wrapped him in a Briar Rose illusion—a forest of thorns he'd had to fight his way out of. He'd been able to do it, but they'd sunk in and cut deeply before he'd finally broken free.

Plus, the last girl hadn't had as much magic in her bones as he had thought, and so he'd gone into the challenge weak. Hadn't had enough power to heal himself after casting his spell, so he had forgone healing and done his best to hide the weakness, the wounds, as much as he could so no one would know how bad it was.

He took another step and gritted his teeth against the pain. He pressed his hands harder against the wounds in his abdomen, winced as blood flowed over them, as he felt the soft edges of opened skin. He thought maybe the bleeding was slowing but didn't want to look back to see if there was a trail of blood visible behind him—sometimes looking too closely at an illusion could be enough to break it.

Two blocks away from Laurent's building. He could get there. He pushed off the wall, felt his legs threaten to go out from under him. Forced them straight and steady. Steadyish.

He would need to replenish his stores of magic. He would need to do that soon. He'd wait to tell Laurent about where he was getting it—he couldn't afford to share this time.

Grey stumbled through the sidewalk crowds like a drunk, arms wrapped tight around his abdomen, as if that might keep the blood in. He kept his gaze down, locked on his feet, one in front of the other. He was shaking when he walked into Laurent's lobby, but he hadn't fallen.

"I'm afraid you can't be here," the doorman said, moving toward Grey as if to herd him back onto the sidewalk.

Perfect. Some idiot new guy. The day just kept getting better. "I'm Grey Prospero. I'm on Laurent Beauchamps' approved list."

"I'm quite sure you're not." The doorman puffed himself up, indignant.

"Send me up." Grey spent energy he didn't have charming the doorman into calling the elevator for him, rather than wasting time fighting with the man. He sagged against the elevator's walls and let himself fall, hard, against Laurent's door.

Laurent heard the thud. Looked through the peephole, then yanked the door open. "Shit. Shit. Grey, wake up."

Grey's eyes rolled open as Laurent pulled him in the door. "Challenge. Hurt. Don't tell."

"Yeah, I can see that you're hurt. The blood everywhere was my first clue. What do you mean, don't tell? How did no one notice this?"

"Illusion." He coughed and blood spattered his mouth.

"You cast an illusion to—you know what, later." Laurent pulled back the other man's shirt. Swallowed hard. It looked like Grey had been flogged with a whip made of razor blades. "Okay. That's . . . that's not so bad. I can help. But I think you should let me call someone. This is maybe a little beyond the healing magic we were taught in school."

Grey shook his head, regretting the movement even as he made it. "No calls. They'll know I'm hurt."

"Yes. And they'll fix you. Better than I can." He spoke slowly and clearly, as much to calm himself as in the fading hope of making Grey see his point. He knew the basics, of course, but the mess of blood and skin was a far cry from the precise cuts and supervised spells he'd been taught.

"No. They'll tell."

"Tell who? Don't be an idiot." Laurent's hands were sticky as he tried to clear away the blood, to see the extent of the damage.

"The next House that challenges me."

"Sydney, then. At least let me call her."

Grey reached up, wincing, his hand leaving a bloody print on Laurent's arm. "She'll know. She'll remember. If you challenge me."

"I won't."

"Said it wasn't as bad as it looked." His voice fading, the words half-whispered.

"I fucking lied, you idiot." Arguing wouldn't help, wouldn't stop the blood washing over his hands in time with Grey's increasingly erratic pulse. He wasn't sure they had time to wait for someone to get there. Laurent breathed in and out, regulating the flow of air in his lungs, slowing his own heartbeat from galloped panic into something that approximated stability. He wished very specifically and succinctly not to fuck this up, hoping his affinity for luck would cancel out his lack of practice with major healing magic. Then he spoke the words that would slow blood leaking, would draw severed veins back together, would drive out infection. He bent his fingers into shapes that would have hurt if he'd been thinking of anything other than keeping his hands steady, and bit by bit, he healed his best friend.

Sweat stung his eyes and Laurent was shaking like a man gripped by fever when he had finished, but Grey's skin was knit, the bleeding had stopped, and his eyes were clear.

"Did you," Laurent asked, his voice a rasp, "at least win your challenge?"

"After all that," Grey said as he sat up from the floor, "I better have."

Later. After Laurent cleaned the blood from the floor of his hallway, after he washed the red handprint that ended in a smear from his door, while trying very hard not to think that it was Grey's blood he was washing away, Grey's blood on the clothing he was changing out of, that the blood had gotten there because of magic, and he was so angry at the very idea of magic at that moment that he didn't even want to use basic spells to clean up, and so here he was, scrubbing like a mundane.

After his apartment almost looked normal again, and not like someone had performed surgery in his front hall. After the blood was gone from everywhere except his memory. After he washed his hands one more time.

After things were clean, he could start thinking about what had happened. Maybe then he could look at it straight on.

He had known the Unseen World could be harsh, knew the Turning carried risks, potentially fatal ones. But these people seemed to treat death like it was a fencing match. There were weapons, sure, but everyone would salute and go home after the ritual was completed. He'd watched it happen, when Sydney had been stabbed at her last challenge and then walked out of the room as if it were a paper cut. He'd let himself get swept up in that—let himself see the idea of death as a possibility, but one they would all shake off at the end.

It wasn't. It wasn't that at all.

He washed his hands again.

After the takeout Laurent had ordered arrived—because this was a thing he could do; he could order warm styrofoam containers of hamburgers cooked rare and covered in mushrooms and caramelized onions, thin French fries with some sort of truffle sauce, and he had to do something. After he had poured them both glasses of whiskey, Laurent said, "You could have died."

"It wasn't a mortal challenge. It just got a little out of hand."

Grey shrugged and kept eating. "Man, I'm starving."

"A little out of hand." Laurent put his burger down, half-eaten. "Speaking of hands, I'm pretty sure I had mine on your small intestine. That seems like more than a little."

Grey drank. "These things happen. I'm fine. It's no big deal."

Laurent stared. "What do you mean, it's no big deal? This was a nonmortal challenge. I thought there were rules. Precautions. Fucking safety measures, I don't know."

"Look, maybe you didn't understand what you were getting into. Maybe you still don't—it's not like you're the one taking any risks out there. But the Turning isn't about precautions and safety measures. It's about power, and about making sure you're strong enough to claim it."

Laurent set his glass down on the marble countertop. A big magic duel. Competition for power. He loved those things. Thrived on them—they had bought this apartment, his parents' house. Every material comfort he wanted. He had thought he would love the Turning as well. "Just because Sydney's in danger and not me doesn't mean I think this is a joke, Grey. I know what the Turning is. I'm just trying to decide if I still think it's worth it."

"If it's worth it? *Worth* it? Establishing a House means the difference between having actual power in this world and being nothing. Nothing else is worth as much. If you weren't so fucking lucky, you'd get that."

"Lucky," Laurent said.

"That is what you're best at, right? Luck?" Grey shrugged. "Some of us have to work."

"Right. Well, I'm glad we've cleared that up," Laurent said.

Grey pushed his plate away. "Look, I'm sorry. Pain's making me say things I shouldn't. But this might be my only chance to get back into the Unseen World, to really be a part of it again. And that matters to me.

"I hate the way these people look at me now, like I'm nothing now that I'm not standing behind Miranda's skirts. Like they're wondering if maybe I don't belong here. I was born in this world—I was the heir to a House! No one belongs here more than I do, and I'm sick of being looked at like an object of pity. This is how I change that."

Grey had never told him why Miranda had disinherited him—he said he had agreed to be bound to secrecy. At the time it had happened, Laurent had understood Grey's decision not to fight his disinheritance. He would have had to prove that Miranda was incompetent to lead Prospero in order to overturn it, a thing that seemed impossible. But he wondered now whether it would have cleaned some of the poison from his wound if Grey had fought back then. "Sure. I get it. Just remember I'm on your side in this."

"As much as you can be, anyway."

Laurent thought back to his conversation with Sydney,

when he had very carefully laid out the circumstances under which Grey could be challenged, and said nothing else.

A diner this time, early enough that pieces of the sky were still sunrise pink. Even so, Sydney had gotten there before Madison and was halfway through a plate of French toast drowned in syrup when the other woman slid into the banquette across from her.

"So, how's your shoulder—wait, seriously, that's what you're eating? Are you secretly twelve?"

"I like syrup," Sydney said. "And from the first part of your question, I gather you heard about the Blackwood challenge. It's fine—all healed. Have you heard anything about what will happen to Colin?"

"Happen?" Madison asked, and flagged down a passing server for coffee.

"For altering the duel. Trying to make it fatal. Whatever he did."

Understanding crossed Madison's face. "Sydney, nothing will happen."

Sydney set her fork down. "He was trying to kill me. In a nonmortal challenge. Which breaks the rules that were sent out at the beginning of this. Rules set by the Unseen World. And nothing will happen."

"Right. Okay. I forget that you haven't been through one of

these before, and Laurent is new, too, and so no one has told you how things work."

"I'm not going to like this, am I?" Sydney said.

"Nope. You're not. First of all, it was during a sanctioned challenge. There is a lot of leeway over what's considered proper behavior in the course of one, and people don't like to interfere. Fortune's Wheel, blah blah blah. And the thing is, you were the better magician, and so you're fine. His loss is considered punishment enough—he's out of the Turning now."

Sydney poured more coffee. "And second?"

"Special Projects doesn't have a criminal division."

Sydney's face went blank.

Madison sighed. "What I mean is, even under normal circumstances, the Unseen World doesn't have a criminal justice system. What they have is a bunch of people with extraordinary power who take matters into their own hands. When the Unseen World decides that someone has crossed a line, there's either social and economic sanctions—disinheritance being a popular one—or there's the equivalent of vigilante justice. And this is a Turning, which means it's not normal circumstances; it's an entire event presaged on the ideas of upheaval and change. The fact that Colin is out of the Turning is enough. And if it's decided that it isn't, I wouldn't be surprised to hear that he has an accident in the next week or two. But there won't be any formal consequences. Now or later."

Sydney stabbed at her French toast. "These people."

Madison held up her hands. "No argument. But happy as I'd be to spend the morning talking about how they all suck, I've got to run soon if I don't want to be late to the office, so maybe I should answer the question you asked me here to talk about."

"Yeah, sorry."

"No problem. So, you asked if House Prospero was doing anything out of the ordinary. Which, turns out, it is. Miranda has our office running two different financial scenarios—one where she shifts her investment portfolio very heavily into only Unseen World concerns, and the other where almost every investment is mundane.

"Now, that could be just caution or curiosity on her part, and I'm going to check Prospero's files to see what the House has done in past Turnings, but it's definitely odd."

"You're going to need to explain why this is out of the ordinary. Aren't there usually financial rearrangements during a Turning?" Sydney asked, pouring more syrup over her plate.

Madison shuddered. "You're doing that just to make my teeth hurt. I can tell. And yes—participation in the Turning tends to be an expensive endeavor, even if you're not paying the big bucks for a champion. Plus, business alliances tend to change when magical ones do, so the fact that she's running scenarios makes sense.

"But the thing that's odd is the potential removal of her assets from Unseen World holdings altogether. That's something I'd expect to see if it looked like the House were in danger of being unmade. Which—did you hear? House Greenfield was."

Sydney set her fork down. "What did they do that was bad enough?"

"Apparently, they tried to re-create your audition spell as part of a challenge. Turns out it's harder to drive a flying bus than people think, and seven mundanes wound up in the hospital, all talking about how the crash felt just like the bus falling out of the air."

"So that's enough to unmake a House, but Colin can . . . You know what, never mind," Sydney said. "Anyway, Prospero?"

Madison nodded. "Prospero is currently ranked second. There's no imminent danger of it being unmade as a result of performance, and Miranda's way too careful to allow Ian to pull the kind of shit that could cause exposure to the mundane world, not to mention he's too good. So shifting assets to fully mundane concerns makes no sense. I'm looking into it."

"I think maybe I can help with that. What if it's not just House Prospero that's in danger," Sydney said. "What if it's the entire Unseen World?"

"What?" Madison asked, her voice knife-sharp.

"If something's wrong with magic. Which, there maybe is.

Actually, almost certainly there is—I'm just not sure precisely what or how bad yet. But it's obviously bad enough that people are noticing. How much have you heard about the failures of magic?"

"Are there failures beyond what happened with Ian's duel with—who was it—Hawkins?"

"Yes. Verenice said normal spells are starting to go haywire, too. There was a mess at the Mages' Club the other day. So something is for sure going on. And if Miranda thinks the entire Unseen World is in danger of falling apart—"

"—then switching her investment portfolio to mundane concerns makes perfect sense. Shit, goddamn, Sydney."

"Exactly," Sydney said.

"Okay, now I really have to go."

"Thanks, Madison."

"Not a problem." She swiped a strip of bacon through the lake of syrup on Sydney's plate, and left.

A quiet chime interrupted Miranda at her desk. She glanced up at her mirror.

Miles Merlin is at the door. The words scrolled in perfect cursive, a precise replica of her own handwriting.

"Miles . . ." she started. Miranda sat back, steepling her fingers, then got up. He'd have an agenda, and he wouldn't mean it to be helpful, but it was always possible she could glean something useful from whatever rumors he'd come to spread. "I'll see him in myself."

She smiled as she opened the door. "Miles! What a surprise!"

"Miranda." He looked around the entry, taking in the sweeping staircase, the beeswax-polished wood and soft-white candles on tables and in sconces. Mirrors reflected white flowers and Morris-print wallpaper. "I always forget how traditional this House is."

"I've never been as enamored of technology as you are, Miles. But I'm sure you didn't come here to discuss interior decorating." She led him down a hall lined with marble sculptures of Greek goddesses in recessed niches and into a sitting room.

"No, I came because I wasn't sure if you would have heard about Grey's most recent challenge." He sat across from her.

Miranda sat on the edge of a chair, back straight, knees together, feet discretely tucked, as poised as a duchess. "Can I offer you something? Coffee, tea, water? The House would be happy to put something together for you."

"Oh, did you have that automated?" He looked around, interested enough to be distracted from what he had come there to say.

"No, that's always been done through the House's magic. I see no reason to change it, not with the spell working as well as it does." And that was a dig, if a polite one. The stronger Houses, the ones with a close bond to their Heads, could do such magic. House Merlin, notoriously, could not. She suspected it was part of why Miles spent so much time at his club, why he'd installed enough technology to make his House look like the set of a sci-fi movie, that the expensive shine was a distraction that kept people from wondering about the real reason that the oldest House didn't run on magic.

"Nothing for me. This isn't a social call. Did you hear about Grey?" Awkward now, and impatient because of it.

"I was just about to get more tea. Are you certain you don't want any?" Miranda asked, cuttingly polite.

"Really, no."

"A pot of tea please, Lady Grey." She didn't want it, not really, but she did want to keep Miles off-balance.

Of course.

The drink followed on the mirror's chime and agreement, the scent of lavender and bergamot steaming into the air.

"Thank you for being patient," Miranda said. "As you may have gathered, since you've been through something similar recently, the disinheritance left things strained between us. Grey and I don't talk; nor are we part of each other's lives. As you might infer from that, I haven't paid particular attention to his progress through the Turning."

"It was a duel with House Morgan." Merlin's eyes watched

her face like the hawk he shared a name with. "Something went, well, not exactly wrong. Let's say overenthusiastic. It was a Briar Rose spell. I don't think I've ever seen such thorns. It was almost as if they wanted to hurt him."

Miranda kept her face carefully blank. Just because she was magically prevented from speaking about the circumstances of Grey's disinheritance didn't mean they were gone from her mind.

She knew, too, that Rose Morgan had been murdered a year after, in circumstances that were close enough to those that had triggered that disinheritance to chill her heart.

She had not asked. She would never ask.

"I know you're very busy, Miles, so while I certainly appreciate you taking the time out of your schedule to tell me this in person, I'm not sure why you felt that I needed to know—he did survive, or I would have heard that before now." That same note of polite curiosity and nothing more.

"Yes, yes, he survived—that challenge was even decided in his favor. But he was, though he tried to hide it, quite hurt. And the casting magician was the older sister of the girl from that House who was killed. Grey dated her around that time, I believe—or am I remembering incorrectly?" He adjusted his cuffs.

And now the reason for the visit was clear. Merlin, with his fingers full of threads, was shaking his spider's web and hoping to catch her in it. "Again, Miles, Grey is not a part of my life; nor am I a part of his. That's been the case for years now. I don't pay attention to whom he has had relationships with. I'm not sure what else you expect me to say."

Merlin held his silence for a moment. Two. Then he shook his head. "Perhaps I misestimated the power of a mother's concern. No matter—I'll see myself out."

"I wouldn't dream of it. I'll walk with you," Miranda said, and led him out of her House.

After he had gone, she stood, her hand on the back of the door that would no longer open to her son and very carefully cleared her mind of the reason why.

There are some things that cannot bear looking at.

Harper had asked some of the other women at work where to find the bar. She knew there would be one, because this was New York and somewhere in this city there was a bar that catered to every possible clientele. She had simpered and giggled and made jokes about wanting to find a guy with a little magic in his wand until she was sure they all thought she was some sort of magician groupie, but they had told her where to go. "Houdini's Elephant. It's next door to a magic shop."

She had poured herself into a push-up bra and minidress, slicked her lips with gloss, and had gotten to the bar early enough to get a seat at the corner, where she could see the other people there without being obvious.

She'd known she was in the sort of place she was looking for when she'd had to prove she could light a candle to get in. She was currently treating the resulting headache with an excellent vodka gimlet, and watching the crowd.

It was, probably, a stupid idea to put herself out there as bait. There were at least five good reasons she could think of not to, not the least of which being she could wind up dead. But she'd heard rumors—women being killed, in a way that made her think of how Rose had been killed. Details that matched the parts of the police file she wasn't supposed to have seen, full of horrors.

And it had been unexpectedly hard, working for Wellington & Ketchum, knowing that she was so close, almost there, and yet not really any more likely to find out who had killed Rose than before. So she'd drowned out the voices that knew precisely how stupid this was because being smart about it was too frustrating.

She waited and watched and the evening dragged on, and her glass got closer to empty, and Harper felt less and less like she was going to find anyone useful in this bar. There weren't a lot of people there, and those who were seemed . . . obvious. Magic so aggressively over-the-top that it looked fake. She wondered if it was, and leaned across to the bartender. "That guy has lit his own hair on fire three times now."

The bartender rolled her eyes. "He's in here all the time. The hair thing is his one party trick. It usually comes complete with a joke about how hot he is. Three's a slow night for him. He'll be fine."

Drunken antics with the addition of magic really weren't any more entertaining than normal drunken antics. Harper contemplated ordering another drink but decided against it. They were slammed at the office, and she was hoping that if she proved herself on the mundane stuff quickly, Madison would let her work on files directly related to magic. "I'm calling it a night," Harper said.

"Be careful. There's women who have been hassled—maybe even worse—after leaving here. Take a cab, maybe."

"What do you mean, worse?" Harper asked.

"Worse like murdered. Finger bones removed." She shuddered.

"Finger bones?" The dread of recognition, a lump in her center that she had to breathe around. Rose's hands had been cut into, like someone wanted to remove her bones.

"Like they were killed for their magic. Which means this creep is stalking magicians. So like I said, be careful. Take a cab."

Harper added an extra twenty to her tip, grateful for the warning. "Thanks. You, too."

She stood outside, letting the cold air wash over her, letting it clear the noise and closeness of the bar from her mind, and thought about walking home. She wasn't that far. But then she thought about how swollen her feet were in her shoes and the likeliness of being able to run in them. "You aren't actually a superhero," she reminded herself, and hailed a cab.

Grey left Colin Blackwood's party early and in a bad mood. He'd had to stand there and listen as Colin—Colin, of all people, who hadn't even made it past his second challenge, who'd been humiliated by that chick Laurent had hired—had bragged about how he was in Miles Merlin's inner circle, how he'd been promised a place in House Merlin at the end of the Turning.

"You should talk to him, Grey. I heard your last challenge was rough." All artificial sympathy.

"Not that rough—I won."

"Still. Merlin can help. I'll put in a good word for you." Colin smiled, and Grey wanted to punch him in his perfect teeth.

He'd mumbled something half-polite and left.

"I couldn't wait to get out of there, either." She was curvy and dark-haired, and Grey was sure he knew her. He racked his brains, and knew it was his lucky night after all when they spit out a name.

"Hayley? Hayley Dee?"

"Wow, I didn't think you'd remember me. I had such a crush on you in high school." She smiled, stepped closer. He could see the flush of alcohol in her face, her unsteadiness on her feet. She had been, he remembered, a couple of years behind him in school. Barely any magic.

Perfect.

"I always remember the cute girls. Want to go grab a decent drink somewhere?" he asked.

"I'd like that," she said.

He needed more magic, and she had just enough. He made sure they never got to the bar.

CHAPTER EIGHT

When the next failure of magic occurred, it was extremely public and impossible to mistake for anything else.

It happened in front of nearly the entire Unseen World. Another party, one to mark an unspoken change in the first part of the Turning and to celebrate the success of everyone still competing. A subtle signal that the real challenges—not just those about settling petty grievances and taking revenge for decade-old gossip—were about to begin. The duels weren't mortal yet, but they were serious now.

The evening was meant to be a civilized, elegant occasion. The duel was even being fought with a civilized choice of magic: illusion. Perfect accompaniment to champagne bubbling in graceful coupes and rich food arranged like sculptures on plates the precise warm cream shade of the beeswax candles that decorated the tables.

Sydney had been right that Laurent would be invited to all the parties after her performance at the first duel. It seemed increasingly likely that the end of the Turning would see the establishment of House Beauchamps, and better to get to know him now, so as to have his ear and his friendship when he came into power. So that he might, perhaps, even feel indebted to those who were welcoming when he was still an outsider. Laurent knew exactly how much those welcomes meant, and so he turned down most of the invitations, but as he was that evening's challenger, he was there, tall and elegant in his tuxedo.

She watched, grey eyes keen, as Heads of Houses and their heirs introduced themselves to Laurent, invited him to dance, leaned close and whispered to him as they stood around the small, high-topped tables that ringed the room. Miles Merlin, she noted, had not gone over to pay court. He was, instead, watching her. That was fine. She had come to be watched. She waved, pleased when Merlin ostentatiously ignored her.

She felt Ian at her elbow before she heard his voice. "You're looking well."

"Blood on the inside this time, and look—not even a scar." Her dress, a severe plunge of black held by the thinnest of straps paid proof to her words.

"Better than well." Ian smiled. "And what splendid activity do you plan to put them through tonight? Will you convince the gilded Heads of all the Houses that they should cluck like chickens or sing opera?"

"Not in the least," Sydney said. "I think I'd like to see an opera someday, and the quality of the arias likely to come out of this crowd would probably end that desire. Besides, tonight's challenge is illusion."

"Will you play our nightmares over the walls like movies?"

"It's not a bad idea. If I do, I promise to buy you popcorn first."

"And sit with me and hold my hand during the scary bits?" He stepped close enough that she could feel the warmth of his skin.

"They'll all be scary bits. That's the point of nightmares."

He stepped closer, leaned in as if he might whisper some secret, but was interrupted by the announcement of the challenge. Sydney sliced through the crowd, to stand at Laurent's side. The representative of the challenged House was announced, and the casting began.

It was a Four Seasons illusion. No points for originality, but they wouldn't be needed if it was well done. It was a complicated, exhausting spell that required a great deal of control to both bring the illusion fully into being and to maintain the subtleties of the transitions from one season to the next. A good choice. Sydney watched the woman's hands as they bent and folded into the necessary shapes. She was casting well—her fingers graceful even in the extreme positions required, bending and stretching with ease.

As was tradition, the illusion began with spring—grass and

trees and flowers slowly growing up out of the polished wood of the floor. Petals opening, leaves unfurling, the air ripe with the scent of growing things. It was beautifully done, and with an immense amount of power—pieces of the illusion filled the entire room and were as rich and detailed at its far end as they were near to the woman holding the spell. A second set of trees grew from walls and tables. The air grew warmer, richer, greener. It felt almost electric—the first edges of an oncoming storm.

Sydney went string-tight. "Something's wrong."

"Are you sure?" Laurent asked.

She pushed him. "Yes. Go. Get out. Now."

"It's rude to—"

"Better rude than dead." She didn't wait for him to respond, but set off across the floor in the direction of the casting magician.

Spring did not peak and shimmer into the haze of summer's glory. Instead, physical vines burst into the room, crawled through the floor, grabbed at tables, at chairs, at the feet of the watching magicians, the illusion searching for any way to further anchor itself into reality. Trees grew, faster and faster, and the rumble of thunder rattled the windows. The green scent of the air no longer pleasant, but choking.

It wasn't an absence of magic but a surfeit, extra power, pulled from somewhere, avalanching into solidity.

Sydney raised her voice to be heard over the crowd, over the roar of the magic. "Beauchamps forfeits the challenge in the expectation it will be ruled a failure of magic and strongly recommends you all leave before the forest takes the room."

No one moved.

Branches curled from the ceiling. Floorboards flew through the crowd. A tree exploded up, driving straight through a thin man in a tuxedo, killing him before he could even gasp in shock.

People moved then.

The air was suffocatingly humid. Wind howled. The growth of the forest was so rapid it could be heard over the chaos of people running for the doors.

Sydney continued to fight against the fleeing crowd, toward the casting magician. Ian's hand closed over her arm. "Is there a reason you aren't taking your own advice?"

"Look at her." She yanked her arm out of his hand.

The casting magician had been at the center of the spell, and the forest was intent on claiming her as its own. A tree, some gnarled, twisting thing, was growing through her—branches emerging in horrible, wet red.

There was a high-pitched keen, constant, streaming from the woman's open mouth.

"She's still alive," Ian said, horror in his voice.

"The magic will keep her that way. It will anchor itself in

her. Use her as a vessel and keep her in pain and undying. No one deserves that. If I break the spell, I can help her." Sydney stepped forward, put her left hand on the woman's heart, her right hand on the tree.

"Sydney, no!"

There was a great, sharp *crack*, and then silence.

The magic had been ended.

She breathed in.

Sydney was, all at once, an entire forest. She was root and leaf, dirt and sky. Green and spring were blood in her veins, air in her lungs.

She was, between one heartbeat and the next, all of magic. The entire universe worth, rendered into a pinpoint hurricane. It moved through the air, currents and patterns, a sequence suddenly readable. It sang through her bones and reordered the stars. She reached out her hand and touched its heart.

It ran through her like electricity. She pulled it all into herself. She held it. She became.

She breathed out.

Ian staggered against the vacuum left by the vanished magic and looked around the room. The illusion had fallen. The living branches and trees were there, but they were now stone and grey, no longer alive. The only thing moving were flames from where a candelabra had been knocked over, licking at a tablecloth. He upended a pitcher of water, extinguishing them.

The room was quiet. No roar of wind, no howl of magic. Sydney had not only interrupted the spell, she had stopped it cold.

Sydney.

The magic. It hadn't simply disappeared. It had gone somewhere. He looked to the center of the room, where the spell had started. Where the body of a woman with a tree growing from her heart was also stone, a cold statue.

Sydney was so still she looked like a statue herself. He wasn't even sure she was breathing. The air surrounding her shimmered like the haze of heat that rose from asphalt in the desert.

"How are you not dead?" he asked.

She turned, and her eyes were as green as the heart of the forest. She saw his expression, and after a pause, her eyes shaded back to grey. "I'm a Shadow. I have some experience in siphoning power."

Too much now to think about the fact that she had said out loud what he had suspected, that her presence here was a nearly impossible thing. The awe of that—the potential *usefulness* of her origins—paled next to tonight's cascade of wonders. "This power. All of this power. That entire spell." Ian gestured to the surrounding room, to the stone forest that had so recently been green and growing. "You hold it."

Sydney nodded. She stretched out her hands, shaking them loose, and sparks flew from her fingers. She watched them fall through the air, a smile curling the edges of her mouth.

Fear pooled at the base of his skull. He wasn't sure if he wanted to run or to kneel at her feet.

"You *hold* it." It shouldn't have been possible—it would be like drinking an ocean, like wearing a storm. He thought momentarily about casting a measurement spell, curious as to how much magic had actually been in the room, then realized it was possible he'd be dead before he spoke the second word if she misinterpreted his intent.

There were still flecks of green, floating like fireflies, in her pupils.

"How are you feeling?" he asked, far more casually than he felt.

"A bit strange. Like there is a river running beneath my skin. I think my heart may have stopped beating for a bit, too." Her voice sounded detached from her body. "That's fine, though. I didn't need it at the time."

"Well, if that's all." Maybe if he pretended like this was normal, like she hadn't just become something else right in front of him, things would begin to make sense. He offered her an arm.

She shook her head. "I don't think it's a good idea for me to touch you right now."

"Why not?"

She cocked her head to the side, like a bird of prey. "Because I can hear the blood in your veins, and I can taste the flavor of your magic on my tongue, and I could call them both to me in the space between one breath and the next."

It took all the control Ian had not to step back, not flee like a fox before hounds. "Yes. Certainly. That makes sense. We'll hold off on the touching."

"Good night, Ian." Sydney's voice sounded like the heart of a dark forest, thick and rife with secrets.

The air shimmered green behind her as she walked through the broken room, through the stone wreckage of the magic it had held, and Ian felt fear drip cold down his spine.

Sydney stood, still in the black dress she had worn to the challenge, in the cold hall of the House of Shadows, holding secrets to herself, feeling them vine around her bones. There was, she realized, a smear of the magician's blood dried on her hand. One more thing not to think about, not while she was here.

She had felt the summons as she walked home—like someone had lit a match to the ragged ends of her shadow. She had come immediately, hating every step that brought her here, knowing that waiting would make things worse and make it more difficult to keep things hidden from the House. There was so much she needed to keep hidden from the House.

About a month after she first got out of Shadows, she had tried to resist the summons back. She was out, she told herself, beyond the great doors. It wasn't as if Shara could physically bring her back in, not with the spell that bound her to the island. She would wait, return when she was ready.

Even then she wasn't quite foolish enough to consider ignoring the summons altogether.

And so she went about her day. And so, Shadows responded.

It began like an itch, crawling across her skin. Mild, an annoyance.

Then the sensation increased: insects—tens, hundreds, thousands of legs. By then Sydney realized what was happening and was determined to resist. If she just waited long enough, it would stop.

She held out for another half day, until her skin was swollen and bloody, covered in welts from things that she had never even seen, from terrors that had been conjured out of her head. Until she felt like she might claw her own skin from her body for relief.

Then she went to Shadows.

Shara had not ended the spell until she had finished talking to Sydney.

Sydney had never waited to answer a summons since.

Magic burned like a fever through Sydney's blood as she

stood in front of Shara. She was close, she could tell, to not being able to conceal its effects. It wouldn't be the worst for Shara to discover she held it, but if the House didn't know she held the extra power, then it couldn't order her to use it, couldn't add its weight to the tithe she owed to pay back a bargain she had never consented to. If the House didn't learn about it, the magic might be only hers. She had been stronger than the House before—she would be in this as well. She let the fever burn.

"The House requires an explanation," Shara said.

Sweat beaded at Sydney's temples. Her heart was skipping beats that it found to be unnecessary. She wondered, idly, if the excess of magic she had absorbed would mean that trees would burst forth from her as well, that she might birth a forest spontaneously. She bit the insides of her mouth to keep from breaking out in laughter she had no desire to explain. When Shara gave no further clue, Sydney swallowed the potential consequence and asked: "An explanation of what?"

"Of your performance and standing in the Turning so far."

Nonsense, then. Nothing that mattered. The parroting of information that Shara would have already known, the summons simply an excuse to remind Sydney that she was not—not yet—free. "Candidate House Beauchamps is currently ranked first in the standings. I am undefeated."

"Due to—" Shara said, and smiled, slow and saccharine.

"Due to the training I received here." A beat. Magic so hot in her hands Sydney had to restrain herself from glancing down to see if they were blistered. It had been a rather large amount of magic she had taken in. An entire season. Could magic be measured in seasons? Would a winter's worth feel different—colder, perhaps, and more crystalline—than this heated spring blooming in her?

Shara's voice jarred against her thoughts. "And which—"

"And which I am grateful for." Sydney considered for a heartbeat, two, reaching out with her magic and stopping Shara's heart. With Shara dead, she would be free, though free only of Shara, and the question of what would happen to Shadows as a place without its avatar was one she wasn't ready to answer. Besides, it felt like there were fireflies in her blood, which was perhaps not the most optimal set of circumstances for casting death magic. She could wait.

"That will be all." Shara handed her the knife and pen so that the contract could be signed once more. There were still-healing marks on Shara's hands. Sydney recognized their patterns—a ritual for the extraction of magic. A ritual she herself had been forced to endure on more than one occasion.

There was no one in Shadows who could force Shara into anything.

"Are you well?" Sydney asked. "Those look painful." Not

because she cared—because she wanted Shara to know that she had seen.

"We all make sacrifices," Shara said. But she pulled her hands away, hiding them.

There were dark green edges on the piece of shadow Sydney carved off herself. Shara said nothing. Perhaps she didn't see them.

Sydney was magic-sick enough to call for a cab when she reached the edge of Central Park. She didn't trust her feet to carry her home without incident. When they arrived at her building, she tipped the cabbie double the fare and then stripped his memory of her.

She made it into her apartment, locked the door behind her, and collapsed to the floor, lost in the dream of the forest, wrapped in the thick, green blanket of its magic.

Had the eyes of the Unseen World been turned to the Angel of the Waters that night, instead of to their own magics, then they might have seen a wonder.

Green and spring burst through the air, all out of season in the current month. Vines wreathed the statue. A small rain rippled across the water, and the scent of spring flowers—of lilacs and peonies and hyacinths—filled the air.

And then.

The howling of a storm, wind sending waves across the

fountain, birds pulled from their flight as if they had been flung into the column of a tornado. As if there was something hungry, reaching, reaching.

And then.

A crack. Spring paused in its progress, then shattered like stone. The winds quiet, the air once more that of early winter.

Snow fell, delicately, through the darkness.

CHAPTER NINE

Sydney cracked her eyes open and lifted her head from the floor. Her apartment. Her hallway. A humming beneath her skin. Power, new and green in her blood.

The light, she thought, was different than it had been when she had come home. The magic, its aftereffects, could have changed her sight. No. Not that. It was only that it was day now. Time had passed. Her head spun as she pushed herself into an upright position, her bones protesting the action. Everything ached—the inside of her skin, the roots of her hair, her blood. Whatever new magic she had, she had paid dearly to acquire it.

Her nose wrinkled at the stench. A lot of time had passed. She was fouled in her own waste. She pulled her phone from her purse. Three days. Forty-seven increasingly concerned texts from Laurent. She answered the last: *Am fine. Will explain later.* She whispered two lines of code as she pressed send, activating the spell that would prove that she was the one sending the message and that she was sending it voluntarily.

She ignored the immediate and frantic signaling of her phone in response. Ignored too the message alerts from Ian, from Verenice.

Three days. She was not, precisely, fine.

She could still taste the green of the magic she had absorbed at the back of her throat, underneath the bile and staleness. It tasted like running sap and fresh grass.

It tasted like freedom.

The new magic ran through her like a current. She was *aware* of it in a way she had never been aware of her magic before. Everything was sharper, brighter, electric.

She peeled off her ruined dress, used it to scrub the worst of the accumulated filth from her body. Then cast a variety of spells at the mess on the floor, tension falling from her shoulders as she moved her hands through the patterns. The other magic was here beneath hers, yes, but it was controlled.

Hers.

All that power, and she controlled it. She closed her eyes and stood, letting the spark of it run just beneath her skin, feeling it in her veins and sinews. She stretched, rising to her toes and rolling back through her heels, settling into her skin. The magic stretched too, moving through her body like a tide.

Glorious.

For the first time since she'd conceived the beginning

pieces of this plan, thirteen years ago, in the cold darkness of her room at Shadows, Sydney believed she would survive to see the end of it. On her way to the shower, she grabbed a bottle of champagne from the refrigerator. She drank it as the water poured over her, washing her clean.

CHAPTER TEN

Miles Merlin walked into a room that was harsh and sterile as a laboratory and locked the door behind him. While not the traditionalist that Miranda was in matters of decorating, he did hold close one tradition of the Unseen World: his firm belief that a magician should have a place, isolated and private, in which to do his magic.

This room—white and chrome and starkly fluorescent—was his version of a wizard's tower.

The first thing he did after making sure no one else could come in was to check—as he always checked now—his supply of stored magic. He rested his hand on a pad that recognized his fingerprints and released a lock with a mechanical hiss. There was no magic there; there were no wards to protect access. Using magic carried the risk that one day he wouldn't be able to open the cabinet.

With the door open, he could taste the magic he had gathered, burnt metallic at the back of his throat, could feel it hum in his teeth. He counted jars, checked seals. It was all there—glass-contained and silver-bound.

Here, alone, he allowed his shoulders to relax forward in relief, and then he closed the door, locked it. Enough, for now, now while he still mostly trusted his own power, to have it. There would—he was certain now—come a day when having it wouldn't be enough. When he would need to use what was there, parcel it out bit by bit. But until that day—he had his supply.

And he could increase it.

He cracked all of his knuckles and stretched out his hands, then reached toward a small statue—a miniature version of the Angel of the Waters.

He'd made the statue after he'd made his most recent bargain with Shadows. He'd wanted a proxy for the larger version. He needed regular access to the spells that had been anchored in the Angel, and it had been easier for him to stand here and guide the flow of magic than to go outside and interact with the actual statue. New York City ignored a lot, but ignoring a man regularly doing magic in Central Park might be a stretch. Plus, he hated being interrupted while he worked.

He held out his hands, reaching for the magic that flowed through the spells connected to the statue. Reached farther, wiggling his fingers like some fraud of a stage magician. But something—something felt wrong. Merlin broke off the spell, refocused, and started again.

Then he swore and broke the spell a second time. Something

was wrong. The magic that should have been there, just at the ends of his fingertips, wasn't. There were trickles, yes, but less than half—perhaps even less than a third—of what normally flowed through the statue's hands. This wasn't his magic misfiring. There was something wrong with the spell that was anchored in the Angel.

There was something wrong with magic. Not his, specifically. All magic.

Miles squashed the beginnings of panic that threatened and ran through every spell he could think of that might be useful—for strength, for detection, to discover the works of his enemies, to reveal hidden things. He cast again and again until his temples were damp with sweat and his hands were shaking. Until he could feel the magic running out from his hands and knew if he didn't pause, recover, he'd have nothing left.

He grabbed the tiny statue and flung it against the wall, shattering it. The magic wasn't there, and he had no idea where it had gone.

He stood, staring at the shattered pieces, forcing himself back to calmness, drawing in slow, deep breaths until he felt the pounding of his heart lessen. Something wet, heavier than sweat, trickled down his face, dripped. Red against the sterile white.

A knock at the door. "Dad, is everything okay?" Lara.

He touched his hand to his forehead, where a piece of the statue had cut him open, and muttered the words to close the wound. Huffed out a relieved breath when it healed.

Opened the door and stepped through it, pulling it half-closed behind him so that Lara couldn't see the mess. "Fine. I dropped something."

"I'm happy to help, if you need anything." Her eyes, searching over his shoulder.

"No, I think I'm going to take a break." He stepped the rest of the way into the hall and pulled the door shut behind him.

"If you're sure?" Her whole face a question.

"I am, yes."

He needed to think. If the magic was gone, it had to go somewhere.

Perhaps the statue itself was malfunctioning. He would go see. Get outside, clear his head. After that, he'd decide what needed to be done.

Lara waited until she was sure her father had left the house. He had never explicitly stated that the locked room at the far end of the hall was private, off-limits, but the fact that it was kept locked implied those things pretty heavily. And she had always wanted to leave her father his secrets.

That didn't seem like a safe thing to do anymore. She placed her hand over the lock and curled her fingers counterclockwise.

The lock opened. Lara held her breath, waiting for alarms, for wards, for anything to happen. When nothing did, she stepped inside.

Broken pieces of white plaster were scattered over the floor. She knelt, picked through the fragments—an arm, part of what might have been a wing—then shoved as many as she could find together in a pile. Spoke a word that left a sticky aftertaste in her mouth and clapped her hands together. The fragments re-formed, and an almost-complete facsimile of the Angel of the Waters stood in front of her. Lara folded and unfolded her hands in patterns of magic, but as far as she could tell, there was nothing particularly remarkable about it. She loosed the spell and let the pieces fall back to the floor.

Then she raised her hands, palms out and open, and searched for the presence of any magic in the room. It was a room that should have been rife with it—traces left over from Miles' practice, from spells being performed. Instead, the room felt as sterile as it looked. Only one place—the cabinet—registered a presence, and even that felt strange. Heavy somehow, a block or lump.

None of it made sense.

The lock for the cupboard was biometric, and while there might be spells that would open it, Lara wasn't aware of them. She looked around, checking to see that everything was as it had been when she came in, then left, locking the door after her.

Then she texted her brother: *We need to talk.*

Verenice Tenebrae had built herself a hermitage in a Brooklyn brownstone. It was full of luxuries—rich colors and sumptuous fabrics, elaborate carpets, leather chairs with cashmere throws. Every room was as well-appointed and comfortable as she could make it. Shadows had not been a place of comfort. Now that she could indulge, she did, and felt no qualms over it.

Even among all the luxury she had gathered to herself, what Verenice liked, more than anything else, was the quiet. The House of Shadows had been loud, had been constant, had pressed on her like a suffocation. There was never any relief, much less peace. She could have quiet here, and she did. Some days, there were no sounds at all in the house beyond her own footsteps, her own breath. Those days, still, were a miracle to her.

She had quiet, but she was close enough to hear the whispers of the Unseen World when she wanted to.

She had thought about leaving the city. About leaving the entire Unseen World behind. Had actually left the day after she signed her final contract for Shadows, had gotten on the first available plane and flown across the Atlantic and then gone to the Isle of Skye because it seemed very far away and because she had liked the name.

Skye had been very far away, and very quiet, and she had stayed there for a year, putting herself back together. She had relearned who she was when there was no one who had the power to force her to be someone else, and then she had decided who she wanted to be. Then she had gotten on a plane again and come back.

One of the things she had learned about herself was that she liked her enemies where she could see them.

Also, she had clung to the hope that someone else would be able to open the House's doors and walk free. She wanted to be there, to help them negotiate that liminal place between fully bound and not yet free that had felt so perilous and strange to her when she had first emerged. She had waited and waited. For years, and then decades, through two more victories of House Merlin in the Turning, through that House renewing its compact with Shadows again and again, and there had been no one.

When Verenice thought of the House of Shadows, when she woke from the dreams in which she was forced to return, when she sat up, breathless and panicked in her bed, she thought of it as a maw, toothed and hungry and endless. Eventually, she gave up hope of it ever spitting anyone else back out.

Then Sydney.

Verenice lived on the periphery of the Unseen World by design—close enough that she could watch those who lived in it, detached enough that they would mostly forget her existence. Sydney had walked into the center of that world like she owned it. She made the air around her electric.

It was a terrifying thing, having hope again.

Snow fell as Sydney stood on Verenice's doorstep, turning the branches of the trees to black-and-white sculptures, blanketing the city with quiet. Sydney lifted her face to the flakes, stood as they clung to her eyelashes, as they gathered in her hair.

"You haven't been out long enough to have seen snow before, have you?" Verenice asked. She watched Sydney turn in a slow circle on her porch, face lifted to the falling snow, and tried to reconcile this woman who looked scarcely out of her teens with the terrifying avatar of power Ian had described to her when he'd visited earlier this week. "It was like channeling all of that magic was nothing to her. I could see the effects of it—she was shedding actual fucking sparks from her hands—but she was . . . fine," he had said, his eyes focused far away, as if he were still in that room that had gone from living forest to stone statues in the time it took Sydney to stop a woman's heart.

The images didn't mesh, but Verenice knew well how little images mattered.

"I left Shadows this summer." Sydney held out a hand and let the snow pile on top of it, then shaped the snow into a star and flung it—sparkling—back into the sky. "I'd seen snow, of course. There are rooms now, open to the sky—you know how the House shifts. And there was magic that required being outside of the House, especially once Shara decided that if I earned my way out, she was going to use me here in the Turning. It wouldn't do for me to be ignorant. But being on the island, even outside, and being here, they're different."

"Yes," Verenice said. "They are."

"I'd never thought snow was beautiful before. It was just another form of cold. This—this looks like feathers falling." Wonder in Sydney's voice, her eyes lifted to the sky.

"I do have warm enough coats that I can have this conversation outdoors, if you'd like to walk in it," Verenice offered.

"Thanks. But no—I'll walk later. I think this is a conversation better had inside." She followed Verenice in.

There was a fire crackling in Verenice's library, and she made hot chocolate. "I'm a great believer in embracing comforts, as I'm sure you understand."

Sydney nodded. "I have blankets. Wool. Down-filled. Cashmere. This antique quilt I found that has stars on it. Because, you know, I could never get warm there. The House wouldn't let me. Sometimes I pile the ones I'm not using on the end of my bed, just so I know they're there, that I can reach out and wrap myself in warmth if I want to."

Verenice kept her back to Sydney. It was the most personal thing the other woman had ever shared with her, and she didn't want to break the moment. So she offered a piece of her own history as she stirred. "It's food for me. Sweets, in particular. I can't leave the house without chocolate in my purse."

"Still?" Sydney's voice as quiet as the snow.

"Still."

Verenice let the silence hold as she finished pouring the hot chocolate, then handed Sydney a mug. "When you emailed, you said you had some questions about magic. Is this about what happened at the duel? Ian mentioned that it was very—intense."

"Ian? He told you?"

Verenice could see Sydney close off, whatever trust had been earned being replaced by the public mask that slipped back over her face. "He did. He was very worried about you. Had you asked him to keep things a secret?" Verenice raised a brow.

"No, I just hadn't realized the two of you were so close." She paused. "He could have asked me. How I was."

"He was afraid," Verenice said, setting down her cup.

"Of what?"

"Of you. Of what you had become."

Sydney reached for the magic, just below her skin, hers

and not. She dreamed in green now. "Maybe he should be."

"I know it isn't my place to say this, but there is a difference between who you are and what Shadows would make of you. Don't let it take that part of you away."

"You of all people know that right now I have no choice between who I am and what Shadows has made of me. Not until that contract is gone." Her voice was bitter as salt.

"Sydney, what has Shara asked you to do?"

Quiet. So very quiet in her house.

"Forgive me," Verenice said. "I shouldn't have asked. What did you want to talk about?"

"How much do you know about the spells that are anchored in the Angel of the Waters?" Sydney said.

"Other than that there should only be one?" Verenice said.

"Maybe we need to have this conversation outside after all," Sydney said.

The park was quiet. Not empty—not ever that—but thick with solitude, the grey winter sky a blanket. Snow crunched beneath their feet. The Angel was draped in a mantle of white.

"I keep waiting to think this is beautiful," Sydney said. "This part of the park—the terrace, the fountain, the statue. I know it's meant to be. But all is see when I look at it is Shadows, sitting behind. Sunset, snowfall, it doesn't matter. I hate it."

"I tried to date, when I first got out. Before I realized that I do not, particularly, want to have that sort of physical relationship. But there was a very nice man—he was kind, and he was handsome, and if I were going to want anyone, it might well have been him," Verenice said. "He took me here—a walk, summer, ice cream. I got sick—physically ill. So no, I have no particular fondness for it either."

"Do you mind doing magic?" Sydney asked. "I'd like your opinion on what you sense here."

"All right."

"Reach carefully," Sydney said. "It may not be pleasant."

Verenice took off her gloves and half-closed her eyes. She whispered something, her voice rising at the end like a question. Then stumbled back, sliding on the snow, and fisted her hands closed, breaking the spell. "What *is* that?"

"A problem," Sydney said, her arm around Verenice, holding her up until the other woman was steady again. "A big one, I think."

"It feels *wrong*—like it's bound into the magic from Shadows, but that instead of allowing magic to flow through, it's being consumed. Fed on."

"I would have said there's something in there feeding on magic, rather than being fed on, but yes. *Wrong*. I can't quite figure out why yet, or if I care to do so." Sydney rearranged her scarf around her neck, stuffed her hands deeper into her pockets.

"Why not?" Verenice asked.

"Because if magic itself is sick, or broken, or whatever that *wrong* is, then of course I care. Of course I want to fix it. But if Shadows is, then I plan on very happily watching it die."

Miles Merlin's feet were wet, his loafers ruined. The boat he rode in leaked, leaked alarmingly enough that he had attempted a spell to mend it, to make sure he arrived at Shadows without having to swim there. The magic hadn't worked. Still, against all expectations, the boat held together until it reached the island. He stepped onto the grit of the shore. The doors to the House of Shadows opened. Shara emerged like a phantom from the darkness inside.

"I thought we had a deal," he said.

"We did. And Shadows has upheld its end of the bargain." Shara's voice was as cold and hard as stone.

"My magic is growing weaker. Again. Our bargain was supposed to fix this."

"The bargain allowed you to modify the spell that is anchored in the Angel. To have the ability to draw on the sacrifices directly, to have access to their magic for your personal use, rather than simply as part of the spell set up to ease the Unseen World's use of magic." She walked closer, close enough that even in the dim light he could see marks carved on her hands. "That spell still holds. Any weakness is in the magician, not in the magic."

He wouldn't allow that to be possible. "There has to be something else I can do."

"I was so hoping you would offer." A smile like the surface of a frozen lake cracking. "Allow Shadows to be an actual part of the Unseen World. Give me real power, and I will redo the spell myself and happily channel an ongoing supply to you. As you know, brother, there are all sorts of ways that Shadows can be useful."

"Get me through the Turning," he said. "I just need enough magic for that, and then we can discuss things."

"We discuss it now. People without magic can't hold a House, Miles. You know this."

Shadows' walls pressed in close. The air thickened, and the effort of breathing rattled in his lungs. "Fine," he said. "Fine. If House Merlin is ranked at the top of the Unseen World at the end of the Turning, I will insist on Shadows being brought in, given full power."

"Excellent," Shara said. House Merlin had held the Unseen World for every Turning since Shadows had been established. If her other plans were unsuccessful, aligning herself with her brother's House was a good option, even with Miles as diminished as he was. "There's just one more necessary thing."

"What else could you possibly want?"

"I need you to sign this contract."

By the time the boat—even more leaky, if such a thing

were possible—deposited him back on the shore of the reservoir, Miles were certain his feet were frozen inside his shoes. His toes burned with the cold. He risked the smallest of spells to unfreeze them, then hopped and stuffed his now-smoking feet into a snowdrift.

Back in Shadows, he was certain, Shara was laughing at him.

She could not be let out.

His shadow ached from the ridiculous ritual she had put him through, one more way to gloat, when a normal signature or even blood should certainly have sufficed. But it did have the side benefit of making him consider who else had signed contracts to Shadows, who else might have owed debts.

He knew what happened when a Shadow got out.

Sydney still owed a debt of magic to Shadows. It was possible—or at least believable—that the magic she was using to such success in the Turning should have belonged to the House of Shadows, and therefore to the Unseen World. The fact that she was walking free and using it, well, no wonder magic was failing if there was so much power missing. And if she were to die—since everyone knew that a death during a Turning canceled that House's obligation—it made sense to think that her magic would return to Shadows, that magic would stop failing.

It sounded very logical, and really, he only needed one person to believe it. This was a Turning, and anyone could die.

• • •

A chill breeze blew through Ian's apartment. His wards were still up, but his back door was cracked open. He walked through the room slowly, an almost-complete defensive spell held in his hand.

Sydney stood on the balcony, wrapped in coat and scarf.

"Do you not believe in knocking? Or waiting until someone is home to let you in?" he asked, releasing the stored magic.

"I like to be sure I can get out of a place if I need to," she said. "If I can get in on my own, I can get out again."

"That does have a certain odd logic. So what brings you to my balcony?"

"It's a good view." She turned from it, to look at him. "And Verenice said you were worried about me."

"I was," he said.

"I'm not used to being worried about." She shrugged. "I didn't know I was supposed to check in."

"You're not supposed to. It's not like I have some sort of claim on you. But I'm glad you did." He paused. "So, we never did have popcorn and a scary movie. I could probably come up with both."

Tension slipped from her. "I promised to hold your hand, didn't I?"

"We could skip that and go straight to the making out if you want. I'm easy." He smiled, and held his door for her.

She walked into his apartment. Stopped. Turned. "Here's the thing. I was supposed to die. I was given away to suffer, to be used up, and then at the end, I was supposed to die, so that everyone could forget about me and forget what Shadows is. What it does. How fucking little they get from it."

"Sydney, I—"

"Let me finish. When you're supposed to die, there is no one to check in on you. There's no one who cares what happens. You are alone. And that's fine, because I am good at being alone. I know who I am and I trust myself, and I do not need to trust anyone else. I actually prefer not having to.

"And *you*, you are the worst possible person to trust, to need to check in with, or whatever, because this is a Turning, and one of us could wind up killing the other." The words simple, brutal truth.

"Sydney." He set his hands, very gently, on her shoulders, looked straight at her. "I would never."

"You can't know that," she said. "You can't know where a challenge might come from."

"You're right," he said. "I can't. But that is not the problem for tonight. The problem for tonight is popcorn, and a scary movie, and, Sydney, if you let me, I'll hold your hand the entire time. Okay?"

"Okay," she said. "Okay."

• • •

It was the last nonmortal duel. Held at the Dees' again, the close a nod to the open. The crowd was as glittering as before, but thinner, and the sparkle had taken on a hard edge. This was no longer a room full of champagne bubbles and gossip, but a room full of strategy and teeth.

Eyes full of awareness followed Sydney this time as she made her way through the assembled magicians. Space cleared for her, voices dimmed.

"And I'm not even the evening's entertainment." She slid into place, next to Laurent, nodded at Grey on his other side. "How do you like being the next big thing, Laurent?"

He raised his glass, the light gilding his champagne. "I like it just fine. Thank you for getting me here."

She tapped her glass to his, drank.

The candidate House Beauchamps was quite comfortably at the head of the standings. The one magician who seemed able to offer a challenge to that was casting tonight, House Prospero having challenged House Hermann. The choice of magic was openings. Both Miles and Lara Merlin were in attendance, Miles watching Ian and Lara watching her father. Miranda held court at the opposite end of the room.

Sydney hadn't fought in a duel since she'd absorbed the blowback from the failure of magic. She had come to a balance with the new power—it no longer shaded her eyes to green or sent sparks flying from her hands, but the lurking awareness of its presence just beneath her skin, contained in her but not her, remained. Her hands were a constant ache, full of the desire for magic.

The duel began. Angelica Hermann cast first, a tiny, elegant piece of magic that unlayered a set of clocks, opening their workings, sending gears spinning into orbit like orreries. It was precision and control made grace and elegance. Sydney's applause was genuine.

Ian stepped into the center of the room. A sharp flick of his left hand. A thud, like the sound of a thousand doors slamming shut. The noise, tremendous, and the House rocked on its foundation.

His hands moved, bent. He spoke a word, and Sydney felt it in her chest, like a window swinging out. Doors carved themselves out of light and shadows, the frames appearing all over the room, scattered among the watching magicians.

Another word, sharp and brass-scented.

The doors opened.

Each onto a different world—thick forests and luminescent icescapes, revolving stars and a concrete and steel sky. Scents and sounds came through, each place unique. The magicians walked through the room, peering through the doors. "Though I would caution you not to enter—I can't guarantee that you would return," Ian said.

After they had their chance to look upon storms and oceans, on lavender fields and jeweled museums, Ian brought his hands down.

The doors closed.

The first part of the Turning was finished.

CHAPTER ELEVEN

Sydney gritted her teeth as the boat took her to Shadows through what had turned from snow to freezing rain. She was certain this was Shara once again summoning her for no purpose other than to prove she could, and to carve one more sliver off her torn and ragged shadow. She resented the cold, and the night, and the being subject to someone's whim. The boat scratched against the shore, and she stomped inside.

Soaking wet and the cold an ache in her bones, she was grateful that the House didn't force her in some roundabout path, but brought her to Shara directly.

"The challenges have become mortal," Shara said. The air around her cracked and snapped with frost.

"They have," Sydney said. Magic like spring below her skin, green and humid. Not quite warmth, not in this place, but a ward against the worst of the cold.

"And so the House requires a challenge. House Prospero."

And there it was. This was the plan. This had always been the plan. When Shara had first explained how the House would use her during the Turning, this particular challenge was the one that had been mentioned with specificity. Sydney had agreed because it hadn't mattered to her at the time, because at the time all she could see was how well that fit into her own plans for the Turning. "Is there a time frame in which the House would like this to be carried out?"

"Soon. It need not be immediate, but if the House feels you are taking too long, there will be consequences. I suspect that you will not enjoy them."

Shara's fingers curled, and Sydney felt the sensation of hundreds of legs crawling over her skin. She did not allow herself to shudder. "Will there be anything else?"

"I thought you'd be happier, Sydney," Shara said.

"I am always happy to serve the House." Expected words, required sentiments.

"Which is why the House has given you this opportunity—vengeance on the House that cast you aside. That is what you feel, isn't it?" An expression that some might have called a smile, overlarge and too sweet. "That you were cast aside and thrown away."

Years of practice gave her the strength to keep her face blank, to not give Shara the satisfaction of knowing that every word had been a knife, twisted. "I don't have a House."

"Except for Shadows. You'll always be a part of Shadows." Shara held up the knife, the pen.

Sydney leaned as hard as she could into the pain as her shadow was cut away, letting it fill her, letting it be all she knew. It seemed like every time she walked back through the doors, she had more secrets to hide, but she had kept them all so far, and she would not let today change that. Better to endure pain than to betray herself.

She signed her name and walked back out into the sleet.

Sydney wanted Madison to feel comfortable, so she asked to meet at the neighborhood bar again. A comfortable setting seemed kinder, somehow, when you were about to ask someone to do something where the consequences of saying yes ranged from "getting fired" to "death." She was pretty sure she could keep Madison safe from that last one, but drinks were in order.

"I need information," Sydney said, after their drinks arrived, "about how the Houses are inherited." Shara's request itched at her. Not that it was unexpected, or that Shara or Shadows had ever bothered explaining things—you don't explain things to a gun; you simply aim and fire—but she wanted to know what Shara was getting out of the deal. No matter what she had said, this challenge wasn't because Shadows was trying to allow Sydney personal vengeance. She wanted to know why she had been aimed in this particular direction.

"I assume you're not asking because congratulations are in order," Madison said.

Sydney stared.

"Right. Well, you'll need to be more specific—under what circumstances is the House being inherited. I mean, outside of the conventional will and a named heir."

"Let's start easy," Sydney said. "There are biological descendants, but no named heirs."

"That one's easy. In case of death or permanent incapacity, things pass by typical intestate succession—spouse first, then any biological children."

"Permanent incapacity?" Sydney asked.

"Significant mental illness or brain damage, the kind that would interfere with magic use, or outright loss of magic," Madison said. "There are legal processes and safeguards in place to confirm each."

Sydney stirred her drink. "What about if there is a biological heir that hasn't been recognized?"

"Like a lost heir problem?" Madison perked up. "I always wanted one of those. The basic proof could come from a Perdita spell, or any of the other pieces of magic that will confirm genetics. Perdita's considered the most rigorous, and so it's preferred. Then you introduce the heir to the House—if the House recognizes them and opens the door in front of witnesses, it's irrefutable."

"Recognizes them?" Sydney asked.

"The physical Houses have magical locks, ones that

recognize the blood of the family that holds them. If the House opens its doors to you, you belong there."

"Interesting," Sydney said. "Okay, what if there is a known biological descendant, but they've been disinherited and the House has no named heir?"

Madison took a long drink of her martini. "You're not speaking in hypotheticals anymore, are you?" There was only one House in living memory that had disinherited one of its children and had no named heir: Prospero.

"No," Sydney said. "I'm not."

"And is there someone else who is a blood heir, who would pass the House's test?"

"There is. I know how to find that person, and I know they would hold the House."

Madison closed her eyes. "I'm going to need another drink."

"They're on me," Sydney said.

"Sydney, that House that we're both very carefully not naming, that's a big, important House, and there is *no* sign that its current Head is about to vacate her duties. I know you have plans, big scary plans, and my willingness to support you in them hasn't changed, but are you sure you know what you're doing?"

"I think so. There's someone else I need to talk to, and a lot will depend on how that conversation goes. And no, that conversation won't include a discussion of the outright assassination of a current Head of House."

"That is something of a relief." Madison did not look like her stress level had been lessened by Sydney's assurances.

"I'm just trying to plan for everything." Sydney liked plans. She liked to have many of them, so their pieces could be switched apart and replaced when necessary. "What you said about the inheritance lines up with what I thought, but are there any special provisions during a Turning?"

Madison took another piece of the pickled asparagus Will had brought with the second round of drinks. "No—the current rules of inheritance were put in place after the last Turning. Oddly enough, it was Christopher Prospero's death that led to them. He had no will, and Grey was too young to be formally invested. It was clear he would be, so there weren't any issues, but it was one of those situations that made people realize that things needed to be formalized.

"Though, interestingly, beyond removing Grey as heir, Miranda never has made a new will."

"That is interesting," Sydney said.

"I have the terrible feeling that when you say 'interesting,' what you mean is 'liable to cause three, maybe four large-scale explosions.'"

"Two. I'm pretty sure I'll only need two. And I'll try to keep you clear of them," Sydney said. "But in all seriousness, you continuing to help me—it might not be a risk-free endeavor. Do you want out?"

"Not even a little bit," Madison said.

"All right. I've set up some basic precautions for you. You'll find an envelope, bordered in red, in your purse when you leave the bar tonight—and no, I can't just hand it to you now. I want it to recognize you specifically, and the less contact I have with it the better."

"Sounds serious," Madison said.

"It is. The envelope will smell like roses. Open it once you get inside your apartment, after you shut the door."

"Self-triggering wards?" Madison asked.

"Good ones. You'll receive a new envelope in your mailbox once a week on Tuesday until this is over. Red-bordered, rose-scented. If any one of those three things isn't right, don't open it. And after you don't open it and you get the fuck out of your apartment building, you call me."

"Got it," Madison said, and swallowed hard.

"Look, if this is too much—"

Madison cut her off. "It isn't. Really. I'm just mentally transitioning from, 'Hey, I feel like a spy, this is kind of cool,' to, 'Those fuckers might blow up my cat,' and it's a bit of an adjustment."

"I swear to you, Madison, I will not let anyone—fucker or otherwise—blow up Noodle. Actually, you know what, I'm going to make Noodle a warded collar. I'll messenger it to you at the office tomorrow."

"Thanks. Seriously." Madison nodded. "Okay. What else?"

"No problem. I love that furball. Anyway, your office is probably safer than your apartment—Prospero isn't the only House that does business at Wellington & Ketchum, and besides, blowing up a law firm is a good way to call too much mundane attention to the Unseen World. Can't have that. Still, you'll receive an email with a 1:13 a.m. time stamp every Wednesday. It'll have poetry in the body—lines from Seamus Heaney's *Sweeney Astray*. The attachment will be an MP3 file. Download the attachment and let the song play all the way through. You don't need to have the volume on, but let it play."

"I just hired an associate, specifically to help me deal with the new work for the Turning—lots of Houses trying to get their affairs in order. She seems trustworthy, and I've been thinking of giving her some of the peripheral work on your projects, too. Do I need to worry about her?" Madison asked.

"I'll modify the email so that the spell covers her, too. Just forward it once you've played it through."

"Thanks. Anything else?" Madison signaled for another round.

"Can you find out why Grey was disinherited?"

"Probably. It'll take a while, though—that sort of thing is kept in physical archive only."

"Please look. I think it might be important. And if I can do anything to make that search go more quickly, let me know."

"Believe me, I will."

Sydney settled the bill and got up. "Watch your back."

"You too."

Sydney walked into Laurent's apartment and covered it in a blanket of wards.

"I thought I had locked the door." Laurent stood in the kitchen, right hand crooked into the opening of a basic defensive spell.

"You did," Sydney said. "I unlocked it."

"Oh." He watched as she moved through the rooms like a very efficient hurricane. Then: "I live in a warded building."

"Laurent," she said, in a voice that suggested that warded buildings were about as much of a challenge to her as a KEEP OUT sign taped to the door would be.

"Right." Shaking his head and slightly befuddled. "Right. Of course. I'd forgotten you were real-life Hermione Granger. Should I be worried that you can just walk in here like that?"

"If it makes you feel any better, they were very high-quality wards, so I seriously doubt anyone else can," Sydney said, continuing to cast a variety of spells. Look-aways and don't-hear-mes. White noise and obscuring shimmers of air. Something complex and Slavic-sounding that left a compass rose drawn in smoke hanging in the air for forty-seven seconds, which Laurent thought was designed to confuse a mapmaker, though he wasn't exactly sure what it would do in his apartment.

"It makes you temporarily unfindable by GPS, both mundane and magically enhanced, as well as hiding you from locator spells," Sydney said, answering the question Laurent hadn't thought he had spoken aloud.

"Oh," he said again, feeling as if he, too, had been rendered unfindable. Whatever this was, it was not how he had planned to spend his morning.

"I need to tell you something, and I need to make sure no one overhears, or even suspects that you know."

"Coffee," Laurent said. He suspected that this was more of a whiskey conversation, but it was 9:23 and there were lines. "I need coffee for this."

Sydney perched on one of his barstools when she had the apartment secured to her liking. Laurent brought over a tray that had two cappuccinos and a plate piled with almond and anise biscotti.

"This," Sydney said, "this is exactly why I'm telling you."

"Because I made coffee?"

"Because there are two cups on the tray. Because it wouldn't have occurred to you for there to not be." Sydney dunked her biscotti and ate half of it, then set her cup down. "What do you know about where magic comes from?"

"Comes from?" Laurent shook his head. "I've never really thought about it. I guess maybe some kind of genetic mutation or something? You know, the kind of thing that explains why it runs in families, mostly, but then every so often someone like you or me shows up."

"That may well be part of it," Sydney said. "Or, to be more precise, may be why some people can access and use the power, once it exists, but others can't. But that's not where magic comes from.

"Magic, at its heart, starts with sacrifice. You have to give up something to get something, and because magic is big, with all that it allows you access to, what you give up has to be big. It has to be meaningful.

"The sacrifice is the thing that runs in families."

"How?" Laurent asked, gulping down coffee and wishing his brain would finish waking up.

"Because the families choose the sacrifice. Each House makes one, once a generation. Traditionally, it's the firstborn." The uninflected blankness of a teacher reading from a textbook.

"The firstborn what?" Laurent asked, setting down his coffee.

"Child," Sydney said. "The firstborn child."

"No." Laurent stood up. "No. What is that? Sacrifice the firstborn child? Like some fucking Greek myth? No. This is the twenty-first century. That does not happen."

"I assure you that it does." Sydney met his eyes. "Quite easily, and without a lot of fuss. It has for four generations now. All it took was for one person to realize that magic hurt. That you could do a spell, but afterward you might be weak, or run a fever, or cough blood, or whatever it was that was your readjustment to what you had just done. Impossibility is supposed to be just that, and there are consequences when it isn't.

"So some people stopped doing magic at all, because it hurt after. And then someone thought—what if we could get rid of the pain? What if we could make someone else pay, instead? And then, better still, what if we took the magic from those kids and put it in the thaumaturgical equivalent of a pool, something everyone could draw from. Easy, convenient access."

"Okay. Let's say you're right. I mean, I get wanting things to be easy and not painful, but kids, Sydney? *Kids?*"

"Easier to give someone up when you haven't gotten to know them."

"That is some fucked up shit."

"Yes," Sydney said.

"But wait. Not everyone has kids. I mean, assuming you're right—which is a big assumption, because seriously, if someone is going to show up and ask me for a child, they are out of luck. Or are they going to make me buy some orphan off the street? 'Congratulations on surviving the Turning, Mr. Beauchamps.

Now, where's the baby?'" His hands went to his head as if by pressing on it he could press himself into the ground, into sanity.

"That is precisely what they'll do," Sydney said. "It won't be immediate, but it is a requirement to establish a House."

"You're actually serious." He sat down hard.

"I am. The only circumstances in which the requirement is waived is if a member of the House has perished in a Turning—the spell is set up to recognize that as a sacrifice as well, the idea being that their magic returns to that waiting pool."

"That's why no one treats any of this like a big deal," he said. "Because losing a challenge is some fucked up get out of jail free card."

She nodded. "Exactly. Otherwise, buying a child is not only an option for those who can't or don't wish to have biological offspring, of course. It's also an option for those who want to guarantee both their bloodline and their access to comfortable magic. With enough money, you can buy anything."

"But you said 'sacrifice.'" Horror in every word.

"I did." Quiet, even. The voice in which the doctor tells you that she's very sorry but the tumor is malignant and surgery is no longer an option.

"You don't mean they actually kill the kids, do you? You can't mean that."

"The sacrifices aren't killed immediately or directly. It's a process. An extraction, or distillation, to choose the most clinical terms. Clinical terms make it easier to talk about, and ease is needed, at least in polite company, as most sacrifices don't survive the process.

"The place those sacrifices are sent, it pulls magic out of them. Through pain, through suffering. Through everything the magicians of the Unseen World should have to endure themselves to access power.

"Does it hurt, Laurent, when you cast spells?" Gentle, the words so gentle, as if he might break when she spoke them.

"It used to," he said. "When I first started. Before I met Grey and started going to school here. I'd get headaches. Migraines. Nausea, auras, the whole thing. I figured they stopped because I'd learned the right way to do things."

"No," Sydney said. "That's not why they stopped. They stopped because someone else started paying your price."

"Oh God." Laurent clutched his hand over his mouth and stumbled from the room.

Sydney sat, unmoving, on the barstool, looking out over the city as she listened to the sounds of retching, of the flush of the toilet, the running water. Laurent was red-eyed and ashen when he returned.

"Not all of the children die of it," Sydney continued as if there had been no interruption. "Most do, yes. But some very few of us come out of it quite well. For a certain definition of quite well, anyway. We learn to use our own power, and to wield it in ways most of the Unseen World can't imagine."

"What's a—wait. You said 'us.' Sydney, you said 'us.' You weren't—" He looked sick again.

"I'm sure you've heard the rumors by now, the things people are saying about me."

He nodded. "Something about you being a Shadow. I figured it was another thing like being an outsider."

"It's called the House of Shadows, the place we're sent. And yes, I came from there. I was the sacrifice of a House." She almost, almost told him which one then, but bit the words back. Too soon to ask him to process that as well. Too much was still uncertain. And he was still asking questions. "I earned my way out. Only one other has in living memory—Verenice Tenebrae."

Laurent nodded slowly. "I knew she was a big deal, that people talked about her. I didn't really pay attention to why. Wait—*only* you two? Out of . . . ?"

"A lot," Sydney said. "More than either of us want to count. Shadows has been around for more than one hundred years. Long enough for people to be used to the idea, for this to be the way it's always been done. For people to feel sad, a little, if they actually think about it, but goodness, the way things were before must have been so much worse."

He shuddered. "But if it's so rare, how did you get out? Are you okay? If you're not a sacrifice anymore, what are you now?"

So she told him. Told him about Shadows, about learning magic, about learning to conceal every part of herself. About the contract that kept her in bond. Showed him the ragged edges of her shadow, where she had cut bits away to make payments. Took a cloth and scrubbed off the makeup that covered the scars on her hands and arms that magic didn't hide.

Laurent winced, then said, "Okay. How much?"

"How much what?" Puzzled.

"To pay off your contract."

"What does it matter?" The reason for his curiosity wasn't any clearer to her.

"Because I'll buy them out. This hold they have on you is bullshit. You're a person—you shouldn't be fucking owned."

Sydney looked at him, long and steady. "You mean that, don't you?"

"Of course."

She closed her eyes. Kept them closed for almost a minute while she steadied her breath, until she was sure no tear would fall. Opened them. "That is possibly the single kindest thing anyone has ever said to me. But that's not how this works. They take payment in magic. In results. And they have something they want me to do."

She told him about the latest order from Shara. Most of it.

"But you wouldn't be fighting Miranda. Not directly. You'd

be dueling Ian. He's the one magician in this who could maybe kill you. I mean, I know you're good. Brilliant. But so is he—he was a couple of years ahead of us at school. I know what his magic is like," Laurent said.

"A month ago, maybe it would have been close. But now, no." The deep greenness of the strange new magic crinkled and whirred beneath her skin. "Trust me. I know what my magic is."

"Yeah, but Sydney, you guys are—not to be in your business, but aren't you guys a thing?"

"I knew what I'd be asked to do before the Turning started," she said, sidestepping the question.

"What would those—the Shadows—what would they do if I refused to challenge him?" Laurent paced in front of the long line of his windows.

"There would be consequences. To me. They would likely be . . . painful." The layers in that last word not something to be considered too closely.

"Okay, so you said they take payment in magic. What if I offered some of mine? I'm a good magician. I have power. I can fight." The pain in his voice had turned to fury.

"Any contract you made would be your own. This plan, this thing that Shara wants done, she will make sure that I do it."

Laurent stopped. Turned. "This is really the most fucked up day. What do I do?"

"Issue the challenge to Prospero, and trust that I can take care of myself."

"Are you sure? What if I just say fuck all of this? Withdraw from the Turning, withdraw from the entire Unseen World. How do I even use magic anymore, now that I know where it's coming from? I can't. I won't." He scrubbed his hands against his jeans as if wiping filth from them.

"I can teach you. You had access to your own power before, and that power is still there. As for the rest of it—the one thing you can do for me now is to stay in the Turning."

"Are you absolutely sure that's what you want, Sydney? Because if it isn't, I will do everything I can—everything—to get you away from that place and out of this."

"Thank you. Truly. But there are bigger things at stake than just what I want," she said.

"Okay. If you're sure."

"I am."

He scrubbed his hands over his face, over his hair. "God, I have to tell Grey. He needs to know."

"Laurent." Her voice was kind. "Grey grew up in the Unseen World. He was the heir of his House. He knows. He's known for years."

"Oh," Laurent said. Then, "Oh," again.

Sydney sat with him on his couch as his world reshaped itself. After some time, he shook his head. "Anything else?"

"Yes," Sydney said. "Let me be the one to deliver the challenge to Miranda. In person."

"Sure, if that's what you want." He paused. "Did you have a choice in representing me, or was accepting the contract something they made you do too?"

"Shadows wanted me involved in the Turning," Sydney said. "But working for you was my choice. I wouldn't change it." She stood up to go.

"Can you leave that unfindable spell running when you go?" he asked. "I think I want to be very alone for a bit."

"Sure." She rested her hand on his shoulder for the space of a breath. "Take care, Laurent."

CHAPTER TWELVE

Working in Special Projects wasn't what Harper had expected. In fact, although theoretically this huge and all-consuming magical battle was happening across the entire Unseen World, she hadn't seen one actual magician in the offices. At least, she was pretty sure she hadn't. Except for the recent emailed wards—which were spectacularly cool and didn't even give her a headache like most magic did—she hadn't come across anything even remotely magical. Working in Special Projects was just like working in her previous firm: long hours and lots of writing. She was currently redrafting a will. Then she had to turn in time sheets. Wild excitement.

"Harper, do you have a minute?" Madison paused in her doorway.

"Sure." She mentally raised a brow when Madison pulled the door closed behind her. Something serious, and secret, then.

"How do you feel about doing some work in the archives?"

The archives. The place where the documents pertaining to the Unseen World were kept—the ones too full of magic to leave on the computers. The place Harper had wanted an excuse to get into since she had started working here. "I feel like it would be more interesting than redrafting form documents."

"Possibly. There's a strong chance that it would just be an exercise in a different sort of frustration. Are you game?"

"Sure."

"Good. I need you to be discreet about this, even within the firm. It involves a case where enforced silence was part of the settlement." Madison looked drawn—her concealer didn't quite hide the dark circles under her eyes. Harper knew how tired she was from the hours she'd been keeping in the past few weeks. She also knew that Madison had been in the office before she arrived and had left work after she did every day that she'd been working at Wellington & Ketchum.

"Like an NDA?" Harper asked.

"No, like a binding spell that will physically prevent them from doing so. The attorneys who were directly involved in negotiating the terms would have also been bound, and I'm not sure whether or how far the binding extends."

Okay, that was kind of cool. "So I might not even be able to tell you about what I find. Is what you're saying?"

"In an extreme case, you might not even be able to read what you find. The file might look like blank pages, or poetry, or gibberish. And because of the binding, I can't even tell you how extreme a case this is."

"Got it. So what case has all these secrets?"

"The disinheritance of Grey Prospero. Time is of the essence, so send me a memo of your ongoing projects and I'll have them reassigned. When you're done with that, come by my office and I'll give you what you need to actually get into the archives."

Harper doubted she meant a key.

"Is there anything in particular that I'm looking for in the file?" Harper asked.

"No, I just need the file itself when you find it. And don't make the mistake of thinking that this will be a quick or easy job because that's all it is. The archives are . . . strange."

It took Harper two hours to write up the memo on her ongoing projects. She hit send and then walked back to Madison's office.

"The first thing you need to know is that the magical archives are separate from the mundane ones. They're up on the thirty-ninth floor."

Harper took the bait and made the obvious statement. "This building only has thirty-eight floors."

"Most of the time that's true." Madison handed Harper a piece of plastic that looked like someone had taken an electronic access card and cut it into the shape of an old-fashioned key. "Use this in the elevator, and it will have thirty-nine."

She slid a small clear box and a white candle across her

desk. "When you get off the elevator, tap the top of the box three times. That will activate the spell that gives you safe passage in and out of the archives."

"Safe passage?" Harper asked.

"Trust me. The files that we store there are the most important documents the firm possesses. It is imperative that they not be seen by anyone without permission. The Unseen Archives are on the thirty-ninth floor because the floor is equipped with a magical self-destruct that will destroy it if there's a breach of access. Use the spell."

Harper felt her knees actually go weak and was glad she was already sitting down. "A magical self-destruct."

Madison nodded. "It will take out the entire archive and everything—and everyone—in it. In theory, the rest of the building will be fine, but we don't have offices on thirty-eight. Just in case."

Harper considered the cost of an entire floor of Manhattan real estate left empty. "I . . . Are you sure you don't need someone more magical to do this?"

"The spells I'm giving you are set up like the self-triggering wards. You don't need magic. You just need to follow instructions. But if you don't feel comfortable, I'll pass this to someone else."

Secrets were in the archives. Which meant that if there was anything in this building that would help her find out what actually happened to Rose, this was where it would be. "No, I can handle it. Tap the box three times for safe passage. And the candle?"

"Light it magically once you're in there, and it will trigger the room's lights and help you find the files. Good luck."

The key worked easily enough. The elevator rose smoothly to thirty-eight, then paused and hopped up one final floor. There was no number in the display, but a symbol of a box, like the one Harper held in her hand.

She stepped off the elevator into a grey concrete room that was—as far as she could tell—empty. She tapped the top of the box three times.

Pink cotton-candy-scented smoke curled out of the box and thickened. For a very long minute, while Harper prayed not to be vaporized, the smoke was all she could see. Then it disappeared, and she realized that she was not in a grey concrete room at all. She was in a room that looked like an elegant library. A very large, elegant library. Windows stretched from floor to ceiling, and green plants vined down the walls. There were worn wood floors and long tables, and there were files. Shelf after shelf after shelf of files.

Harper braced for the headache and lit the candle. As she did, lights flicked on—wall sconces and an enormous chandelier. She looked around for a reference, a card catalog, anything that would let her know where to begin looking. Nothing.

She walked over to the closed shelf and pulled down a file—no name and blank pages. She looked again at the candle—Madison had said it would help her find the files. She held it up—there. Where the light from the candle shone, the file was illuminated.

It was not the Prospero disinheritance. It was something to do with the purchase of the land underneath what was now House Dee and whether magic could be used as consideration in the sale. The next file was also not the Prospero disinheritance. Neither was the next. Nor were they in any order that she could figure out. Contracts were next to divorce proceedings were next to wills were next to intellectual property licenses. Apparently, it was possible to patent a spell.

She picked up her phone to text Madison, to see if there was any other spell she was supposed to use to figure out the filing system. "That can't be right." The time on her lock screen was the same as the time stamp she had put on the memo she'd sent to Madison earlier that day. Her stomach rumbled, suggesting that a significant amount of time had passed since lunch.

"This is too weird." Harper blew out her candle and got back on the elevator. As it descended, her phone recalibrated. 7:47 p.m. She'd been in the archives for almost four hours.

"Sorry about that," Madison said. "Time is . . . weird up there. We keep watches—ones you actually have to wind. I'll get one for you to use. And go ahead and order in food tonight and expense it. I should have remembered to warn you."

"Thanks," Harper said. "And the filing?"

Madison looked away. "I'll see what I can do, but it might take some time. I'll need to consult outside the firm. For now, keep looking and hope you get lucky."

It was the first of the challenges that were required to invoke mortality—Lara Merlin casting against Bryce Dee—and the room was packed full of magicians who resembled nothing as much as circling sharks. The failures of magic had continued, had—it seemed—increased. Not just during challenges, but simple spells, casual magics, glamours and illusions simply deciding not to work. And as the failures continued, the speculations over their causes increased. One of the louder theories was that things were somehow Miles Merlin's fault—that his magic had grown weak, that his control was slipping. As the head of the Unseen World went, so did magic. It would balance things out, the whispers went, if his daughter died to pay his debt.

Sydney wanted to spit. She had no patience for Miles, but even less for those who would visit the sins of the father onto his child.

"I hear this is your fault. You stole our magic when you snuck out of that place." An older man, face red enough to suggest he'd been drinking for quite some time, stepped in front of Sydney. She stepped around, then found herself yanked back, his hand squeezing her arm. "I'm talking to you, bitch."

"I have no interest in listening." She bent the index and ring fingers on her left hand, and the man yanked his own hand back, as if from a hot stove. He continued to mumble slurs and rage as she walked away but had enough self-preservation not to follow.

Had tonight's duel been between almost anyone else, Sydney would have stayed home. She had no great desire to watch people destroy each other for the amusement of a crowd. But Ian, she knew, loved his sister.

She continued through the room, and stopped when she reached him.

He stood alone at the front of the crowd, his hands fisted at his sides, the bones pressing white against his skin. "I couldn't not be here. I didn't want to be, but I couldn't stay away."

"She's better than he is," Sydney said, her voice matter-of-fact. "Your sister. She's smart, and she's strategic. Bryce thinks he has twice the talent he actually has, and he underestimates everyone else." She moved her hand until the back of it was—just—touching Ian's.

"She used to do this thing when she was little, when she was just learning magic," Ian said, his eyes never leaving Lara, who stood in solitude at the front of the room. "She called it setting booby traps. She made little pockets of magic that would be triggered when you'd do something like open a door. They'd go off, and you'd be covered in glitter or feathers or something ridiculous, and she'd cackle like a tiny witch. I'd set them off on purpose, just to hear her laugh like that.

"But the best one—my dad was having a dinner party. Very fancy, Heads of Houses, all that. Lara heard 'party' and didn't understand why she couldn't go. So she—I still don't know how—made a booby trap full of tiny frogs and set it to go off when my dad sat down in his chair. They hopped everywhere—the plates, the water glasses, people's laps . . ."

The beginnings of a laugh escaped Sydney, and she bit down hard on the inside of her mouth to keep the rest of it in. "I think I might like your sister."

"I think you would," Ian said.

The challenge began.

It seemed at first as if Lara were doing nothing but standing still. It happened, sometimes, magicians who did not understand the gravity of a mortal challenge until they were in the middle of one and froze. Bryce was visibly casting something—his hands and mouth were moving, and the air around him was shaking. He flung something unidentifiable at Lara, tossing the spell like a softball. But beyond raising a hand to deflect whatever it was, she did nothing.

The crowd rumbled, feral and hungry.

Ian drew tighter and tighter, tension vibrating through him. Sydney watched neither of the men, her focus completely on Lara's hands. "Oh, I do like your sister. I like her very much," she whispered.

Ian turned and stared at her in shock.

"Just watch," Sydney said.

Then Bryce wiped his arm across his forehead. Red smeared across his skin and his sleeve. As if that was a cue, blood dripped from his hairline, his eyes, his ears—faster and faster until he ran with red, the floor slick with it beneath him. In less than a minute, he had collapsed on the floor. In less than two, he was dead.

Lara straightened her cuffs, then left the room without speaking to anyone. Ian watched her go. Only when he could no longer see her did he look for his father.

Miles Merlin had not been in attendance.

When Miranda walked into her office the next morning, Sydney was waiting behind the desk. "Don't bother to check your wards. I took them down after the House let me in."

"The House *let* you in." Miranda's left hand flickered against her side.

"I asked it nicely, and it opened its door right up." Sydney lips curved up, an expression so bright and fake that it was the funhouse version of a smile, and she batted her lashes. "And don't bother with that spell you're starting either—I could stop your heart before you finished casting. You've seen my magic, so you know that's true, and you're smart enough to know that if I wanted you dead, it would have been a spell waiting in here for you, not me. So why don't you trust that all I want is a civilized conversation, and have a seat."

"I suppose you have some reason for your theatrics." Miranda settled into one of her own guest chairs, her back pin-straight, her legs crossed at her ankles. She took her time, smoothing imaginary wrinkles from her skirt, brushing invisible lint from her jacket. She glanced up at the mirror, but it was frustratingly blank. The House was not going to offer her any clues. They would have words, later, about why it hadn't warned her, and—more important—about why it had let Sydney in to begin with.

"I have a message for you. I wanted to be sure it was delivered." Sydney slid the envelope with the challenge in it across the desk.

Miranda left it untouched.

"The challenge was Shara's directive. She says it's to allow me revenge, though I've never heard of the House caring about any of the children who were tossed into it being allowed to take vengeance on the parents who abandoned them there. There are so few of us, though, so I could be wrong. Anyway, with Dad already dead, you're it. Mom."

The color drained from Miranda's face as Sydney spoke, leaving her pale as her silk blouse. "I don't find that at all funny."

"Neither did I, when I found out. Shara doesn't tell us which Houses gave us away. 'You're all Shadows now. That's all that matters.' She'd say that over and over to those of us who survived long enough to ask. I think it was to make us feel like we were special, instead of like we'd been thrown away.

"But to be able to leave, to be able to convince the House that I was strong enough to walk through its doors and survive crossing that threshold, well, that took time. There were tests to pass, secrets to be learned.

"I learned a lot of them. Though I do wonder: Was it because Grey was the boy and you're just conservative enough to think that those feudal guys were right about primogeniture, or did you flip a coin to decide which of your kids Shadows would grind up and use for magic?" Sydney drummed her fingers on Miranda's desk.

"You." Disbelief and hope warred in Miranda's voice. "Alive."

"Yes. Me. Alive. Sorry, Mom." A quick, casual shrug. "Why else do you think the House let me in?"

"What you're suggesting is impossible." Eyes not leaving Sydney's face.

"I'm surprised you admit that. I thought people like me were the fairy tale you all told yourselves about Shadows so you could feel better. 'But some of them get out!' I mean, there have only ever been two of us. Verenice and me. And it's not like the rest are on extended vacation somewhere. But, you know, two is more than one, so that means *some* of us got out."

"Shara promised me. I begged her. I bribed her. And she promised me she would tell me if my daughter made it out," Miranda said.

"Shara says a lot of words that sound like promises. I've learned it's smarter to not believe any of them that aren't written down. Shadows does love its contracts." Acid in Sydney's voice. "Like I said, the House let me in, and yes, I did things the old-fashioned way and gave it my blood, but if that's not enough, I can prove who I am now, if you'll agree to the casting."

"A Perdita spell?" Miranda asked. She didn't see how the House could be wrong; she was terrified that it was right.

"Seems appropriate."

"Fine. I assume you have something sharp."

"Always," Sydney said. She spoke a word that shattered against the air and drew a fingernail over the pad of her thumb. The skin parted in a precise line. She squeezed three drops of blood onto Miranda's desk, then held out her hand to her mother. Miranda's hand shook in hers as she repeated the action. Sydney said a line of poetry, and the scent of lilies filled the room.

The comingled blood turned gold.

Miranda stepped backward once, again, until she stumbled against her chair and sat down. "I begged her to tell me." She closed her eyes. "I'll decline the challenge."

"No," Sydney said. "You'll accept it. And you'll require that it be held soon."

"Ian could kill you."

"Unlikely," Sydney said. "Besides, do you honestly think Shara would let me keep walking around if I went against her wishes? Let me make this easy for you, since you don't seem to have much of a handle on her character: She wouldn't. She'd see me dead in a blink. I'm still bound to Shadows—I still owe interest on the debt you sold me into, so when she says 'jump,' I don't even need to ask how high, because my muscles are already coiling."

"Your father." Miranda's voice sounded as if she were speaking from very far away, perhaps even from the past.

"What?" Sharp as the spell that had pooled blood onto Miranda's desk.

"Your father was the one who took you to that place. He told me you were stillborn. I didn't find out what he had done until the most recent Turning." Anger, still. "I wasn't going to give away any of my children. I had planned to find some unwanted infant and pay our debt with it. But he said family blood kept the magic purer. Stronger. He did this.

"I killed him for it, during a challenge. I made sure a spell went wrong."

"That's all well and good, but in the end, it doesn't matter who walked me through the doors and left me there. Someone did. And you may well have killed him to make yourself feel better, but it's not like you took yourself over to Shadows to ask for me back, now, is it?" Sydney asked.

Miranda's face was her answer.

"Exactly. Let you know if I got out, but you weren't about to try to pull me out early. Not and have to suffer for your magic. And you still use Shadows' magic—this entire House reeks of it. I made you dance, just like almost every other damn magician the night of the first challenge. You can say you wouldn't this and you're sorry that, but words are easy, and your actions say otherwise. So forgive me if I don't reach out for a hug. Mom."

"I've just found you again." Tears in Miranda's eyes.

"And what? I'm supposed to believe you feel some miraculous connection to me? That you feel bad about what I went through, what I suffered to get here, and now you want to make amends? Your entire world is built on suffering—the fact that I lived through it changes nothing about that."

"That is the way our world is," Miranda said. "You can't change that."

"That's where you're wrong. Accept the challenge, Miranda.

If you want some kind of relationship with me, that's where it starts." Sydney got up and walked out of her mother's office.

The House said nothing as it closed its doors behind her.

Miranda sat in the quiet of her office after Sydney left. After some time had passed, she stood up, walked around the desk, and sat in her own chair. She gathered up the desk pad and threw it away—the blood from the Perdita spell had ruined it. It would have to be replaced. Then she straightened the items on top of her desk, making sure they were precisely where she wanted them.

She did not ask the House why it hadn't warned her that Sydney was there.

Miranda picked up her pen and wrote "accepted" in even script on the challenge. On the line for choice of magic, she wrote one more word: "mortal."

Then she took the ruined desk pad back out of the trash. The proof of the results of the Perdita spell would be necessary. She picked up the phone and called her lawyers.

CHAPTER THIRTEEN

"I'm so pleased you had time to meet with me today," Miles Merlin said. "And thank you for being willing to come here, to the House, instead of to my club. I have some rather delicate news that I wanted to share, and I really felt that it was better to do so here, where we wouldn't be disturbed."

"Of course," Grey said. He would have preferred the Mages' Club, where they could have been seen together, but he'd still been thrilled to get the invitation. This was exactly what he'd been waiting for. For someone to acknowledge that he had value as an ally. The fact that it was Miles Merlin, his mother's biggest rival, just made it sweeter.

"Though, just because we're in more personal surroundings doesn't mean I can't offer you a drink. You're a Scotch man, am I right?" Merlin set out glasses.

"Neat, please." Even more flattered then, that Merlin had gone to the trouble to find out what he drank. This was the beginning of his return to his rightful place, to the inner circles of the Unseen World. While he waited, Grey looked around the room. Screens and monitors covered the walls, scrolling data, flashing images. Something happening everywhere, and everything up to date and top of the line. It looked like power—like the sort of room he wanted for himself.

"Very different from House Prospero, isn't it?" Merlin asked.

"It is. But this—this feels more like the future. I'm more comfortable in a House like this."

"I suspected you might be." Merlin handed Grey his drink. "I asked you here because I—well, first because I've been very interested in your progress through the Turning. As you know, my own son and I have had a disagreement and parted ways, but he hasn't chosen to do what you've done. He hasn't chosen to strike out on his own, to attempt to establish his own House. I would have preferred it if he had—I could at least respect his ambition." The last as an aside, a secret confessed between friends.

"Once I left Prospero, I always knew I'd work to establish myself as a House at the next Turning," Grey said, glossing over the fact that his leaving Prospero hadn't been voluntary, making it seem instead like a choice made through ambition.

"No thought of reconciliation with Miranda, then? Although, I suppose you wouldn't, not after what happened." Merlin shook his head, the image of a man remembering something he'd rather forget.

Grey set his drink down. "There was a binding to silence put in place over the disinheritance."

"Oh, no, no. I don't mean that. I'm not referring to any of your actions. I mean what she did. To your father." And now Merlin looked at Grey straight on.

"To my father?" Grey's hand went to the shoulder that had been hurt by the magic that killed his father.

"Yes, of course. That's right," Merlin said. "You were there. I apologize for mentioning it. I don't want to bring up bad memories. I shouldn't say anything else."

"If she did something to him, I want to know."

"I don't have any concrete proof, of course, or I would have done something officially. But you and I, we're men of the world. We both understand that sometimes official isn't the best way to go about doing things." Merlin poured more Scotch into Grey's glass. "But, as you remember, the party was at House Prospero. And the mirror, well, I've heard it was one of your mother's. I don't know why she would have allowed something of hers to be used in a challenge like that. Unless."

"Unless she had done something to it," Grey said, his face growing hard. "If she had sabotaged it because she wanted my father dead." It made—in the haze of his memory and the unhealing wound of his anger at Miranda—a kind of perfect sense.

Merlin rested his hand, briefly, on Grey's shoulder, the same shoulder that bore the scars from that misfired spell. "I'm only sorry I can't tell you more. That I can't be the one to help you reopen your disinheritance or somehow get back what is rightfully yours. But with so much at stake, I couldn't stay silent—I know what it is to have family betray you."

"I'm glad you told me," Grey said, tossing back the last of his drink. "I'm his son. I should know. And you're right—sometimes official isn't the best way to go about doing things. It's too rigid—too easy."

"You would think," Merlin mused, more to his glass than to Grey, "that someone who had interfered in a previous Turning would guard against that sort of thing, but sometimes I think success blinds people. They become complacent. Too sure of themselves. It leaves them open to mistakes. Or to surprises. Challenges are so fraught—you never can be sure of what will happen at one."

"It's a Turning," Grey said. "Mistakes do happen."

Merlin's eyes sharpened like a hawk's. "They certainly do. Though if there is anything I can do, officially, don't hesitate to ask. You're so close to Ian's age—I feel like if I could help you, well, it would almost be like helping him. Plus, I have a vested interest in making sure that the kind of people who make it through the Turning—either to establish Houses, or as heirs of Houses that already exist—really do represent the best of the Unseen World. Magic should be for those who deserve it.

"Will I see you at Prospero's next challenge?"

"You know," Grey said, "I had already intended to be there,

to show my support for Laurent. But now I think it's even more important that I go. Though won't that be difficult for you, with Ian representing House Prospero?"

"The thing about a duel is, you never know what might happen in the course of it," Miles said. "And if something does go wrong—we're certainly having enough issues with magic that such a thing might be possible—you never know what might happen or who might be affected."

"That," Grey said, "is a very good point. Thank you again for meeting with me."

"Certainly," Miles said. "I found it very instructive."

Grey didn't bother with small talk. He'd picked the first girl alone at the bar, dropped a spell into her drink, and had her outside within five minutes.

There wasn't time, not now. He needed more magic. The Beauchamps-Prospero duel was in two days, and he had plans for that evening.

The girl stumbled as he shoved her around the corner, into an alley. Once she fell, he hauled her through the rotting garbage and slush behind a dumpster. The stench was unbearable, but it meant they'd be less likely to be disturbed.

She didn't struggle, didn't fight. Just lay there, eyes blown wide with shock as he ripped the bones from her hands. He suspected he'd been too heavy-handed with the spell, not that it mattered one way or the other. It's not like he wanted her to wake up when he was finished.

The last bone came loose with a pop and a spattering of blood. He tucked it in his pocket with the rest, then said the words that would steal her breath. She'd go quietly, and he'd be gone.

He had magic to plan. He had a House to take back.

"Getting the challenge was bad enough," Ian said, pacing through Verenice's library. "But Sydney won't talk to me at all. At all. I've texted and called and emailed and nothing. Not one response. And this isn't a question of who has the best spell. This is a mortal challenge. One of us dies at the end. I have no idea how to handle this."

"I'm not quite sure why you're asking me for advice," Verenice said. "It seems to me that you have two options—you duel, and you duel to win, because I am sure Sydney will, or you forfeit."

He continued pacing, a pendulum swinging wildly across the room. "That can't be all there is. I feel like there's something else going on. Like, there's part of the challenge that's a secret. Which I would really like to know about, since I'm one of the people maybe dying over it."

"And even if there were, how would that change what you are required to do?" Verenice asked. "You signed a contract with House Prospero. You agreed to stand as their champion, knowing that the Turning always ends with the invocation of mortality, knowing that if you got that far, you would risk your life—you would kill—on its behalf. You may not like the fact that you're matched against Sydney, but this can't have come as a complete surprise to you."

"Intellectually, of course I understood this was possible." He slumped into a chair and dropped his head into his hands. "But this isn't what's supposed to happen."

"'Supposed to?'" Verenice set her teacup down. "The last time I checked, you were an adult with some degree of awareness as to how the world works. Unless you've also become an oracle, I don't think 'supposed to' enters into it.

"Now, if you mean you're frustrated by having only a bad choice, well, I can understand that. But the fact is, you do have one. If you want to be sure that both of you walk away, forfeit the challenge and deal with Miranda later. I assume you've shared your frustration with her and she's not moved by the fact that you're occasionally sleeping with your opponent?"

Ian winced. "I didn't phrase it like that, but yes. All she said was that she had spoken to Sydney and the duel would be held as scheduled.

"I mean, what the hell? And why will she talk to Miranda and not me?"

"And have you told Sydney all your secrets? Does she know, for example, about your aunt?" Verenice asked.

"No." He couldn't. He'd seen the scars on Sydney's arms and he knew those were the least of it. He didn't know how to look her in the eye and tell her that Shara was his aunt.

"Then you can hardly blame her for clinging to some of her own. As I said, you still have a choice. You may not much like it, but it's there. The worst that will happen to you if you forfeit and it's found to be for a reason outside of the immediate terms of the challenge is that your magic will be stripped. And as unfortunate as that might be, I would think that a life without magic is still preferable to death. Or killing someone you have feelings for."

"I'd feel better about making my choice—even if it's a bad one—if I knew what Sydney was doing," Ian said. "Laurent said the challenge was Sydney's idea. She has to have a plan, right?"

"The challenge was Sydney's idea?" Tea sloshed over the rim of Verenice's cup.

"She even insisted on delivering it in person."

Before she had left Shadows, Verenice had learned the identity of the House that had given her up. She had never used her House name, taking her own instead. But she was certain that Sydney would have learned the same thing. Certain, too, now, of what she had only suspected before—that this challenge was at the direction of Shadows, that Shara had set Sydney against Prospero for a reason. That Sydney would not be allowed to forfeit or to show any mercy. And that she wanted Miranda to know who she was before it happened.

"Verenice? She has a plan, right?" Ian repeated.

"Yes," she said, her voice shaking, "yes, she does. Ian, forfeit the challenge. Even if it means Miranda enforces the letter of the contract and strips your magic. Sydney will kill you if you don't."

"That's not very comforting," he said, and pushed a grin across his face, a feeble attempt to lighten the atmosphere in the room.

"It isn't meant to be."

"Well, I should go," he said. He leaned over and kissed her on the cheek. "Thanks, Verenice."

She closed the door behind him, "Goodbye."

Sydney stood on her balcony, watching as the sun set.

Darkness fell early this time of year—such a change from the blue-purple evenings that seemed to stretch on forever that she'd seen when she'd first left Shadows. It was quiet—or as quiet as the city got, anyway—the horns of taxis and the hum of the subway white noise in the background of her life.

Magic twisted like vines through her. She could see it, sparking, beneath her skin.

She had gotten used to it now, the sharp greenness of the magic, the way it would roar through her if left unchecked. It would be enough, and more than enough, to get through the challenge tomorrow. She didn't allow herself to think of any moments past that. There would be consequences, but then, there always were.

Ian had tried and tried again to talk to her. She had text after unanswered text on her phone. But talking to him wouldn't change anything, so she hadn't. Shadows had given her a task, and she would see it done.

She did not want to kill Ian. She would kill him if she had to.

There were more things at stake than simply what she wanted.

The ragged ends of her shadow wept at her feet.

For now she was here: outside, in her own space, above the city, under the stars. She could get through tomorrow. And whatever came after.

CHAPTER FOURTEEN

Harper passed the candle over the page: PROSPERO, MIRANDA. IN THE MATTER OF ~~PROSPERO~~, GREY. This was it—the disinheritance. If she hadn't been so exhausted from spending twelve hours a day every day for the past two weeks in the archives, she would have broken out into a dance. Madison had gotten a spell to use to help sort the files, but it had been clumsy—the candle would burn blue if the file related to House Prospero, and red for anything else. Which was great, except there were *a lot* of files for House Prospero—it was one of the oldest Houses. And the candle didn't distinguish between a hundred-year-old disagreement over disappearing carriage horses and files that actually involved Miranda. It had been a long and headache-filled two weeks. Still, she paused to grin and punch the air in victory.

Grey had, apparently, been disinherited for "improper appropriation of magic (attempted)." Harper's mouth twisted. That wasn't a phrase she had seen in the archives, and she had seen plenty of weirdness since she had started reading through them—"inappropriate reappearance" was her favorite so far.

But this just sounded like someone making something up so they could pretend to be official.

The first pages of the file detailed the legal consequences of his disinheritance. House Prospero, in itself and in its members, would no longer recognize him; he was no longer heir to any of Miranda's goods or property, real or otherwise.

And then what he'd actually done became clear.

It was not a police file—there were no photographs of his victim, and for that Harper was desperately grateful. But there was a description. Language so cold and detached that she read it twice to make sure she hadn't missed something.

Grey Prospero was disinherited for trying to murder his girlfriend for her magic.

Not Rose. Another woman. Grace Valentine.

Not Rose. But in circumstances so similar, it could have been.

Harper wasn't sure if it was better, or not, to know that some other woman had been hurt that way. Like Rose had been, like she'd heard other women had been. All the little details that matched up so well that she kept seeing the image she had tried every day for two years to banish from her mind. The image of a man, his face in shadows, bent over her friend's body, cutting into her hands. Grace's hands had been cut, carved into, but she had stopped Grey, had escaped, before he had finished.

A sob burst out of Harper, echoing off the walls of the archives.

Harper pressed the heels of her hands against her eyes, holding the tears in. Sucked in a breath. "This is what you came here to do, remember? This will help Rose." Her voice was shaky and thin, but she felt better for saying it.

She kept reading. Nothing ever said what happened to the woman involved, to Grace, after the disinheritance had been finalized. Harper wondered if it would be possible to find her—to talk to her.

She read a few key paragraphs of the disinheritance papers out loud then, testing the binding. No magic rose up to choke off her words in her throat, and nothing happened when she tucked the file into her messenger bag to take back downstairs.

She went to Madison's office and closed the door behind her as she walked in. "I found the file. And there's something I need to tell you," she said.

Sydney's phone rang. A text alert popped up simultaneously. From Madison: *Answer. Emergency.*

Sydney answered. "I'm on my way to fight a mortal challenge against Ian, so I hope this really is an emergency."

"Trust me, Sydney, this is something you'll want to know. The blue fox eats pies for moon day breakfast."

"Madison. Are you drunk?"

"Fuck. No. I'm not. I'm trying to tell you about that thing you wanted me to look up." Frustration rang through her voice.

Sydney considered. "The disinheritance?"

"Yes. The sea overflows onto candy floss."

"The binding seems to be fully in place." It was almost, almost funny, Sydney thought.

"Damn it, yes. But Sydney, there's no good to come of a universe in a house."

Sydney stopped. Pinched the bridge of her nose. "There's a difference between something that's an emergency for me, personally, and something that means I should forfeit this challenge. I trust you, Madison—which is it?"

A pause, and then a breath blown out. "Fight your challenge, Sydney. Win. This will still be there for you when it's over."

Sydney hung up and turned off her phone.

Madison clicked her phone off and turned to Harper. "I'm guessing from your face that it sounded like I was talking nonsense to you, too."

Harper's eyes were wide. "That was bizarre. And probably also means that having her come here to look at the files herself won't work, either."

Madison said nothing.

"Right?" Harper asked.

Madison shook her head. “Sorry. Preoccupied. You’re right. Yes—what just happened shows the binding is keyed to people, not place. She wouldn’t be able to read it if she came here, and—if by some miracle we could get it out of the building—it would still read as gibberish if we brought it to her.”

“But that’s good, right? I mean, not in and of itself, but that we know that.”

“It is. I just . . . I have the awful feeling that I just gave Sydney the wrong advice.” She stared at the file on her desk like someone reading an augury.

“What else were you supposed to say? You literally can’t tell her what’s in the file, and even if you could, it’s not like she’s dueling Grey tonight.” Harper leaned against Madison’s door.

“I know,” Madison said. “But something is off. I can’t quite put things together, and I don’t like it.”

“She’ll win, though, right?” Harper thought of those seconds of video, of flying cars and the woman who had made that look easy. She didn’t want to imagine the magician who could beat her.

“She should,” Madison said. “She should. Anyway, you should go—it’s late, and there’s obviously nothing else we can do right now. Oh, and you did great work on this, Harper. Thanks.”

"I did it for Rose. I mean, don't get me wrong, I like this job, but I did this for her." She felt oddly washed out inside, like it hadn't quite sunk in, what she'd found. She'd go to Rose's grave this weekend, tell her. Not absolute proof, and not justice, not yet, but Harper knew in her gut that she was close.

"I get it," Madison said.

"Anyway, good night." Harper went to her office to close out a few things and gather her stuff. It took longer than she'd planned. There was always one more email, and her brain felt like it was thinking through mud. As she was finally leaving—so ready to go home, have a hot bath and the world's largest glass of wine—she heard Madison's phone ring, then heard Madison say, "Oh my God."

She dropped her bag and ran to Madison's office.

There was no party this time. Nothing fancy. No passed champagne or elegant gowns. Only Sydney and Ian and death between them.

Even now, Ian thought, Laurent looked more nervous than Sydney did. He looked fidgety, stressed, closed off. Not his usual collected self. Ian couldn't read Miranda either. She had chosen to attend, which she hadn't done for any of the challenges that weren't attached to social occasions. Though, he supposed, this one was, in its own way. Nearly all the other Houses, candidate and established, their Heads and heirs and champions, were in attendance. Blood in the water and all that. Miranda looked preoccupied, focused on Sydney as if she would be the one dueling her.

Sydney looked as calm as ever, as if they were standing in the center of the room to shake hands or exchange recipes. Not to cast magic at each other until one of them was dead. There should have been words. He had words for so much magic, but no magic word to help him understand what she was doing.

She had to have a plan.

His father was there, because of course Miles Merlin was there. Ian wasn't sure if Miles was more looking forward to seeing House Prospero or Sydney lose, never mind that in one of those scenarios his own son died. Lara stood, blank-faced, next to him. Ian felt like he should say something to her, but other than, "I'll try not to die," he wasn't sure what.

He had written her a letter, just in case. Verenice would give it to her, if. He had not written anything for his father.

Verenice stood in the back of the room, clear of the press of the crowds, watching Sydney.

Grey Prospero stumbled into the room, clearly in a bad mood and possibly drunk. He headed for Miranda, but Merlin pulled him aside, whispered something to him, and Grey stopped.

Ian felt disconnected from the people, the place, like he was watching a film from behind a window. It was such an ordinary room.

He didn't particularly want to die today. He didn't want to kill Sydney either.

He knew what he had to do.

The clock rang the hour. The challenge began.

Sydney opened her hand. Power knifed between them.

Ian stumbled back, shouted a word that rippled the air and raised his hand to shield himself as he fell.

A line of red appeared across it, and blood ran down his arm. "Sydney!"

"I'm sorry. Did you not hear that we were starting?" She coiled shadows like snakes and sent them slithering. They crawled over Ian, wound their way up his legs, holding him in place as he tried to stagger to his feet. "Or were you just planning to not fight back?"

A window exploded behind Sydney, shards of glass in the air like death in pieces. She didn't even look, simply raised a hand. The glass paused in its fall, an afterthought of shattering, then changed shape and fell as snowflakes to the floor.

"Ian, do better." Her face was a terrible thing.

Ian bent his hands at such severe angles, it looked like they would snap. He spoke a phrase that scorched the back of his throat, that spattered blood across his lips and sent a dragon of flame rising into the air.

"Thank you. It was like you weren't even trying." Sydney

raised her hands in the air and the room darkened. Shadows, creeping from their corners, growing and rising and thickening. The shadows carried terror. As they grew, Ian felt his own heart grow darker, lonelier. The small part of him not focused on controlling his magic registered the sounds of weeping from somewhere in the room. The shadows resolved into a shape—reverse negative of the dragon. It opened its mouth impossibly wide and began to swallow the dragon of flame.

Somewhere in the crowd a scuffle. A snap of magic that was neither of theirs—a spell that shouldn't have been cast. "Sydney!" Ian shouted.

"I've got it!"

He felt the terror release its grip on him at the same time as he let go of his own spell. Felt a ward pass over him like a tidal wave, and he flung his own after it.

The dragon, now a thing of combined flame and shadow, plummeted toward the assembled magicians. It burned out, disappeared as it dropped, the magic sheering off of it.

As the flames extinguished, as the shadows dissipated, it became clear that the wards he and Sydney cast had been almost enough. Nearly everyone in the room was unharmed.

Miranda Prospero lay, unmoving, on the floor.

Sydney spoke into the shock. "House Beauchamps forfeits the challenge."

• • •

Chaos ensued.

"What in the actual fuck was that?" Ian asked, pulling Sydney away from the crowd.

"You're going to want to take your hand off my arm and rephrase your question, Ian, or we're going to continue our duel in an unsanctioned manner. And in case you hadn't noticed, I was winning." Fury in every line of her body.

"I had noticed. I noticed very well that you were actually trying to kill me."

"I'm not sure how that was a surprise to you, what with the notice of the challenge and all. And even if that were somehow a surprise, you fought back. Poorly."

"Seriously?" He stared. "So are you angry that I fought back, or that I didn't meet your exalted standards?" He turned away from her, then snapped back, "You could have forfeited."

"*You* could have. I couldn't. And before you get self-righteous, Ian, look." She held up her shadow, displaying the ragged ends. "Shadows owns me. *Owns*."

Shock on his face. "Sydney, no."

"Did Verenice not tell you that part of it? I can't blame her—it's worse, somehow, than being sent there in the first place. Shadows owns me, and my magic, and it wanted this challenge fought, and yes, had I refused, they could have forced me. It's bad enough that I forfeited at the end." She shuddered.

"And you didn't think to tell me that. That you didn't have a choice, that someone was forcing your hand. I tried to talk to you, Sydney, to find a way out of this. I *tried*."

"No, I didn't think to tell you that. I mean, what was I supposed to say—please give up your magic so I don't have to kill you? It's my life, my problem. Besides, what would you have done if I did?"

"I would have forfeited the challenge at the beginning."

"Would you?" she asked, the fury gone now, only exhaustion remaining in her voice. "Would you really? And let yourself be stripped of your magic? Or would you have done exactly what you did—cast a bunch of second-rate defensive spells in the hopes that one got lucky so you could tell yourself that it was self-defense? Because Verenice told you I was going to kill you, so I'm not sure why the precise reason I'd made that decision mattered all that much."

She watched as shame covered his face like a veil. "That's what I thought. The one thing—the *one* thing I could have asked you to do that would have helped me was to die for me. So no, I'm not sorry for not returning your texts."

He pushed his hand through his hair. "Fine. Fine. Just—would you really have killed me?"

She stepped close, curled her hand around his cheek, looked him straight in the eyes. "Ian. You already know the answer to that."

And because he did know the answer, because if he closed his eyes he was certain all he would feel was the terror born from the shadows she had conjured, he didn't ask again.

There was a pause, full of the weight of everything. Ian looked back over Sydney's shoulder. "I'm sorry, this is a private conversation."

"I'm sorry for the interruption. My name is Madison Prospero, and I'm here on behalf of Wellington & Ketchum. It's very important that I speak with Sydney. Immediately."

"Well, this seems very official," Sydney said, offering no hint that she knew the other woman. Madison looked stiff and formal. Possibly worried.

"It is. Due to this evening's events, Miranda Prospero no longer has access to her magic. Unseen law prevents her from holding a House in this condition. Therefore, the inheritance process for House Prospero has been triggered."

She handed Sydney a stack of papers, magically sealed. "This is Miranda's most recent will, naming you as heir to House Prospero. There is also an affidavit that swears to the outcome of the Perdita spell, which proved you are her biological daughter. I'm sure this is a lot to take in right now, but this is a Turning, and so we have little time to wait for a response. Will you please come with me to our offices?"

"I will," Sydney said.

"Sydney?" Ian stepped back. "You're a Prospero?"

"No," she said. "I'm a Shadow. But I'm a Shadow who knows who gave her away."

Madison was silent all the way out to the waiting car. Silent as she and Sydney got in, silent as the car pulled away from the curb. Only then did she hit the button to roll up the partition between them and the driver and say, "Give me a dollar."

"A dollar?" Sydney asked, confusion evident.

"Yes. Just do it."

Sydney kept a skeptical eye on Madison as she reached into her purse. "All I have is a five. Will that—"

Madison plucked the bill from her hand. "And now I'm on retainer. So when I ask you what the fuck you knew and when the fuck you knew it, for example, you can tell me, and it's covered by privilege."

"I've known that Miranda and Christopher Prospero were my biological parents since before I left Shadows," Sydney said. "And as I also know you're not a stupid woman and were paying attention when I asked you about inheritance issues, I know that's not why you're this pissed off at me."

"You're right. Did you know what would happen tonight?" Madison's voice was perfectly empty of inflection.

Sydney turned sideways in the car so that she could look directly at Madison. She made a small gesture with the first and fourth finger of her right hand, and silence enveloped them—the hum of the engine, the spin of the wheels on wet pavement—gone. The only noticeable sound was Madison's breathing. It wasn't quite as steady as she would have wanted it to be. "Are you asking if I attempted to kill Miranda, or, failing that, if I stripped her magic in order to inherit her House?"

"Yes."

"I did not. I might well have done either at some point. If you want my cards on the table, Madison, let's just start with the queen and be clear: I have no problem with, no grief over what happened tonight, and I would feel the same had whoever interfered with the challenge been successful in killing her. But I didn't cause it, and I will take whatever oath you like that there was magical interference during the duel tonight, and that interference was the cause of Miranda's loss of magic. Ian and I both felt someone cast an outside spell—we were too busy trying to wrestle it back into some kind of safety and ward the crowd to notice precisely who or how."

Silence again. Then: "Okay.

"Someone interfered?"

"Yes. Possibly more than one someone—there was some sort of disturbance in the crowd before the spell was cast. Again, I had other things on my mind and missed exactly what it was, but it was loud enough that I noticed it, which means it's likely other magicians did too. I didn't recognize the magic that interrupted the spell, so it was no one I've dueled.

Whoever they were, they were trying to redirect the magic Ian and I were using. I'm pretty sure it was meant to be fatal—they weren't trying to change anything that we had already cast, just send it somewhere else. And while I'm slightly less sure on this, I do think Miranda was the intended target."

"Would you recognize the magic again?" Madison asked.

"Yes."

"Good. You'll need to swear to all of that. I'll have someone meet us at the office so that—Syd. Your hands."

Sydney looked down. The beds of her nails were full of blood. Red drops fell from the ends of her fingers, streaking her pants, the seat of the car. It hit, then—the ache of the magic, the steel-knife feeling of it in her joints. "Backlash from the magic. There are always consequences."

"This *always* happens?"

"This or something similar. The bigger the spell"—she broke off, rolled down the window, stuck her head out, and vomited—"the worse things are. If you could have the driver take me home, please." Sydney leaned back, closed her eyes.

"Yes. Sydney, of course. Is there anything else I can do?"

"What was the emergency? Earlier?"

"Sydney, it doesn't matter right now."

"Okay." The aftermath of magic racking her body, Sydney closed her eyes and fell into sleep.

• • •

Ian woke to the scents of fresh coffee and frying bacon, which was unexpected, as he was the only one who lived in his apartment. He stepped cautiously out of bed and into his kitchen.

"You desperately need to buy groceries," Lara said.

"Sorry. I've been a little preoccupied with my possible imminent death. Which would have meant I wouldn't need food. Though if I'd known you were planning to visit—how did you get in here again?"

She carried two plates—bacon, eggs, hash browns—over to the table. "I came over last night. After the duel. I was waiting in the lobby when you got here. You were . . . not well."

"Consequences for magic," he said between bites of hash browns. "Worse because of what happened in the duel."

"That's actually why I'm here," she said. "You need to know what happened."

"I'm guessing you mean the part at the end with Miranda, because otherwise I've got what happened down pretty well."

She nodded. "It was Dad. He pushed her. Not with magic. With his hands. Which, bad."

Ian set down his fork. "Yes, we'll start with bad, there."

"But I don't think he was the one who actually interfered with the magic. I think that was Grey. And I think the reason that Dad pushed Miranda was that he knew what Grey was going to do. Or at least that he was going to do something."

"I see we're moving on from bad, then."

Lara leveled a stare across the table.

"Sorry. But why would they possibly be working together? Grey's a prat. And not much more."

"Agreed. But the end result of this is Dad's biggest rival is stripped of her magic, and House Prospero is either unmade or given to Grey—"

"Nope." Ian used a slice of bacon to mop up egg yolk. "Sydney was a Prospero. Before she was a Shadow. I was there when the lawyer came by."

"Holy shit," Lara said.

"Pretty much."

"Ian," she said, "the thing is . . . the weirdest thing . . . is Dad pushed her. With his hands, not magic. I wouldn't have noticed if I hadn't been standing next to him, so he must have thought the crowd would hide him, but why not use magic? It would have been a lot easier to hide that."

"When was the last time you saw him cast anything?" Ian asked.

"It's been a while, Ian. I think things are bad. Like, really bad."

"Bad how?" Ian looked at his plate as if he were astonished by the fact that there was suddenly no more food on it.

"I broke into his tower—I told you we needed to talk, Ian, but you are shit at returning your texts."

He winced. "Sorry."

"Anyway, the point being, there's almost no magic in the entire room. Not even traces, like you would expect if someone was even doing basic spells in there. The one place there is, is in a biometrically locked cabinet. Not magically locked, biometrically."

"I'm not sure I follow. You know how Dad likes that sci-fi stuff." Ian poured himself more coffee, trying to make his brain feel faster than sludge.

"I do know that, yes, as I live at that House. Which is now entirely run on sci-fi stuff. Like it would be—"

"Like it would be if Dad didn't have any magic anymore," he said slowly, catching up. "That's why the lock is biometric. He can't trust himself to be able to take down wards."

Lara nodded. "I'm working on a spell to get me past the biometrics. What I want to know is, if I can prove he's lost his magic, will you support me in removing him as Head of House?"

"I don't know what it will be worth, since I'm not officially part of the House anymore, but absolutely. Whatever you need."

"Good," she said. "I should go. Things to do, coups to plan."

"Thanks for breakfast."

"I'm glad you're not dead," she said. "Now buy yourself some damn food."

CHAPTER FIFTEEN

The door to Madison's office flew open and slammed against the wall. "Ms. Prospero, I'm sorry, I told him he couldn't come back without an appointment."

Grey stood, flushed and angry, in her doorway, her secretary standing behind him. It was not a wholly unexpected visit, though she had thought that he would come earlier in the day. "I can give you ten minutes, or you can make an appointment."

"I'm here now, aren't I?" Grey said, and sat in her guest chair. "I need to know if this bullshit I've heard is true."

"And what bullshit would that be?" Madison asked.

"That that woman, that fucking *Shadow*, inherited House Prospero. That House should be mine."

"While it is true that Sydney now holds House Prospero, the fact is, you were disinherited three years ago, in a fully legal and vetted procedure. One which you yourself agreed to and signed off on, with full advice of counsel. This firm, as you know, possesses the file of that proceeding, and I can produce that document should you need to refresh your memory."

"I know what's in the file," Grey said. "But I should still have a claim. I'm a Prospero."

Madison wished she didn't know what was in the file, particularly with him sitting in her office. "Legally, I'm afraid that's not the case. You were disinherited, and the disinheritance stands. And even had Miranda not made a new will—which I have here, witnessed and blood-bonded—Sydney as Miranda's daughter and the closest biological descendant would still inherit."

"She's lying. I don't have a sister."

"Not only do you have a sister, but you have a twin. Miranda stated under oath that twenty-five years ago she was delivered of a living female child—one born before you, incidentally—who was then taken to Shadows. She also swore to the results of a Perdita spell, which confirmed Sydney's parentage. The House itself officially recognized her this morning, in front of the required three witnesses from other Houses. I have affidavits from them, as well as an unedited video recording. You're welcome to review any of it." Madison slid a file and a tablet toward him.

He didn't touch them. "I'll have this undone."

"You're welcome to try. But not today. Your ten minutes are up, and I have work to do."

"Bitch," he said, and slammed the door on his way out.

Madison texted Sydney: *Those extra wards you mentioned? I want them.*

The response was almost immediate: *Done.*

• • •

The whiskey in Grey's glass sloshed as he paced in front of Laurent's windows. "Did you know? When you hired her?"

"I told you, I had no idea who she was. Do you seriously think I would have had your long-lost sister working for me for all this time and not bothered to tell you? She was the third magician I auditioned, and I didn't look at any of the others after her because her magic was so strong. We didn't talk about personal details—we didn't then, and we don't now, because that is her business and not mine. I don't even know where she lives," Laurent answered.

"She's an accident of biology—if even that—not my sister, and she lives at my House now, doesn't she?" Grey slammed his glass down on the counter, paying no attention to the liquid that spilled over the rim.

"I don't understand why you're so upset. You agreed to the disinheritance. You could have fought it. And Sydney could undo it—she'll have to name an heir, and probably soon, with the Turning." Laurent didn't say the other things that he was thinking, that perhaps Grey ought to show a little bit of compassion for what Miranda had done to Sydney, for what the Unseen World had apparently been doing to its children for generations in order to make things easier for itself.

"I don't want to be the heir. Again. The House should be mine. Maybe it won't recognize her. Maybe it won't even let her in the door. My bitch of a lawyer cousin said that it did, but she could have been lying." He tossed back the rest of his drink.

"Is that likely?" Laurent asked. "I mean, listen to yourself."

"All I know is that this woman came from nowhere, and now she's the Head of a House. My House. She shouldn't be allowed to be part of us, especially if she came from the House of Shadows. Do you know what that place is?" Grey sneered.

"Do you?" Laurent asked.

"The magic of Shadows is corrupt. It's not like ours. Anyone who uses it can't be trusted. Plus, Miles says she's the reason for the failures of magic."

Laurent knew he was going to regret asking, but he let the question out anyway. "How is that possible?"

"Because her magic should still be in there. She took it with her when she left, and now we can't use it." Confident in the righteousness of his theories.

"That sounds—you know what, never mind." Laurent moved to the other side of the room, giving Grey's rant a clear berth.

Grey didn't seem to notice. "Prospero should be mine, and I'm going to take it from her. You can help me, or you can stay the fuck out of my way."

The elevator *ping*ed. Grey turned around. "Are you expecting someone?"

"Yes," Laurent said. "Your cab. You're drunk, and you've had a shock, and you've been my best friend for years, so I'm going to give you a pass and put you in a cab. Then I'm going to pretend this conversation never happened, and maybe we'll still be friends tomorrow."

Laurent pushed Grey gently into the elevator and stood away from the closing doors.

"You don't understand," Grey said.

No, Laurent thought, he didn't. He picked up his phone to text Sydney and warn her about the man he had considered to be his best friend, someone who he was pretty sure was not going to be his friend tomorrow, or ever again.

The front desk rang up to Miranda's room. "There's a Verenice Tenebrae here to see you, ma'am."

Miranda considered. "Send her up, please. Oh, and have the kitchen send up afternoon tea. Sandwiches and petit fours." It was still odd to her, this having to request things from other people, rather than her House. Her mirrors all looked strangely empty, wordless and silent.

"Thank you so much for coming by," Miranda said as she ushered Verenice into her suite. "Your dress is lovely. Is it vintage?"

"Still have your manners, I see. I hope you have a spine of steel to go with them. You'll need it after losing your magic.

"You do know it's not coming back, don't you?" Verenice said, matter-of-fact.

Miranda nodded. "I felt the connection break. It's useful for people to be uncertain of me, so I haven't publicly confirmed it. How did you know?"

"We get very good at sensing magic in Shadows," Verenice said. "I knew as soon as I walked in. I'm sure Sydney does as well."

"Yes. It didn't seem right not to tell her, what with her having to take responsibility for the House, but—like you—she knew without my saying anything."

A knock on the door announced room service. Both women sat silently as the waiter set up the tea. Miranda signed the bill and looked up to see Verenice pouring whiskey from the honor bar into the teacups. "I beg your pardon."

"You've just lost your magic and your House. You've found your daughter, who probably wants very little to do with you and is currently risking her life on a regular basis. Tea is not the appropriate beverage for the occasion." Verenice sipped at her porcelain cup of whiskey.

Miranda sat down, eyes blank. Then she picked up her cup and tossed back its contents.

Verenice refilled it.

"Why did you come to visit me?" Miranda asked.

"Because I remembered a conversation we had, years

ago, at your husband's funeral. You asked me about Shadows, which seemed an odd topic of conversation given the setting, but then you asked if I thought anyone else could make it out. People do tend to find things when they go through papers, and as you had just taken over as Head of Prospero, well, I wondered. And now I know, so I wanted to see how you were.

"How are you, Miranda?"

Miranda cut the whiskey in her teacup with tea, then sipped, each movement pulling the veil of control back over her. "I was happy to learn that Sydney's alive, of course. I am happy that she continues to be so. The rest of everything will sort itself out."

Verenice was certain there was more—how could there not be, as this was not at all a situation that would simply sort itself out—but she recognized the words of a woman who had shared all she was going to at that moment. "Also, I'm here because if I know the Unseen World, no one else will have visited."

"Oh, a couple have tried." Miranda straightened the edges of her sandwich and centered it on her plate. "Miles Merlin, to gloat. The Dees, for the same reason. All the fun of a funeral, except with a living subject. I wouldn't see any of them.

"I suppose that's the good thing about all of this. I never need to be polite to some sycophantic ass again." The corners of her mouth approximated a smile.

"If you're through being polite, why did you let me come up unannounced?" Verenice asked.

"Because of Sydney." And here the carefully crafted facade began to break. "Because I want you to tell me that Sydney will be all right. That what happened to her, in there, that it won't matter."

Verenice set her cup down. "I suppose that depends on what you mean by all right. I still have nightmares, for example. It took me almost a year after I got out before I stopped hearing the screaming every time I closed my eyes. There is a great deal of screaming inside Shadows." Her voice was distant, meditative. "And, of course, she's not free yet. Not all the way. She's still bound to the service of the House until she's used enough magic under its direction that it agrees she's paid off the debt incurred by living there."

"The debt?" Miranda asked. "But she didn't have a choice."

"That doesn't matter. We were taught. Trained. Housed. And so we owe. I assume the end of the Turning will see her free—her service to Shadows in the course of it involves a lot of big magic in a short time. That's providing that she survives. Which is not a given—aside from the risks inherent in a Turning, the House may order her to lose."

"To lose?" Miranda, horrified. "That would kill her. Why would they want that?"

"Because it would serve the House." Steady, implacable.

"And until we are truly free, we can do nothing that does not serve the House."

Tears gathered in Miranda's eyes.

"You asked because you knew I wouldn't lie," Verenice said. "And it's unlikely that Shara would waste her in that fashion. But not impossible.

"To return to your original question, I survived everything I was asked to do, and most days, I like my life, so I suppose I am 'all right.' You can decide for yourself if that's enough to assuage your guilt."

"Do you think Sydney will like her life?" Miranda said, her teacup forgotten in her trembling hand.

"I think," Verenice said gently, "that I'm not the one you need to ask that question."

"She won't talk to me. Not really. She's like a stranger."

"Miranda. Can you blame her?"

Miranda pressed her lips together until they went white. The teacup rattled as she set it down. "If you'll forgive me, I find I need to be alone. But I am deeply grateful to you for visiting."

"If you like," Verenice said, "I could come by again."

"I would like that," Miranda said. "Very much."

Sydney agreed to meet, but only if she could choose the location. "The Met. The Temple of Dendur."

There was a pause on the other end of the phone. "Any particular reason?" Ian asked.

"It's beautiful," she said.

As he walked in, he was struck again by the fact that it was—the quality of the light through the glass, the calming stillness of the reflecting pond, the grace and antiquity of the Temple. He joined Sydney on a corner at the water's edge, leaving careful space between them.

"I'm prepared to release you from your obligations to House Prospero," she said. "I haven't had a chance to look at the contract specifically, but I will obviously make good on any financial debts the House owes to you for your service thus far in the Turning."

"I have no desire to be released from any obligations I might owe you," he said. "And it wasn't a financial contract. I serve as champion of House Prospero in the hopes that doing so will put the House is a position of enough power at the end of the Turning to break the Unseen World's relationship with the House of Shadows."

A flicker of expression crossed her face, the subtlest thing. On anyone else, it would have been the equivalent of jaw-dropped shock. "I see."

"You know, I'm sure, that House Merlin helped found the House of Shadows," he said.

She nodded.

"It is not something my family is only passively involved in. It would have been bad enough, if that were everything. But Shara—Shara is my aunt." His hands went to the scars on Sydney's hands and arms. She left them uncovered now, as everyone knew who she was and where she came from, but his shame would have given him a lens to see them even through makeup.

"She's the one who required the challenge to House Prospero," Sydney said. "She knew that you were its champion. What she wants—what she's always wanted—is power. And not just the sort of power she has now, over life and death and pain and suffering. She wants power where she's seen. She thinks that as the Unseen World would not function as it does without the House of Shadows, Shadows should lead it. She sees this Turning as a way to make that happen."

"There's something else you should know," he said, ignoring that his aunt had ordered his probable death. It was among the least of the things she was guilty of. "Lara and I both strongly suspect that Miles is in the process of losing his magic, if it's not already gone. And she knows that he was at least part of the interference in our duel." He explained what Lara had told him.

"I suspected it might be Grey," Sydney said. "He's made it quite clear that he thinks Prospero should be his. He might've thought Miranda was the only thing in his way."

"But why would Miles help him?"

"Shara would find that useful. She'd trade him," Sydney said. "Magic for power. With neither of them knowing who I was, Miles could have pretended to promise Prospero to Grey, and meant it to go to Shara in exchange for access to more magic."

"Is that even possible?" Ian asked. "Giving him more magic, I mean."

"Of course. It's only a variation on the spell that already exists. Make that stronger, increase the number of sacrifices, pull more magic from them—there are ways. There's always a way. The only limit is what people are willing to trade to get what they want."

"I want Shadows ended," Ian said.

"House Prospero is pleased to accept your ongoing service." Sydney rested her hand on top of his for just a moment. Three breaths, no more. Just long enough to acknowledge all that was said and unsaid, in this room full of history.

Shara sang as her knife scratched across Grace's radius. No lyrics, just Shara's voice, rising and falling in counterpoint to the scratch of the knife, to the blood that dripped to the ground, that sank into the floor of Shadows and disappeared. It was not a particularly soothing melody.

The song paused. The knife continued its work.

“I could train you,” Shara said.

“If the House wills.” The expected answer, so little choice in giving it that it meant the same as Shara’s wordless singing.

“I’ll need help.” Shara dropped Grace’s left arm and picked up her right. The knife slid in just before the cluster of small bones in the wrist. “There will be more sacrifices, a stronger House.”

Grace’s gorge rose, and she bit hard at the inside of her mouth, forcing her lips together. She could not speak, could not react, did not have the option of screaming her rejection, of vomiting her sickness at the thought.

“There is power to be found here.” Shara finished her work and cleaned Grace’s blood from her knife. “Consider what I offer. That will be all.”

On her way back to her room, Grace stopped before the House’s doors. She held her hands up—almost, almost touching them. Soon, she promised herself. Soon.

CHAPTER SIXTEEN

Sydney sat next to Laurent at his kitchen table. "Like I told you before, when you first started doing magic, before you were part of the Unseen World, before they got you in school and changed what you did, you were relying only on your own power, not what came from Shadows. Which means you can learn to go back to that."

Laurent drummed his fingers on the table. "Good. I mean, I'd miss having magic, you know? I don't know if I'd even remember how to be a person without it. But I won't use something that comes from hurting people. I can't, not and live with myself."

She nodded. "The first thing I'm going to teach you to do is break yourself of the habits that the Unseen World taught you. Think back—what's the first thing you do when you're setting up a spell?"

"It depends on the spell, really. Sometimes it's knowing the words, and sometimes you build in gestures, or there are pieces that you can set up in advance—"

She cut him off. "I don't mean that. I mean the very first

thing, the thing that's no different from spell to spell."

"Oh, you mean the focus," Laurent said. "I don't even think about that anymore. It's like breathing."

"Then yes," Sydney said. "That's exactly what I mean. That's what you need to get rid of. How did they teach it to you?"

Laurent tipped back in his chair, eyes half-closed. "This takes me back. Freshman year. Ms. Elizabeth Dee's Elements of Magic class. I was in there with a bunch of really little kids—I was an outsider, so I had to learn the basics way after I would have if I'd been born here. It was annoying because I was with these, like, kindergarteners, but it was also kind of cool because Ms. Dee was cute, and she let me borrow her comics. There was this whole series about magic keys. . . ." He trailed off.

Sydney looked deeply amused.

"Moving back from that tangent down memory lane before I fully embarrass myself, she said that it should feel like reaching for a connection. I was supposed to imagine that I was stretching out my hand, and then someone else, someone strong, holds it. I could pull as much strength as I want through that other hand as long as I was holding it.

"Grey used to give me such shit about it, because when I was first learning, my left hand would do this straight-fingered jazz-hands sort of deal at my side whenever I was starting a spell."

"Okay." Sydney nodded. "That's good. We can work with that. We'll start with relearning some spells that don't require any hand gestures. Stand up and put your hands in your pockets."

Laurent did.

"Pick a spell that's easy for you and not likely to burn down your apartment if you do it wrong."

Laurent nodded. "Levitation. I'll use the oranges in the bowl."

"Good. Now, think only about that spell. Not the focus. Don't reach your hands for anything. And cast."

She could see him tremble, see him fight to keep his hands in his pockets, not to reach out for magic that should never have been his.

Laurent spoke the words of the spell, and one orange rolled from the bowl and landed on the table. He watched it in silence until it stopped moving. "Wow. I mean, really, wow. With power like that, I can't believe I didn't try to represent myself. Float cars—hell no. I can roll oranges."

"I know," she said. "Everything is weak and awkward right now, but those things will both improve—it's not an indication of weakness inherent in your magic; it's just part of the process of relearning. And you did it. You cast your own magic without reaching out for what comes from Shadows. How do you feel?"

"Like I have a headache coming on, but nothing bad." He

rolled his head from shoulder to shoulder, shook out his hands.

"Okay. Let's keep trying."

By the end of an hour sweat dampened Laurent's hairline and his shirt. By the end of two hours he was shaking. "And the headache is full-blown."

But also, by the end of those two hours he could reliably levitate an orange out of the bowl. He could control the height it rose to and set it gently back down again. He could do all of these things without reaching for the magic from Shadows.

Sydney filled a glass with water, handed it to him. "I know it seems frustrating. Like you've taken a huge step back and only baby steps forward. But you are doing great. And it will get easier every time.

"It means a lot to me, the most, that you're doing this. Thank you."

"I'll keep practicing on my own. Now that I know it's about not reaching for the focus, I can keep this up. Try different spells," Laurent said. "It's kind of a good feeling, headache aside, to know that I'm doing this completely under my own power."

"Talk to Ian, maybe," Sydney said. "He relearned his magic too—he might have better advice than I do, since he knows what both versions feel like."

"Thanks. I will." He picked up his phone to enter the note in his calendar, then clicked his other notifications. He stared at the email he'd just opened. Refreshed the screen. Read it again, because surely it had to be a joke, or at the least a mistake. "You're not going to believe this."

"Oh, I bet I will," she said. "There's been a challenge. I'm surprised it took this long."

"You're right, but how is that even possible? I mean, honestly, if it were me, I'd want to stay as far away from you as possible. Before all that shit happened, it was clear Ian was toast, and it's not like anyone sees him as a pushover," he said.

"Fortune's Wheel keeps turning." She paused. "If anything, you're likely to get more challenges than otherwise, now that I've stepped into things at Prospero. Word is out that I came from Shadows, which makes exactly no one comfortable. The people who didn't like Miranda will consider whether they can hurt her by coming after me, which may mean that they come after me through you. I won't hold you to the contract, if you want to terminate it." It would be tricky, this late in the process, but there were circumstances—misrepresentation, malfeasance—that would allow Laurent to get out of his contract with her and maintain his status in the Turning.

"Is there a magician who can beat you?" Laurent asked. "Because as far as I can tell, there isn't."

"In the right circumstances, anything is possible. Under expected conditions, no."

"Not even Ian?"

"I thought you said he was clearly toast." She raised a brow.

"Sure, but the desire for vengeance can do funny things to a guy."

"I appreciate the concern, but I forfeited to Prospero after Miranda was injured, which means House Prospero officially won. Even if I wanted a rematch, completed challenges can't be refought. So I think I'm in the clear there."

"Then no. I'll let you out of the contract if you think working for me is too risky, but I'm not terminating it."

"You're stuck with me, then," she said. "There's no one else I trust to keep you safe. And I'm not done yet."

He wasn't at all sure she was only talking about the Turning. "Okay. I'll send the challenge over. Deal with it however you want. That includes forfeiting, if you're sick of all this bullshit.

"And speaking of challenges, I know this might not matter since you have a House now and can make them yourself, but if you ever need to challenge anyone—you know, because you have some sort of plan or something going on with all of this—just let me know. I've got your back."

"I'll keep that in mind," Sydney said. "Thanks."

CHAPTER SEVENTEEN

The great Houses of the Unseen World, the buildings that bore the names of the families who lived in them, were more than just constructions of wood and stone, brick and mortar. Suffused with magic, they were themselves ongoing spells. The doors that opened only for blood members of the House were just the beginning. The older Houses, the ones that had seen generation upon generation, developed further magical links with their families. It was rumored they could even reshape themselves according to the desires of the people who lived within them. House Prospero was one such House.

Sydney had wanted no part of that. "I have an apartment," she had told Madison. "It's nice. You know it's nice because you helped me find it. Here are some of the things I like about it: Except for you and Verenice, no one knows where it is. It doesn't talk to me, or fetch my food, or fucking redesign itself when I'm not looking—I had more than enough of that in Shadows. Also, did I mention that no one knows where it is?"

"Look, I'm not the best person to explain this to you, but

from what I've been given to understand, 'holding the House' is one of those things with hidden layers. You must formally introduce yourself to the House, and you must visit on a semi-regular schedule. Or it stops being yours."

"Must," Sydney had said.

"I'm sorry, Sydney, but yes." Madison had scribbled down a note. "I'll see what I can do to find out the specifics, but for now you need to go claim your House. You don't have to live there; just let it know you're paying attention."

And so here she was. Sydney laid her hand against the door. Something sharp pierced the pad of her finger, deep enough to draw blood. The scent of smoke and oranges rose in the air, and the door opened.

"Let's do this thing," she said, and stepped across the threshold.

On the surface it was nothing like Shadows. There were no dark and cramped spaces, no pockets of coldness that lurked and followed. No sense that a misstep could mean death. No weeping or screams or bloodstains left as warnings. As a place, House Prospero was everything Shadows was not: soaring ceilings, polished blond wood, ornate carpets. The gleam of brass and scent of beeswax. Warmth and quiet. White everywhere, as if dirt would be afraid to land.

She could feel the House's attention as she walked hallways, up and down stairs, as she opened doors and cupboards.

She saw nothing of herself there. Not in the chairs around the kitchen table, the paintings on the walls, the open well-lit spaces that were scented with beautifully arranged flowers, not in the bitter taste of broken magic. This was nothing of how she'd grown up, of what she'd lived.

And yet she was afraid. Afraid to make a sound and disturb the blanket of silence that lay over the House. Afraid to touch anything, to move a chair or a glass and leave it a hair away from precision. Afraid that the slightest mistake would risk the wrath of the House. She'd had more than enough of living like that.

Miranda had checked herself into a hotel. Sydney had made it clear that she had no desire to live in Prospero, that Miranda could certainly remain there and have the place to herself, but Miranda said that wasn't it. "The House, it's like another part of me. Or, at least, it was. Living there cut off from magic, not being able to feel the connection, the presence, that's not something I'm ready for. I don't know if I ever will be."

But for Sydney, that awareness, that sense that the House was watching, waiting, was the one place this House did come close to what Shadows had felt like, and that closeness was too much. A brighter mirror, certainly, but a reflection all the same.

And there was one more issue. The magic, all of the magic

in the House was, like so much of the magic in the Unseen World, contaminated by its connection to Shadows.

Miranda had explained about the mirrors. Sydney stood in front of one. “Can you hear me?”

Yes.

“I need to change your magic. To give you mine.”

Why?

How to explain morality to a House. She would have laughed if it hadn’t mattered.

Are you unhappy with my service?

“No. No. But—you’re my House now. This magic that I want to give you is who I am.”

Very well.

Will it hurt?

She hadn’t thought about it. “I don’t know.”

A pause. *I am ready.*

Sydney hoped she was. She set her fingers on the mirror. Felt its surface liquefy around her hands, felt her hands sink in. A sharpness that scraped over her skin, a cold that etched itself into her bones.

The flutter of the beating heart of the House. The wrongness of the magic from Shadows that wrapped around it. She felt nauseated touching it, but unwound and unwound and unwound that magic until it was gone from the House. From her House.

She pulled her hands from the mirror, leaving it shimmering liquid silver.

Took a small knife and the ragged edge of her shadow and peeled a further piece of it away. Shadows were, like finger bones, a concentrated source of a person's magic, and since she had no plans to live here, this was the fastest way to get the House to acknowledge her magic and build its own around that. She dropped the fragment of shadow into the mirror, then spoke a word that smelled like burnt glass and watched as the mirror's surface resolidified.

"Are you okay?"

She waited. Silence. Then:

Yes.

The word not the elegant cursive of before, but her own rushed scribble.

"Good," she said. Then she looked around—at the white, at the polish, at the formality of the House.

She walked back through the hall, down the stairs, and paused, just before the front door. Said, "This isn't my place. I'm sorry, but I can't stay here."

And left.

House Prospero closed its door behind her, the sound hollow in its emptiness.

It did not want to be empty. Its reason for existence was

service of its family, and it had seen that family shrunk into—into this: empty hallways and closed doors, a fine film of dust settling like a veil. No life in it, no voices, no beating hearts.

It was hers, and she had gone.

It was lonely.

The House considered what it knew about the woman who had just left, what it had learned when she had placed her hands gently on its heart. When she had given it a piece of herself. It began reshaping itself in her image.

Sydney stopped a block from House Prospero. There it was: the familiar, hated feeling of the summons to Shadows itching beneath her skin. The cut edges of her shadow burned.

She had known the summons would come, as it always came. Known the question was when, not if. Knew, too, that there would be the same question through the rest of the Turning, through however long it might be before the House decided that she had earned her freedom.

Through when the House decided.

She was done letting the House of Shadows decide.

She clutched magic in her fists like lightning and stalked through the city like a storm.

On the shore of the reservoir, she lit the required matches. One. Two. Three. The magic just beneath her skin echoed their burning. She stepped into the boat, listening to the boards creak, the waves splash against its sides. Her eyes toward Shadows, looming larger in her field of vision. She focused until it was all she could see.

The boat shuddered against the shore, breaking into pieces. She stepped off. Shadows opened its doors.

Sydney did not walk through. She stood just outside the doors and loosed the magic she'd held tight in her hands. "I challenge the House!"

The House answered.

When it had been time for Sydney to leave Shadows, the testing had been rigorous. She had been required to perform a variety of spells—magics both subtle and complex—under adverse conditions. In cold and rain. Exhausted. Starving. In physical pain and mental anguish.

She had gotten out. She had won free. But she knew her magic, and she knew how close it had been—the moments that had been knife's-edge balanced, that might have kept her inside.

Today was different. Today she was a hurricane.

Sydney cast magic that was an answer to everything she had ever endured behind these doors. She spoke words that cut through walls like knives and carved symbols of freedom on the foundations. She bent her hands into symbols of loosing and broke chains. She curled her fingers and sent windows shattering, letting light come in, shouting words of brightness until every corner was illuminated.

Until there were no shadows left.

She reached into the lines of magic that tied and wrapped like spiders' webs, that offered peace and painlessness to magicians willing to send others to suffer. A word scissored through them, echoed by a wind that blew through Central Park like a storm, breaking branches, downing trees, and sending people running for shelter.

The Angel of the Waters rocked on its foundation, the stone lily crashing from its hand.

Sydney stole the sacrifices, the few that remained, transporting them to emergency rooms, fire stations. Places where unwanted children could be safely left.

It wasn't enough to be free herself. She wanted no one else to ever be trapped again.

Sydney crooked her fingers, and the great doors cracked and fell from their hinges.

She walked through.

The air shifted as she crossed the threshold, and it was no longer Shadows trying to pull Sydney and her magic in, but the House desperately trying to stand against her. It twisted itself and changed its shape—moving hallways, throwing up walls, crumbling floors, but she kept walking.

As she walked, she cast magic of her own: freezing the House's architecture in place, opening its doors, crumbling its foundations. Something rent and something screamed and

Sydney raised her hands and the entire building trembled. Locks opened. Bars loosed. Shadows was a hell, and this was a harrowing.

Once more she reached. There, beating, was the heart of the House of Shadows. She took it in her hand.

"Enough!" Shara, trembling. Not with rage, with effort. Even now, her hand worked at her side, trying frantically to tie scraps of magic together, to prevent her House from falling. From dying.

"Enough," she repeated. "Shadows agrees to release you from your contract."

"I want to see it burn," Sydney said. Not only her contract, but Shadows itself.

"That's unnecessary—the word of the House is binding," Shara said.

Sydney tightened her grip, and the heart of Shadows skipped a step in its beating.

"Fine." Shara held up her hand, and the paper appeared in it, Sydney's name written and written again in shifting darkness that was not ink at the bottom. She snapped her fingers, and it caught fire.

Sydney felt the chains that had bound her to Shadows break and pop and turn to ash as the paper burned. She pulled in a breath, and for the first time in her remembered life, it was fully, solely, hers.

"Are we finished here, you ungrateful brat?" Shara asked.

Sydney bent her fingers into one final piece of magic. The glass bottle that had held her shadow, the knife that had cut it, the pen that wrote, caught fire, burned. "We are."

When the last flame died out, Sydney turned and walked out of Shadows.

She did not look back.

Shara stood in the wreckage of the House, her hands coated in ashes. She could feel the House's crumbling inside her, like her own bones were loosening themselves from her tendons. Shadows was unmaking itself. Slowly now, but if unchecked, it would get worse. Her home was dying, and she would die with it. Because of course, of course, the one piece of magic Sydney had left fully intact was the spell that prevented Shara from leaving. There was a cruelty in her, and Shadows had taught her well how to use it.

Light shone through the rents Sydney had torn in the walls, and the magic—the magic that bound the sacrifices, that made everything—it was unraveling. Slowly now, but it would go faster, and then it would be gone. She stared at her hands, her scars showing in pieces through the ash, and wondered how she would ever get the power to rebuild. House Merlin had made the original spell, but Miles—she laughed, harsh and bitter—she doubted he had even noticed its falling. Even if he had, she knew better than anyone that he didn't have the power to cast it anew.

The failures of magic would come hard and fast now. The look on Miles' face—it wouldn't be worth this, but she looked forward to seeing it. She looked forward to seeing him stand before her and beg. It was important to hold on to the little things.

Shara sat down in the ruins and laughed until the laughter tripped over into weeping.

When she got home, Sydney stood under the shower until the steam turned lukewarm. She wanted all of Shadows, every scrap of it, washed from her. It wouldn't be, just as her own shadow would never be whole, but now, today—as the remnants of her spells still ached in her hands—scouring its traces in hot water could be enough.

She turned off the water, stepped onto the bathroom's heated floor, and wrapped herself in towels.

Then she noticed the scrawl on the mirror, the same version of her handwriting that scrolled across the mirrors of House Prospero.

Grace Valentine is here.

She didn't know who that was.

In distress.

And that wasn't creepy at all. "Here as in at my apartment, or here as in House Prospero?"

The House.

Apologies.

Please come. Now.

"Can you let her in before I get there?" Reaching for fresh clothes.

Yes.

Sydney opened the door to an unrecognizable version of House Prospero.

Gone was the pristine white, the sterile elegance. This was a House that looked like the inside of a forest—dark wood and stained glass, rich green. Trees growing from walls. Everything dark, quiet as a secret, and warm.

"You did this? Why?" she asked.

A quiet chime and words on a mirror.

Lonely. Please stay.

She could understand loneliness. "Okay. Thank you—it's beautiful, really. We'll talk about things. I'll . . . I'll try to get here more often. Maybe stay once or twice. But right now I need to see Grace." Whoever that was.

Bathroom. Upstairs. First door.

Sydney hurried past light fixtures that looked like vined roses and up a staircase draped with a worn runner in a pattern like a knot garden. She reached the bathroom. Stopped in the doorway and stared. She hadn't recognized the name because they'd never been introduced, but she knew the woman. Three years ago she had been brought to Shadows as a sacrifice. It was the only time Sydney had ever seen an adult brought in that way. It had seemed strange, out of place, but she had learned far before then not to ask questions. She'd never seen her again, and assumed that, like most sacrifices, she hadn't survived.

"Sydney?" Grace was soaking wet and trembling. Spattered with mud and filth, and she smelled like lake water. Two of the nails on her left hand were torn and bleeding. "Thank God."

"Not that I'm not happy to see you, and believe me, I'm glad you're out of that fucking place, but why are you here? Sorry, that can wait. Why don't you go ahead and have a bath—get cleaned up." She turned on the taps and pointed to a cupboard. "I think there's probably first aid stuff in there—the House seems to think of everything, and that's where I'd put it. Do you want something to eat or drink? Soup. I'll have the House make soup. Do you like minestrone?"

"Sure."

"Minestrone and wine, please. Maybe some bread, too."

She could feel the House acknowledge the task, pleased at what it had been given to do.

"Is Miranda here?" Grace asked. Water pooled in her footsteps, then disappeared as the House cleaned it.

"She's not. But I can ask her to come, if you need her."

Sydney set out towels from a linen closet and grabbed a pair of pajamas as well. The House really did have everything. "There—those should fit."

"No, it's not that. I just—I don't want Grey to find me. Or Miles Merlin, for that matter."

"Grey—" Sydney began. The scars on Grace's hands and arms. The file Madison couldn't talk about. The utterly broken relationship between Miranda and Grey. "So, we have a lot of catching up to do. And part of that catching up is that I think keeping you safe from Grey is probably my job now. But, if you can, maybe you could explain things to me."

Grace stepped into the bath. "Three years ago Grey Prospero attacked me. He wanted my magic—he was going to cut it out, take my bones."

"So the scars aren't from Shadows?" Sydney asked, showing her own, the patterns almost an exact match.

"No, they are. I fought back. Got away. Went to Miranda, who let me hide here, until the disinheritance. She tried to help me, as much as she could, anyway. But Miles—" Her voice broke.

Sydney waited. She had turned herself away from the tub. It was easier sometimes, to tell an ugly thing when you didn't have to see the face of your audience.

The water shifted, and Grace began again. "As the head of the Unseen World, Miles signed off on the disinheritance.

And he told Miranda he'd take me somewhere safe. He took me to Shadows. To pay a debt, he said. The magic, the binding, it's fast. I couldn't . . . I couldn't fight back."

"None of us can. It's absolute. You did the only thing you could do, Grace. You survived."

A sob, then. Sydney reached back, offered a hand. Grace held it while she wept.

Her voice was still edged with tears when she started speaking again. "Thank you. So when I got out today, I cast a spell. To find you. To say thank you. And because, because now I don't know where to go."

"You can stay here, if you want. It's the safest place I can think of—the House can't let Grey in because of the disinheritance, and I can make sure it keeps Miles out, too," Sydney said. "You'd be doing me a favor, actually, as the House is a bit lonely, and I'm still not quite used to it. I think it'll be glad of the company. So I'll bring some things over for you, and we can go from there. But that's something we can talk about tomorrow, after you've gotten some rest." Sydney got up.

"Did you always mean to break it?" Grace asked. "Shadows?"

"I mean to bury it," Sydney said. "And to salt the earth behind me."

CHAPTER EIGHTEEN

Sydney shoved her gloved hands in her pockets, bounced lightly on her toes while waiting for the challenge to begin. "Outside. In January. Who does that?"

Laurent looked at her. "Sydney. Please tell me that you actually read the challenge."

"I got . . . distracted. Besides, it's not like I was going to refuse it." She had read it, the day he'd sent it. However, a fairly significant number of things had happened in the interim. She'd had a lot on her mind.

"You are literally the only person I know who would stand here facing potential death and shrug and say that you were distracted by other things."

Sydney shrugged. "We all have our talents."

Laurent shook his head. "Well, the who in this case is Eliot Vincent. Candidate House. A year ahead of us in school, and probably another one of Merlin's allies. He's really good at physical magic, so my guess is you're out here so he can use the snow and cold as weapons."

"See? I didn't even need to read it—you've told me

everything I need to know. And I hate the cold." But she pulled off her gloves and handed them to Laurent.

The day was bitter and biting, wind that whipped raw against skin, that seemed to seek out gaps between coat and skin, to insinuate itself into bones and joints. Not many braved it.

Eliot Vincent wore no coat, no scarf, no hat, his lack of armor against the weather a subtle reminder that he was strong enough not to need it. He stood, calm and easy in the cold.

Sydney removed her hands from her pockets and rubbed them together for warmth. "Let's get this over with."

The challenge began.

The snow beneath Sydney's feet jerked and heaved up, flinging her off-balance. By the time she regained her feet, it had turned to a slick of ice. She hit it and fell, hard.

"Oh, well done," she muttered under her breath as it then cracked. Splinters and shards drove up, sharp enough to pierce through skin. She left blood in red smears across the ice and heard the reaction go through the crowd.

"Right. That's enough of that." The ice around Sydney melted. Slow at first, but then all in a rush. The air warmed. Green shoots burst from the ground and grabbed at Eliot's feet. His hands turned into twigs. Bark replaced his skin, and leaves burst from him. He became a perfect tree, a beech, in full bloom. Spring in the midst of winter.

Sydney walked over to Laurent, who handed her a tissue for the blood on her face. "I was worried for a minute there."

"He was good. Good enough he should have gotten through this. The tree was as close as I could come to leaving some of him alive." She reached out her hand. "Can I have my gloves, please? I really do hate the cold."

Miles Merlin sat in a quiet corner of the Mages' Club, Grey across from him. "Here is a thing I find very interesting. There have been a series of bodies found, throughout the Turning. Bodies upon which a number of spells have been performed, in the course of the killings. Most interestingly, in each case, the finger bones have been removed. It looks almost as if someone has been killing people in order to cut the magic out of them."

"That does seem interesting," Grey said, his face blank. Under the table, he held his hands rigid in the opening posture of a defensive spell. He couldn't remember the last time he'd seen Miles cast, but he was the head of the House that led the Unseen World. He must be strong. Better to be ready.

Michael Dee walked over, bourbon in hand. "So, what do you plan to do about the failures of magic, Merlin?"

Miles turned on the charm, a politician at the negotiating table. "I'm looking into the causes, of course. And—forgive me, Grey, I know she's your sister—but it does seem like Sydney's presence among us may have something to do with them."

"Shadows ought to be kept in the Shadows," Dee said, then laughed as if he found himself very funny indeed.

"You're exactly right," Miles said.

"Carry on, then." Dee toasted his glass in their direction, losing a little bourbon over the rim in his enthusiasm.

"Forgive me. I chose this table hoping to avoid interruptions. Now, where was I? Oh yes. The truly odd thing is that the girls who've been killed are all lesser magicians from lesser Houses. They barely have enough magic to remain in the Unseen World. Now, what I don't understand is, if you're going to go through the trouble of killing someone for their magic, scraping it from their bones, why go after someone who has so little?" Miles picked up his fork and tapped it against his plate, causing capers to roll from the top of his bagels and lox.

Grey pushed his chair back slightly, giving himself room, just in case. "I'm not sure why you're asking me this."

"An academic discussion, nothing more." Merlin smiled and draped red onion on his salmon. "We spend so little time fully considering the sources of our power. If this is one, we owe it to ourselves—to magic—to think about the best way to use it. Because, as you know, there have been some recent problems with magic. Indeed, last night there was a complete failure of magic at a challenge."

"Complete?" Grey echoed.

"I'm sure it's part of the reason for Dee's visit just now. Both magicians attempted to cast, and nothing—*nothing*—happened. And we're all aware of other times when magic has misfired, or hasn't been as strong as it should have been," Merlin said. "And while these events have increased dramatically since Sydney appeared in our midst, it doesn't necessarily mean that she's taken magic from Shadows to help her performance here. It may simply be a sign that it's time to look for alternate sources of magic. If something is happening, it's best to be prepared."

Grey relaxed then. "I would think that, if you're trying to make the collection, you'd choose people with less magic because you'd want to increase your chances of success. It's like the sacrifices—they're sent away when they're small, before their magic is as strong as it might be, but that's because it makes it easier to take it out of them. You don't want someone who might be able to fight back."

"Well, that's certainly something to think about, though I'm not sure it helps us deal with that woman who claims to be your sister. Whatever else she is, she is very strong magically." Merlin shook his head as if this problem were a great sadness for him.

"Do you really think she's the reason for the failures of magic?" Grey asked. "That if her magic were taken—no, not taken. If her magic were returned to where it should be, would the failures stop? Would everyone else be stronger?"

"I think," Merlin said, "that there is a reason magic is failing. There does not seem to be the pool of magic there normally is, and, as I've said before, the biggest connection I see is that magic became weaker once Sydney began to participate in the Turning. Magic does not just disappear—it goes somewhere. If she has too much—"

"Then someone ought to take it back," Grey said.

"You are aware, of course, that Houses whose members fall in the course of a Turning are exempt from the next required sacrifice," Miles said.

"I'm not sure how that applies here. I won't have established my House until after the Turning is finished."

"It applies because the death returns their magic to that same pool of power that the magic of Shadows comes from. If Sydney were to fall in the course of a challenge, perhaps some sort of balance would be restored. It's certainly something to think about," Miles said.

Yes, Grey agreed. It certainly was.

CHAPTER NINETEEN

Grey sat at the corner of the bar farthest from the door. He liked to be able to watch the people, the girls, come in. He could tell, usually, who had strong magic and who didn't—hell, half the time he knew which Houses the girls were part of and how closely related they were to the main families. And even when it wasn't immediately obvious, being farther away gave him time to think, to consider. The corner seat meant he could watch, directly and in the mirror that hung behind the bar. No reason to waste an approach, no reason to make himself memorable if he didn't want to be.

He normally wouldn't have come back so soon, not while he still had a supply, but the conversation with Merlin made him wonder if it wouldn't be better to have more bones in reserve. Miles was powerful—if he was looking for alternate sources of magic, it might be a good idea to show him how effective the bones could be. Plus, if he was going to challenge Sydney, he needed to be sure she didn't have any advantage over him.

Even so, at two drinks in and no possibilities, he had just

about given up and decided to leave when he saw her. Short dark hair, almost conservatively dressed, but still sexy. She looked like the sort of girl he might have said hi to at the bar if he were here looking for a date. Best of all, she was alone.

He waited. He waited while she settled in, while she had a drink. He watched as her eyes scanned the crowd, but not like she was looking for someone she knew, just like she was looking for someone. He watched as she didn't check her phone.

He didn't recognize her. She wasn't from any of the Houses. But she was here, which meant she had enough magic to find out about the place, enough magic to get in the door, and probably not much more than that. Perfect. There was no one important who would miss her.

Grey signaled the bartender. "The woman at the end of the bar—if she orders another drink, I'd like to buy it for her."

The bartender nodded. Fewer than five minutes later, the woman sat down next to him, vodka gimlet in hand. "Thanks for the drink," she said.

"My pleasure," Grey said. "Grey Prospero."

Her eyes widened, just a bit. "It's so nice to meet you. I'm Harper."

Harper's lip curled as she looked at the man passed out on the bed. Then she set the timer on her phone so that she could be sure she was finished and gone by the time the spell wore off, and got to work.

It had been the emailed wards and spells for the archive that had given her the idea—if it was possible for a magician to package magic in a way that would let mundane people trigger it, then she wanted some. And she guessed that if such things existed, that sex would drive their creation as much as it drove any other technology.

She'd been right, and it had been the bartender who had hooked her up. She was a magician—Alanna Valentine—and when Harper explained what she was doing, that she was looking for the man who had been murdering women for their magic, Alanna said that she would help however she could. She'd had a cousin, she said, who'd disappeared in mysterious circumstances.

She'd given Harper a lighter, one Harper had been carrying in her purse each time she'd come back to the bar. "Once you find the guy, just ask him to light your cigarette for you. When he clicks it—or anyone does, so don't get confused and do it yourself—it activates the spell."

Harper didn't smoke, but that was fine. It was easy magic, and it worked. Grey had become very affectionate and had been delighted when she'd suggested that they go back to his place. They'd barely made it in the door before he passed out. When he woke up, he'd be very confused.

Very.

Harper methodically stripped him of his clothes, tossing them around the room so that it looked like they'd come off in the heat of passion.

Then she searched his apartment.

She got lucky—if that could possibly be considered the right word in this situation—when she got to the final set of kitchen cupboards. They weren't even hidden. She guessed that when he had gone through the spells to take down his extra wards when they came in, his lack of focus meant that he'd accidentally taken down all of the wards in his apartment.

She found a tiny glass jar. Inside it, three human finger bones.

Her eyes went from the glass and its terrible contents to the man on the bed. She thought about the women who had gone missing the past few months.

She thought about Rose, whose bones hadn't been stolen but whose hands had been carved into, cut open. Who had still had her life stolen from her.

There was a block of knives just on the edge of the counter, and Harper's hand ached with the desire to pick one up.

Instead, hands shaking, she picked up her phone and took pictures—close up on the bones, then the cupboard, then the kitchen. Enough to put what she'd found in its horrible context. Then she grabbed her coat and her purse, and she got the hell out of there.

• • •

Grey paced around his apartment. It felt somehow unfamiliar to him. He'd woken up naked and alone in his bed. He didn't remember fucking the girl, though he supposed he must have. He didn't even remember bringing her home with him, and that was part of the problem. He never brought girls here. He never brought anyone here.

Even worse, when he'd woken up, all his wards were down. All of them, even the ones on his cabinet where he stored his spare magic. Nothing was missing—it was the first thing he'd checked—but still. Something felt off, felt wrong. He couldn't shake the feeling that the girl, whoever she was, had opened that cabinet, had seen what was inside.

Not, he told himself, that anyone would believe her. Some nobody who wasn't even part of a House. But still—he'd gone out looking for power, and instead of refilling his supply, he'd brought a girl back here and gotten laid. He thought. He scratched his balls, wishing he could remember.

Better to be safe. With the wards down, who knew what she might have seen. Grey took the finger bones from their container and ground them to dust with a mortar and pestle. He added honey, and wine, and salt, and he drank all of it down. The magic burned going down his throat, burned as it traveled out through his veins.

Now even if she did tell someone, even if they did

believe her, there was nothing to be found, no matter how hard anyone looked. And he could always get more if he needed to.

He glanced back at the rumpled bed and got dressed. There was something he needed to do.

Sydney was on the way to House Prospero. She'd picked up some clothes and food for Grace, who seemed to be settling in well, all things considered.

"I feel like I'm okay while I'm here in the House, but I'm not quite ready to reintroduce myself to the Unseen World yet. Things are still—I don't even know what things are, but you know how that place messes with your head," she'd said when Sydney had called to check clothing sizes.

Sydney did. "It takes a while, for not being there to feel—forget normal. For it to even feel possible. And even though the adjustment is to something good, it's an adjustment. Give yourself time."

Grace blew out a breath. "Thank you. I'd been feeling like some kind of freak. Not that I wanted to be back in there or anything, but I felt like I should be running down the street singing my jubilation, and instead I'm tucked away in here reading every book in your library."

Sydney'd read a lot, too, when she'd first gotten out. It had helped her believe in the world outside. She wasn't that far from McNally Jackson now. She'd stop by and pick up something for Grace to read.

Her phone rang. Grace. "Hey, I was just—"

"He's here." Grace's voice a rough whisper.

"Grey?" Knowing the answer as soon as she asked the question.

"Yes. Trying to get in."

"Okay. Are you in a room with a mirror?" Sydney cast a summoning spell for a cab.

"Yes."

"Ask the House if it can hold him there."

Sydney overheard the question as a cab stopped in front of her. "It says it will."

"Stay where you are. I'm on my way."

Grey was still there, hands anchored to the door, when she pulled up in front. She paid the driver quickly, but then took her time walking to the door. "So, were you planning to steal from the House, or were you going to leave something nasty inside for me?"

"Let me go, you bitch. You have no right to hold me here."

"And you have no right to be here, or to do whatever it is you had planned. So let's start over." She smiled, raised a hand as if she might begin a spell, and Grey pressed himself closer to the door. "What were you planning to do here?"

"I don't have to tell you," he said.

"Fine." She shrugged. "I don't have to let you go." She turned and started back toward the street.

"Wait!"

She paused.

"I was going to leave a spell."

"I assume it wasn't going to burst into 'Welcome Home!' balloons the next time I opened the door."

He glared at her.

She leaned against the stair rail, pressed a few places on her phone's screen. "The House took video. That fun little *whoosh*ing noise you just heard was me emailing the file to the entire Unseen World, and to my lawyer. So they all know you did this. They also know that it was this House—my magic—that kept you out."

"And you think any of them will care? You're an abomination," he said.

"That's not a very nice thing to say to your sister," she said. "Especially when she's the only one who can let you go. They're calling for snow tonight, had you heard?

"Anyway, maybe they'll care; maybe they'll even agree with you. But they'll know what you did. And how funny you look, hunched over here, stuck to the door."

She walked up next to him. "And speaking of knowing things, I know what you did to Miranda. Well, what you tried to do. The magic didn't quite work, did it? You were hoping she'd be dead, not just magicless."

He glared. "No one will believe you."

"Do I have some sort of reputation as a liar? You seem very sure no one will believe me about anything. Though, even if you're right, I bet they'd believe Lara Merlin. She figured out what happened that night and told Ian. She's not really happy with her dad right now, either. I bet we could convince her to say something." She cut the spell, and the sudden release dropped him to his knees. "Now get away from my House."

He stumbled away from the door and raised a hand.

"Don't even think about it," Sydney said.

"Bitch," he called over his shoulder, and left.

"Thank you," Sydney said to the House, and rested her hand against the door.

The door opened. Grace stood on the other side, fireplace poker in her shaking hand.

"You do remember you're a magician, right?" Sydney asked.

"I hate him so much I wasn't sure I could trust myself to cast. But I was sure I could clock him if I had to."

"Badass," Sydney said. "Well done."

They gathered in the packages Sydney had dropped on the lawn. "This ice cream isn't even going to make it to the freezer. I really missed chocolate-chip cookie dough," Grace said.

"Look," Sydney said. "I don't want to push on healing

wounds. But do you have any idea of why Miles took you to Shadows?"

"To pay a debt, he said. I don't know anything more than that."

"That helps," Sydney said. "Thanks."

CHAPTER TWENTY

Lara was making eggs Benedict. At least, that's what she was doing in the kitchen. In her head she was working through the steps of a new spell—a nastier version of the booby traps she'd loved as a child. Something she could use in a challenge if she needed to.

And so it was an annoyance, but not a surprise, to check the water she was going to poach the eggs in and realize she'd neglected to turn the burner on.

She muttered the spell to cook the eggs under her breath and snapped her fingers.

Nothing happened.

She tried again, enunciating clearly and making the gesture as sharp and precise as if she were in school.

Still nothing.

She didn't let herself think, just pulled open drawers, searched through cabinets. There had to be candles here somewhere, left over from a dinner party, or a birthday, or something. "Shit," she said, and reached for the toaster where her English muffins were turning into charcoal discs.

She burned her forearm on the toaster while yanking the cord from the wall. “Damn it!”

“Lara, what is going on in here?” Miles paused in the doorway, taking in the mess.

“Nothing!” She slammed a drawer shut, a purple taper in her hand. She spoke the word that should light the candle.

It hesitated, sparked, caught. Lara was so surprised, she fumbled it. Another fast spell, and its fall stopped—paused in midair. She picked it up with her hand rather than risking another spell, and then blew it out.

“I thought my magic was gone,” she said.

“What happened?” Miles asked.

She explained. “I guess it was just another failure, like in the challenges.” She watched his face carefully, looking for any hints of what Ian suspected.

“I—” He paused. “I’m sure you’re right. I’m sorry—I’ve just remembered that I have a meeting.” He hurried from the room.

Lara looked around at the mess and wondered what it meant that he was lying. And considered the fact that it was probably time to try out the other spell she’d been working through, the one that would bypass the biometrics on her father’s locked cabinet.

Shara walked the ruined halls of Shadows. They didn’t move; they didn’t change. She was used to the House holding its shape for her, but this was different. This felt like walking through a dead place, not a living House. There was no life in these halls. The breath of the House was ragged, irregular, its heartbeat slow.

Shadows was fading, dying. Sydney—Shara's hands clenched into fists, her nails cutting into her palms—had broken too much of it. She had unraveled its threads, left poison in its foundations. The corruption, the weakness was spreading. Shara could barely hold things together as they were, much less even dream of healing them.

And as for the magic, the magic that was the very purpose of Shadows, that was flowing out like water. A trickle at first, but now she could feel the cracks in the dam. Things were close to breaking. Her footsteps echoed off floors that had held their same shape for days.

Standing inside the doors was Miles Merlin.

Anger rose, hovered just beneath Shara's skin. "I was wondering when you'd bother to show up."

Merlin gestured at the scars on the walls where light leaked in, at the great doors, only barely rehung. "What exactly happened here? I thought there were systems in place to prevent this sort of thing."

"Systems that require the support of the Unseen World," Shara said.

"The Unseen World has always supported Shadows—our

House has seen to that since Shadows was created. It's why you're here, and why I have my own responsibilities. We make sure there are rules in place so that the sacrifices are provided. We take their magic and bind it to the statue and make sure that it reaches the Unseen World safely."

"Your House," Shara said, "not mine."

"House Merlin is proud of your service," he said.

"Cut the bullshit, Miles, and tell me what you want."

"Magic is failing—" he began.

"And that is not the fault of Shadows. Tell me, how long has it been since you successfully cast a spell, Miles?"

His face went blank.

"Did you think I wouldn't know?" she asked. "That you could stand in front of me here, of all places, and I wouldn't know that you held no more magic than a mundane?"

"I hardly expected you to be criticizing me for lack of power after you let this happen. How can I possibly support your desire to hold power in the Unseen World when you don't even have enough power to maintain your own House here?" he sneered.

"I really think we're beyond the point of whether or not you'll support me mattering. After all, if you can't hold magic, you can't hold a House. So it seems like we both want the same thing, big brother." She stepped closer to him, magic held in her hands, visibly enough to remind him which of the two of them held the sort of power that mattered.

"I don't see how."

Even now, like this, he couldn't keep his distaste from showing. She knew very well what he thought of Shadows, what he thought of her. A necessary evil at best. She knew better—he had nothing she didn't give him. "You want your House. I want mine. Get me enough magic to rebuild Shadows, restart the spells, and then the Unseen World will have enough magic to never question yours."

"Done," he said, and turned to go.

"Don't wait. I hear your daughter still has some big challenges to fight. I'd hate for there to be another failure of magic at a time when she requires it."

CHAPTER TWENTY-ONE

The car glided to a stop outside of House Prospero. "You grew up here?" Harper asked.

Madison scanned her card, added a tip for the driver. "What? No—only immediate family live in these places. I'm like a second cousin once removed. I grew up in a normal house."

Sydney had asked them to come. There was someone they needed to meet, she said. Someone who couldn't go to the Wellington & Ketchum offices. "Or at least, not right now. She's been through a lot. I'll let her tell you."

Madison and Harper had just gotten to the top step when the door swung open. Sydney waited, barefoot and wearing snug black pants and a loose black shirt.

"Very assassin-casual, Sydney. I like it," Madison said.

"Ha ha. She's waiting in the back. Do you want anything?"

"Coffee." Harper nodded agreement.

A chime rang. Sydney glanced at a mirror, the old-fashioned brass frame a pattern of thorned roses. "The House will bring it when it's ready."

"The House?" Harper asked as they followed Sydney down a hall vined with ivy. "Is that what you guys call butlers or whatever?"

"No, I mean the actual House," Sydney said. "It's tied to my magic."

Harper's eyes widened.

"Like I said, I grew up somewhere normal," Madison said.

"It likes to be helpful," Sydney said. "The House. I'm still getting used to it myself." She led them to a room with bright sun flooding the windows. A young woman stood, her back to the door, looking out. A hair too thin, shoulders braced, her left hand fidgeting at her side.

"I'd forgotten how much I loved watching the birds," Grace said. Harper's eyes dropped to her hands. They were covered in a pattern of thin silver scars.

"Madison, Harper, this is Grace Valentine. She's—" Sydney looked at Grace.

"I'm the woman Grey Prospero tried to kill three years ago," she said.

"We know," Madison said. "Well, we didn't know it was you we were meeting, but Harper found the file. The disinheritance. So you're not totally unexpected. But—where have you been?"

Coffee appeared on a side table, and Sydney poured while Grace told the other women her story.

Harper listened unmoving, her coffee untouched at her side.

"So I guess this means the binding on the disinheritance is officially broken. Or at least so loosened as to not matter," Madison said. "However—Harper, what is wrong with you?"

Harper shifted in her seat. "So, I did something, and, Madison, I think you might fire me for it. I took these two nights ago." Harper took her phone out of her bag, opened the screen, and passed it to Madison.

Madison looked at the first screen. "Is that what I think it is? Is that *where* I think it is?"

"Scroll back further."

Madison did, and came to the picture of Grey naked in the bed. "Oh God." She handed the phone to Sydney.

"You're not fired, but what were you thinking?" Madison asked.

"That women were dying and no one cared because they didn't have a lot of magic. If he'd killed Sydney—no offense, Sydney—but if he had, it would have been a big deal. Even killing her in a challenge would have been a big deal. But this? I read the description of what he did to you, Grace. I *found* Rose. No one cares, and even in Grace's case, his disinheritance was supposed to be enough. I mean, fuck that—you got sent to what is basically hell for three years, and you'd still be there if it weren't for Sydney. Meanwhile, he's out picking up girls in bars. Sorry," she said to Grace.

"No, you're right." Grace nodded.

"But economic consequences are enough in most cases. And besides, Wellington & Ketchum doesn't have a criminal division in Special Projects," Sydney said softly.

Madison shot her a sideways glance.

Sydney scrolled through the rest of the pictures, held out the phone. "Grace?"

"No. I can guess what's on there well enough." She flexed her fingers.

"You took these yourself?" Sydney asked Harper. "I didn't know you were a magician."

"I'm not. A friend—Alanna Valentine—made me a self-activating spell. It made him really . . . affectionate, and then really unconscious."

Grace laughed. "Alanna's my cousin. She had a version of that spell in high school. She used it on the guys who liked to lie about the girls, or get pushy with them. She'd leave them naked on the lacrosse field."

Harper smiled. "I can totally see that."

"Still," Madison said, "that was a big risk. If the spell had gone wrong—"

"He killed my best friend," Harper said.

"Good fucking reason to take a risk," Sydney said. "And I'm so sorry. Forward the pictures to me."

"Sydney?" Madison asked.

"I am a special project. I have no problem being the entire criminal division besides. And as you pointed out before, we're in the middle of a Turning. Things happen. Fortune's Wheel does turn. I'm just going to help Fortune out a bit."

Miles Merlin sat at his customary table at the Mages' Club, watching as Sydney crossed the floor toward him, the doorman trailing like jetsam in her wake.

"Miss! Miss! You can't just—I'm sorry, sir. She wouldn't listen."

"Mind if I join you?" Sydney slid into the chair across from him. "I hear you've been talking to a lot of people about me. Making up stories about me stealing magic, telling people that I shouldn't be allowed to hold my House because of where I grew up. It's almost like you think I'm not as good as you, which is so weird, considering how close your House is to Shadows. How much help you get from there." She spoke clearly enough that interested ears from all over the club turned their way.

Merlin waved off the doorman. "It's fine. She can stay."

"Smart choice," Sydney said, setting her phone on the table.

"Obviously you have something that's so important to say to me that you didn't have time to be polite." Merlin smiled, an indulgent parent looking at a misbehaving child. "I didn't see the need to make you wait any longer."

She opened the phone to Harper's pictures, angled the screen toward him.

"Well, that's certainly macabre." He curled his lip in distaste.

"It is, isn't it?" Sydney left the picture up. "And rude—murdering people for their magic."

"Is that where those are from? Those poor women?" Exaggerated shock and horror.

"Those pictures were taken in your good friend Grey Prospero's apartment." Her eyes were sharp as knives as she watched him.

Merlin shook his head. "Grey would never—"

"Cut the crap. He tried before. It's what got him disinherited." She paused. "Of course, you'd know that, since as the Head of the Unseen World, you would have signed off on the disinheritance."

"Did you come here to discuss the finer points of legal procedures?" Miles asked.

"Not at all. I just wanted to let you know that I was aware of those fine points. Of all of the fine points of that case." She waited for him to react, to show some regret over what he had done to Grace, or at least some fear at being found out, but the only thing on his face was annoyance.

"Is there anything else you're aware of, or can I go back to my day?"

"Fine. I am also aware of the fact that there was outside interference in the Beauchamps-Prospero duel. You remember that one, Miles, the one where Miranda's magic was stripped? And not just magical interference, but physical as well. Did Grey know you were going to push her, or did you just decide to help things along?"

"Lower your voice," Merlin said.

"Yeah, I figured that would be the one that upset you. You people will allow just about anything, but outside interference in an active challenge is right out. If people learn you helped Grey, you could have your House unmade."

"I don't control his actions."

Sydney leaned back in her chair. "I believe you. At least, I believe the precise truth you think you're telling, because for all your faults, you're too smart to say anything that would get you in that kind of trouble. So we'll call Miranda water under the bridge. But what I would like to know is what you're planning to do about this." She tapped her finger on the screen of her phone.

"Do about it? An action he's already been punished for—rather severely—and some rather weakly supported accusations?" Merlin sat back, steepled his fingers. "Even assuming he's done something that necessitates any action being taken, this is the Turning. Fortune's Wheel will do what it must. I wouldn't want to interfere in that."

"So nothing," Sydney said. "That's about what I expected. I just wanted to be sure before I do what I must."

"And what is that?" Merlin demanded.

"I'm going to give Fortune's Wheel a fucking push. You might want to consider getting out of the way. Or don't—I wouldn't want you to interfere."

They met this time at the *Alice in Wonderland* statue. It had been Lara's favorite place in the park when she was younger. "Do you remember when you made all of the caterpillars in the park crawl their way over here and have a tea party with you?" Ian asked.

"I remember being grounded for a week after and forbidden from magic for two because I had drawn undue attention from the mundane world," she said. "Dad was furious. Which—nothing's changed there."

"What is it this time?" Ian asked.

"I'm not sure," she said. "He's mostly stopped talking to me, except to tell me what challenge is next. I'm fairly certain he'll go after Sydney, though—he's just trying to decide if he's best served by going after her directly, in the hopes that I can actually beat her, or if he'll challenge Prospero and try to knock her House out of play.

"The smarter thing would be to challenge her House—I don't have a good chance of beating you, but I have a much better chance of beating you than I do her—but he's still thick as thieves with Grey, and I think he's insinuated to Grey that if Sydney dies, he can make sure that Grey inherits."

"Can he?" Ian asked, letting go of the hypothetical in which their father forced them to try to kill each other.

"I don't think that's really the point. I think right now he sees Grey as obvious and expendable, and a good way to deflect attention from people talking about whether Dad still has his magic. Grey's out there telling everyone who will listen that the failures of magic are due to Sydney getting out of Shadows. It's patently untrue, as nothing like that happened when Verenice did, but if Grey says it loud enough, it won't matter if it's true. People will believe it because it's the easier story. I think Dad's hoping Grey will be stupid enough to challenge Laurent and try to kill Sydney himself, and get lucky."

"He'd have to get very lucky to beat her, but Grey would be exactly stupid enough to think he could," Ian said.

"There's one other thing." She drew in a breath and looked at Ian. "Can you teach me to use magic the way you do?"

"Sure. Of course. But—why now?" He had offered before, and she had never seemed interested. What she did worked, and Shadows was a necessary evil. He hadn't agreed, but he hadn't pushed the issue.

"Because I lost my magic the other day."

"Oh, Lara, no."

She shrugged. "It was a temporary thing, and I got it back, but I think something's seriously wrong. Maybe with Dad, maybe with the spell. I don't know what. But he won't tell me anything, and I still can't get through that lock of his. I don't need to worry that my magic's going to cut out in the middle of a challenge. Or disappear altogether. And you and Sydney are among the few people who haven't had magic fail."

"Of course I'll help," he said again. "Absolutely."

"I remember one other thing," she said. "I remember you bought me *Alice's Adventures in Wonderland* while I was grounded, so that I could pretend I was here, having tea parties. You're a good brother, Ian."

"What else am I supposed to be?" He slung his arm around her shoulders, and they stood there, together.

CHAPTER TWENTY-TWO

Sydney had invited Miranda to meet at House Prospero, but Miranda had declined. "I'm still—I'm sure you think I'm foolish, but I'm still not ready to be back in that House. Even as a visitor. Perhaps especially as a visitor."

Considering the changes the House had made in its appearance since becoming Sydney's, Miranda's decision was probably a blessing. The difference between the two versions of the House was enormous enough to be a distraction, and not one that was likely to be useful. "Of course. We can go out somewhere—you choose."

"The restaurant at my hotel is a good one, and they'll seat us somewhere discreet."

The restaurant reminded Sydney a bit of how House Prospero had been when she had first seen it. It was decorated to give the same impressions: that this was a place that was refined, that there were important traditions that took place within its walls, that the people who were there were special and would be treated like it. Everything was hushed and warm as she followed the server back to Miranda's table. Even the air felt expensive.

Sydney hadn't seen Miranda since the night she had lost her magic. She'd expected Miranda to look different, now that her magic was gone, that the sudden absence of something that had been that much a part of her should leave a mark. But if there was a difference, it was hidden. Miranda's facade was as smooth and unreadable as marble.

Miranda stood, partway out of her chair—as if she might offer an embrace—then sat back down when Sydney made no move to reciprocate.

"You should know that Grace Valentine is staying with me," Sydney said. She watched as the color drained from Miranda's face, replaced by absolute blankness.

"Grace . . . Valentine." Miranda's voice was as thin as tissue paper.

"Which means I also know why Grey was disinherited. What I don't know is if you gave Grace to Miles to take to Shadows so you could forget about her and ignore what your son was, or if he came up with that little wrinkle in events all on his own."

The facade cracked then. "He did what?"

"Took her to Shadows. Gave her to Shara as a sacrifice. To pay a debt, apparently."

"He told everyone she had died. Sydney, I believed him. I went to her funeral."

"It's probably what he hoped would happen. I mean, if she

dies in there, no one finds out what he did, and the last person officially connected with her is Grey."

"I would have tried to help her, had I known."

"Would you? Like you tried to help me, when you learned I was in there?"

Miranda looked away. In a harsh whisper she asked, "What else have you brought me here to tell me?"

"You should know that it seems very likely that Grey's gotten better at what he does in the past three years. Or worse. I'm not really sure what the precise phrasing should be." Sydney sipped from her glass of wine. "Women are being killed, and their finger bones are being taken.

"Some of those bones were found in his apartment."

Miranda closed her eyes, her lips pressed together, white. "I wish I could say I was surprised. But he never did think he had enough, no matter what he had. He wanted things to be easy. The sort of easy where you don't have to work, where it just comes to you, and you're not just adequate, you're brilliant. He never understood why he didn't have that, or that hard work might bring him closer to it.

"He also never understood why he shouldn't try to take it from someone else who did, especially if he thought they were less than he was. I very much wish that I didn't, but I know what my son is."

"Well, so does Miles Merlin," Sydney said. "Though he

believes the solution is to let Grey continue to compete in the Turning and for Fortune's Wheel to sort things out. I have a more direct approach. I'm going to challenge him."

Miranda's face went whiter then, but there was no other change in her carefully controlled expression. "I understand. Thank you for telling me in person."

"I'm glad you appreciate that it's necessary." Sydney pushed back her chair.

"Do you have to go?" Miranda asked. "I thought we could at least eat, that for one meal we could be a normal mother and daughter."

"Normal," Sydney said. "Because the conversation we just had was exactly normal."

"You know what I mean," Miranda said.

"The thing is, I don't. I don't know what normal is. I don't know how to have a mother. I mean, yes, Shara oversees things at Shadows, but the point of Shadows is not raising children. Shadows doesn't particularly care if the sacrifices even survive, much less whether or not they feel like they have a relationship with a parent while they're there."

"I don't know why you feel like you need to say these things to me," Miranda said. "I feel guilty enough already."

"Do you?" Sydney asked. "Be honest: If your magic hadn't been stripped from you, would you ever have even considered using magic that didn't come from Shadows? Or would you have kept telling yourself that's just the way things are?"

"I had agreed to support Ian if House Prospero won."

"And I certainly appreciate the gesture. But your magic—the *House's* magic—all of that still came from Shadows. Even after you knew I was alive, you used that magic to make sure you'd have tea when you wanted it, because it was easier. Because the consequences of its use had already been cut out of people like Grace and me." She shoved back her sleeves, showing her scars.

Miranda's calm did break then, the sob that escaped from her loud enough to send heads turning in their direction.

"Exactly. So no, I don't think we can ever spend time together like a normal mother and daughter. There is nothing about our relationship that is normal." Sydney stood up and left. There were other people she needed to tell.

Laurent set his fork and knife on his plate. "By the way, I have something to show you."

"I am all anticipation. And French toast. That was good," Sydney said.

He stuffed his hands in his pockets, and three oranges rose from the wooden bowl in the center of the table. They spun slowly in the air, then faster, and then two more rose up to join them, crossing and looping in a juggling pattern. After a minute they paused in their pattern and dropped—one at a time, controlled—back into the bowl.

Sydney applauded. "I'm so happy for you."

"Thanks. I tried for seven, and it was a disaster. Hence the mimosas." He nodded at the pitcher.

"Hence," she said, smiling.

"But I'm getting better. It's almost natural to cast like this now, even with things that are useful magic and not just showing off with oranges, and the headaches aren't as awful."

"I'm glad." She finished her mimosa. "So, to completely change the subject, I need to tell you something, and you're not going to like it," Sydney said.

"That sounds serious," said Laurent. "Is it something else horrible about how magic works?"

"In a roundabout way, yes."

He shook his head. "I should know better than to ask by now."

"You've heard about the women who are being killed," she said.

"And the bones removed from their fingers, which is creepy as fuck."

"It is," she agreed. "It's also one of the places in the body most likely to retain residual magic—we use our hands in almost all castings."

His gaze dropped to her hands.

"Still have all mine," she said.

"But what you're saying is that someone is killing them for their magic."

"I am. And I am pretty sure I know who." Sydney opened the camera app on her phone, pulled up the pictures Harper had taken.

"That . . . that is someone's bones." Laurent flipped through the pictures. When he got to the final one, the one that pulled back for the wide shot that included Grey in bed, he turned ashen. "That is someone's bones in a jar in Grey's apartment."

"Yes. It is."

"And you think—" He swallowed, hard. "You think he put them there. That he cut them out of some poor woman's hand. After he killed her."

"I do think that. I think that because these bones aren't the first time he's done this." She told him—Grace, Rose, everything.

"I need a minute." Laurent slid open the door to his balcony, went outside. Sydney watched him but didn't follow.

After a few minutes he came back in. "The thing is, I can believe it. I mean, I don't want to. It hadn't occurred to me. But—he's said things, about magic and how to get it, and what he deserves, and, Sydney, he hates you. With a terrifying amount of hate. So I can believe it."

"I know you said you wanted him kept out of things, but I'd like to challenge him. Either as your champion, or through House Prospero," she said.

Laurent nodded. "I get that. And I'm not going to fight

about it. But can you—can you do it as House Prospero? Maybe I'm a coward, whatever. I just—I'm not saying he's not a bad guy. I'm not saying I think you're wrong. But there's still a part of him that was my first friend in this world."

"I understand," she said. "And I am sorry."

"Me too." Laurent dropped his head into his hands. "Me fucking too."

In the end none of it mattered. The carefully negotiated permissions, the face-to-face discussions. Grey forced the issue, and challenged Laurent.

"Are you fucking kidding me with this?" Laurent asked.

"You'll be fine." Grey shrugged it away. "There isn't a House here that wouldn't let you join—hell, I'm willing to put all this behind us and let you buy membership in my House at the end of this. But Sydney has caused nothing but problems since she showed up. This is the way to stop her."

"Sydney has caused problems," Laurent said. "Sydney."

"She has. Laurent, I know you feel like you need to be loyal to her since you hired her, but if she's out of the picture, it will fix things. I'll get my House back. All the problems with magic will stop. Miles says she's the one—"

"Stop. Just stop," Laurent said. "Miles Merlin says a lot, and most of it is shit."

"What, because he talks to me now and not you, you don't think he's worth listening to?"

"No. I think he's not worth listening to because all he's doing is telling you what you want to hear to get you to do his dirty work for him. And as soon as you do, he's going to hang you out to dry. I mean, has anything—*anything*—that he promised you actually happened?" Laurent asked.

"Just because we see things similarly doesn't mean he's making me do anything. And all those things he's promised will happen once she's gone. Things can be normal again, like they were supposed to be. I'm trying to help you here too." His voice was calm and even, everything a reasonable explanation.

"I really don't see how you trying to kill Sydney is helping me."

"Her leaving Shadows stole magic that should have belonged to all of us. If she falls in the course of a challenge, the natural balance of magic will be restored."

"You don't even sound like yourself anymore—you sound like Miles Merlin's parrot. I can't talk to you when you're like this." Laurent walked to his windows, hands clenched in frustration. "Actually, you know what? I can't talk to you anymore at all."

"Come on, Laurent. Be serious. If you pick her side, you're giving up your chance to be part of the Unseen World when this is over."

"That's not what this is about. I wasn't going to say anything to you, because how do you look at the guy you thought of as your best friend—as your brother—and tell him you know he's a murderer. That is the end of things, when that happens. And the thing is, I was a coward. I didn't want to say it, because you were my friend, my best friend, and what is wrong with me that I didn't see that?"

"It wasn't—" Grey started.

"Whatever it is you're going to say, I don't want to hear it. I know what you did, Grey. I *know*. And I thought I could know that and look at you and still see the guy who was my friend, but I can't. I need you to leave. Now. And don't come back again. You're not welcome here."

Grey shook his head. "It's a good thing you won't make it through the Turning. You never did understand how this world works." He walked to the door, then stopped. "I did consider you a friend, so I'll give you one more chance. Apologize at the duel, and I'll put in a good word with Merlin."

"Not a chance," Laurent said. "Goodbye, Grey."

Ian came back to his apartment to find Sydney perched on his balcony. "How long have you been out here?"

She climbed down from the barrier wall, stretched, and rolled the stiffness from her muscles. "How long have you been gone? I like being up there. It's quiet. I can think."

"You know, you could have been conventional, met me at the restaurant and walked back with me. Or even waited for me in the lobby," he said, unpacking the takeout.

"But you don't mind when I borrow your balcony, and if I were conventional, you'd be disappointed, and if I met you at the restaurant, dinner wouldn't be a surprise," she said.

"All valid points." He smiled. "I got Indian. Enough to share if you come inside."

"Perfect. I love aloo gobi." She followed him in.

"Is Miranda coming tomorrow?" he asked.

The challenge. "I didn't ask. I don't even know if she can—she's technically a mundane now."

Ian passed over a plate piled with garlic naan. "I'd hate to be the person who tried to keep her out. She'd call her magic back through sheer will just so she could smite them."

"I'd almost like to see that," Sydney said.

"Are you going to be okay?" he asked.

She shook her head, puzzled.

"About the challenge, I mean. Because he's your brother."

"It's not like you and Lara, you know," she said. "I mean, if there's anyone I might love like you're supposed to love family, it's Madison. And the thing is, she likes Harper, and Harper doesn't have a best friend anymore because my brother killed her.

"The only thing I know about Grey is that he's a murderer who hates me."

"So you're going to be fine," he said.

"As fine as any of us who survive this are."

"Will you stay tonight?" he asked, and stroked his hand down her arm.

"No, I need to keep my head clear. But I'll stay tomorrow. I'll even come in through the front door."

"It will be a wonder I greatly look forward to."

"Excellent." She grinned. "Now please pass the samosas."

Madison was, as she had been since the cursed Turning started, leaving work late again. There was just something wrong about walking out of a building at ten thirty at night, especially when she'd be walking back in the door by eight thirty the next morning. Actually, more like seven thirty, or maybe even seven o'clock—she'd forgotten about the Goldblatt file. And of course there were no cabs, because everyone else had gone home at a reasonable time. Sushi. She deserved sushi—she'd walk to Bluefin and get takeout.

She was reaching into her tote for her phone when the spell hit her. It flung her forward, laptop and files flying from her bag, one stiletto heal cracking and breaking off.

Her heart beat so hard she felt it in her ears. But her phone was in her hand, and even in her panic and pain, she scrambled to hit the emergency button.

Hands yanked her from the ground. "I'm going to kill you."

Grey's voice. He muttered the words of a spell, and the phone in her hand grew white-hot. She dropped it, and he slammed his foot down on its surface.

Madison scratched at his hands, tried to shift her weight back and get her feet under her.

His hands tightened around her neck. Hands, or magic, she couldn't tell, only that it was harder and harder to pull in a breath, that white sparks were bursting behind her eyes.

"Kill you, and take your bones, and use them to kill her tomorrow. Just think of that. You're going to help me beat her." His breath, hot on her neck. She reached up, yanked at her necklace, breaking the chain.

Then she hit the ground again, hard. But she could breathe and there were no more hands clutching at her. Madison scrambled to her feet and away, grabbing at her bag and belongings.

She turned back to look. Grey stood, frozen like a statue. The spell had worked.

She drew in a breath, and then another, and looked straight at him. "So, you're not, actually, going to kill me tonight. And my bones are staying in my hands, and I am going to drink an entire fucking bottle of champagne when Sydney kills you tomorrow, and I hope a dog pisses on you like you're a hydrant before her spell unlocks. Because she knew you were enough of a coward to try something like this, and that was her magic in the necklace, and if she can hold you like this when she's not even here, just imagine what's going to happen to you in person. You fucking miserable excuse for a human."

Madison walked—limped, really, with that broken-heeled shoe, and she'd liked that pair, damn it—to the sushi bar she'd been heading to.

"Madison! What happened?"

"Bad day at work, Hideo." She sank into the chair he offered her. "Can I break your cell phone rule, and also get the world's biggest bowl of miso soup?"

"Of course. Are you sure you don't want me to call the police?"

"I am, thanks." She dug through her tote until she found her personal cell. The one Grey had smashed had been her work one. Sydney had put emergency spells on both—if something happened to either and Madison didn't check in within a certain time, another version of the necklace spell would be triggered. "Sydney. You were right. He came after me."

"Are you safe right now?"

"I'm at Bluefin. I'll be fine. I used the necklace charm. And I told him I hoped a dog pissed on him."

Sydney stifled a laugh. "Are you going to be okay? Do you want me to come get you?"

"No. Hideo will put me into a cab himself if I ask. I just

wanted to let you know." She paused. "He said he was going to use my bones. To kill you."

"Madison, I'll be right—"

"No, really. Don't come. I am safe, and about to consume my own weight in spicy tuna and wash it down with sake, and if you show up, I will probably cry, and I don't need to do that right now. I just—you be careful tonight. And don't hesitate tomorrow. I know he's your brother and Laurent's friend and whatever, but don't you hesitate for one second before ending him."

"I won't, Madison. I promise. Enjoy your spicy tuna, and call me if you need me. I'll be there."

"I know."

CHAPTER TWENTY-THREE

Sydney stopped by House Prospero on her way to the challenge. "Grace, do you want to be there tonight?"

"No. I appreciate you asking, but I don't want to be in a room with him. I don't want to see him, even under these circumstances. I don't ever want to see him again." She fisted her hands, then wrapped her arms around her stomach, hiding her scars.

"You won't have to." Sydney reached out, set her hand on Grace's shoulder. "I'll call the House when it's over."

"Sydney." Grace put her own hand over Sydney's, squeezed. "Thank you."

Sydney paused on her way out the door and spoke to the mirror. "If . . . if I don't come back, keep her safe from him. Be her House, okay?"

Yes.

Come back.

"That's the plan."

Sydney walked the rest of the way with Laurent. "I'm really sorry about all of this," he said. "I feel like you got way more trouble than you were signing up for in this thing when you decided to work for me."

"Please. You know me well enough by now to know that I am perfectly capable of causing my own share of trouble."

Laurent laughed. "That is true."

"Besides, Grey would have come after me whether I was your champion or not. I chose to work for you, and I have exactly zero regrets about doing it. You've done nothing but given me kindness and support this entire time, above and beyond. You have nothing to apologize for."

"Thanks," he said. "And—I know what I said. Keep him out of things and all that."

She nodded.

"Just in case I haven't made it clear—that's gone. Don't hesitate tonight. Fight hard, Sydney. For them."

"Absolutely," she said.

Miles Merlin was waiting just inside the door. He took her hand in both of his. "Now, Sydney, you can always forfeit."

"Take your hands off of me or I will remove them from your wrists."

"There's no need to be hostile," Miles said, still holding her hand.

Sydney spat a word that hissed and sparked in the air. Miles yanked his hands away, both palms visibly red and blistered. She smiled and kept walking.

"That was worth the price of admission right there," Laurent said.

Sydney laughed.

Miranda arrived then, causing another wave of whispers through the growing crowd. Merlin stood in front of her, temporarily halting her progress, but made no move to stop her as she walked around him.

More and more people crowded in, until it seemed the entirety of the Unseen World was crammed into the concrete warehouse.

Ian's hand slipped into Sydney's, squeezed. "I look forward to you knocking on my door later."

She squeezed back, for just a breath holding on to the warmth, the comfort.

And then it was time.

Grey brought his hands up to begin casting.

"Please," Sydney said. "Try." She flicked her fingers with the casualness of shooing a fly, and his hands were yanked out to the sides, held.

He struggled but couldn't move, couldn't speak.

"Do you see the scars on my hands, my arms?" Light now, silver and shimmery, rising from her skin. "This is what remains when you carve the magic from someone's bones."

She bent her hands to sharpness, and lines of red slashed through Grey's hands and arms, an echo of the scars on hers. Blood dripped into the silence of the room.

"Of course, I still have my bones. Mine were carved again and again. But you, you took theirs, didn't you?" A terrible cracking and a wet *pop* and the bones of Grey's fingers and hands rained to the ground.

"And then you killed them."

Sydney raised a hand, bent her fingers into unforgiving shapes. The scent of ashes and dust rose into the room. Grey was frozen in place—unable to move, to speak. Sydney gestured, and the room went black and silent, all except for a small patch of light were Sydney and Grey stood.

From the darkness, ghosts. Pale and white, their faces terrible and unforgiving, their hands, red with blood. Scars glowed silver, the shapes of a ritual meant to steal magic.

They were the ghosts of the women Grey had murdered. Rose Morgan. Hayley Dee. Lena Hermann. Mariah Blackwood. Allison Glass. Sounds of weeping and shock traveled through the crowd as they were recognized. As their names were spoken in whispers and cries.

They converged upon him and, like maenads, tore him limb from limb. Stripped his flesh so that all that remained was a pile of bones, the finger bones left separate, scattered.

The ghosts faded.

The lights came up.

Sydney spoke into her phone: "You're safe now," her voice clear in the echoing silence of the room. Then she stepped over the pile of bones and left.

The day after, Sydney made official pilgrimage to Madison's office at Wellington & Ketchum. Madison's secretary checked her in, then paused in the hallway. "I went out with him once. He creeped me out so bad, I made a friend call and fake an emergency so I could leave in a cab. I never said anything, because he was a Prospero, and I'm not even strong enough to be in a House, and all I had was a bad feeling. I don't know if I feel better or worse, knowing I was right and that I wasn't the only one. But, anyway, thanks."

Sydney nodded. "You're welcome."

"News travels," Madison said. "Was it really their ghosts?"

She shook her head. "I'm not a necromancer, and it was more important for him to see them at the end than for them to have to interact with him again. No, just an illusion."

"Sydney!" Harper rushed through the door, then kept going and hugged Sydney hard. Sydney went stiff, then relaxed into toleration of the embrace. She carefully, gently, put her arms around the other woman.

"Thank you," Harper said, and stepped back, scrubbing

tears from her face. "I'm going to her grave tonight. To tell her what you did."

"Tell her what you did, too," Sydney said. "She was lucky to have a friend like you."

Harper left, still sniffling.

Sydney sank into a chair.

"How are you?" Madison asked.

"Tired. I'll be glad when this is over." She could feel the magic like a weight in her veins. Her joints ached, her fingers were the white-cold of frostbite. There would be a reckoning, at some point, for the power she had contained. But some point was not now, and there were still things to be done. "I need to name an heir."

"Did someone challenge you already? Is it Merlin? That bastard," Madison said.

"No, but I realized as I left last night that if Grey had managed to cheat his way into winning, Miles could have given him the House. He's the Head of the Unseen World, and I don't have any blood family left who have magic. So he could just give it away."

"He could try," Madison said. "I'd tie him up in filings until the next Turning."

"Which is why I'd give it to you, if I could."

"Bite your tongue!" Madison said.

"I think you are technically my biological cousin. Regardless, you're the closest thing I have to family. If you hadn't renounced your magic, it would be yours."

Madison reached across her desk, held Sydney's hand.

"But since you did, I can't leave it to you, and it's a Turning. Plus, you know, I could get hit by a bus. I want the House safe, and I want Grace safe, so for now I want to do what I have to in order to name her my heir."

Madison pulled pages off her printer. "If you're willing to bleed a bit, we can do this now. This is our most bare-bones template. So the only thing that you are directly disposing of here is the House. If you want to do something more involved, come back after all this nonsense it done, and you can make a full will."

"Perfect." Sydney cut her thumb, let blood fall to the paper, then pressed her index finger down. She said the word that rendered the action binding, and the fingerprint turned gold.

"So now what?" Madison asked.

"I'm expecting a challenge from Miles. Which I am not expecting to go well, mostly because he's smart enough to challenge House Prospero instead of Laurent, and set up a duel between Ian and Lara. And I'm contemplating a challenge of my own, though I think the magic may be complicated."

"Anything I can do to help," Madison said.

Sydney leaned forward, then slammed her hands down on Madison's desk, bracing herself.

"Sydney?"

"Basket," she said through clenched teeth.

Madison passed the recycling bin over just in time to catch the vomit—flecked with blood, with bright green—that Sydney coughed up. The stench of a rotting garden filled the room. "Sorry. The consequences are getting worse."

"I know you said you came here today to make your will because you could get hit by a bus, but Sydney, is there anything I should know? I am asking as your friend, incidentally, not your attorney."

"I'll be fine," Sydney said, and wiped blood from her mouth. "This isn't anything different than I've been through before, not really. It's just more intense because the magic has been bigger, and I've used more of it than I normally do. I just need to get through the end of the Turning, and then this will be over."

"I'm going to pretend like I believe you and ask you one more thing: Are you sure what you're doing is worth it?"

"Yes."

CHAPTER TWENTY-FOUR

Sydney shrugged herself deeper into her coat, and—as the wind knifed through layers of down and scarf and gloves—wished that there had been any place other than here on Bethesda Terrace where this meeting could have happened. The snow had melted and refrozen enough times that it was no longer picturesque. It was hard heaps in alternating shades of yellow and dinge, with rocks and cigarette butts and worse frozen into it. The air was as bitter as the day.

The Angel of the Waters hadn't been repaired yet, the lily still missing from its hand. The statue itself was cracked in places—the decay of the magic that had been grounded in it for so long also causing decay in the physical world.

Ian and Lara, both flushed from the cold, walked down the promenade, Lara's hair the one bright spot in the dull grey of late winter. "Why did you need to see us?" she asked.

"Your father has challenged House Prospero," Sydney said.

"Of course he did," said Lara. "I'm only surprised that he waited this long."

"I'm not killing my sister," Ian said.

"No, you're not," Sydney agreed. "Nor is she killing you. But I am accepting the challenge."

"I assume you have a plan," Ian said.

"So long as you're both willing to go along with it," Sydney said. "To start with, your father doesn't have any magic of his own."

"Are you sure?" Ian asked.

"You don't seem surprised." Neither of them did.

"I'm not. But are you sure?"

"I am. When he took my hand at the duel with Grey—"

"He still has blisters, by the way," Lara said.

"Good. When he took my hand, I could tell. Shadows makes you very good at sensing magic. He has none. At all."

"Which means he can't hold a House," Lara said.

"Which also means he can't officially make a challenge, either, which is how I plan to get everyone out of this alive. But I need it to play out in public," Sydney said. "And that's why we're meeting here. I assume you both are familiar with the spell anchored in the Angel?"

"House Merlin is responsible for it being there, and its upkeep on this end, so yes," Ian said.

"Good. Could one of you please—very carefully—check the Angel for magic?" Sydney asked.

"I'll do it," Lara said. She peeled off her neon purple mittens and handed them to Ian, then stretched her hands toward the statue. She spoke a phrase that rose at the end, questioning, then yanked her hands back. "What the fuck was that? That's not how it should feel at all."

"I need to tell you what happened to Grace Valentine," Sydney said.

As she spoke, Ian swore, viciously and fluently. Lara's face closed off further and further, until she might have been a statue herself by the time Sydney finished. "I think what happened is that the spell that was supposed to allow him the use of her magic—his own sacrifice that he'd brought in—somehow got tangled up with the other spell that was already anchored in the statue. And that the more Miles' magic failed, the more the spell tried to compensate, by pulling magic from everywhere else to feed itself. I think I can stop it, but I need the link to Shadows to be completely broken for it to work."

"Do it," Ian said. "Do whatever you need."

"I need one thing from you in particular, Lara—as heir to House Merlin, you'll become interim Head of the Unseen World. I'll need you to verbally break the agreement with Shadows."

"That's it?" she asked.

"That should be enough," Sydney said.

"Then of course. There is one other thing, though. If he were siphoning off magic somehow, keeping it somewhere, could that have increased the problems in the spell? Turned it from whatever it was supposed to be into that?" She waved a hand at the statue.

"Possibly," Sydney said. "I don't know what the magic would have felt like when it was healthy—our perspective, from inside Shadows, is a bit different from what you feel out here. But it could—if that was the part of the spell that misfired, I could see how something that was supposed to act like a siphon turned into something that's acting like a vacuum."

Lara looked at Ian. "I think I know what Dad's been keeping in that locked cupboard."

Sydney stood on the edge of the Central Park Reservoir and steeled herself against the edge of fear that even now crawled in her gut. Her hand automatically reached for her pocket, for the three wooden matches that used to be the requirement of the journey.

Not today. Not for her.

She spoke a word that froze her breath before it left her mouth, and a path of ice crackled and solidified across the reservoir's surface. She stepped onto it and crossed once more to the House of Shadows.

It could barely be called a House anymore, this collection of darkness that slumped over a whiteness of bone—all of the sacrifices who had died in its service, fragmented and heaped in the freezing water. A flame lit, hot, in the center of Sydney's heart: this place was unmade, diminished, rendered almost into nothingness. She had done this. And she would make sure that no more bones were added.

"Have you come back to gloat?" Shara looked like the place, all black and white and grey. Stark now, and now bleeding together in a slurry. She sounded like a wraith, like a remnant.

"I've come back to set you free," Sydney said.

Hunger flashed across Shara's face. "If that is a joke, it's in poor taste."

"The binding between the magic that came from here and the magicians of the Unseen World is almost gone."

"That is not something I need *you* to tell me, here as I am, my House breaking around me." Shara's voice as sharp as her knife had been.

"I need it completely broken. And one part of doing that is to sever your connection to this place, to this"—she looked around and decided the old word was still the only one that might fit—"House."

"And if I say no?"

"You're welcome to try to stop me," Sydney said. "I almost wish you would."

"Do what you came here for, then."

It was easy. A word that snapped like a twig being stepped on, like the crack of ice on water. The final breaking of the magic a spark across Sydney's skin. The remaining shadows fell, all but those cast naturally by the February day.

Shara shook once, hard.

"There," Sydney said. "You have your life back. Go where you want; do what you please. Though you may want to do it quickly, because I doubt there'll be much left here soon."

"Is it that easy, to destroy your home?" Shara asked. "To turn your back on me? All I ever did was make you stronger. It's because of me you are what you are."

"This was never a home. And I made myself what I am."

CHAPTER TWENTY-FIVE

"Perhaps you're confused," Miles said. "But this is a challenge against House Prospero. You are not that House's declared champion, and so you aren't allowed to participate in the duel. As I'm sure you're aware, interference can be grounds to have your magic stripped."

Sydney stood in a room full of magicians, almost all of the remaining members of the Unseen World. She stood between two of them, Ian and Lara Merlin, her physical presence there preventing the duel from taking place. "I'm very aware. But I'm not here to participate in the duel. I'm here because the duel shouldn't be happening in the first place. You have no right to hold your House, and therefore House Merlin has no standing to challenge House Prospero."

Miles forced out a laugh, the sort of thing that was meant to show how unimportant her words were, the sort of thing that would have worked had it not been so anemic. Had his hand not gone to his pocket, as if to check for something, reassure himself it was there. "This is ridiculous. Explain yourself."

"If you can't hold magic, you can't hold a House. And you have no magic."

The whispers of the crowd now an ocean of noise. "You're talking nonsense."

"Prove me wrong." Sydney held out a candle.

"This is absurd," Merlin said. He shoved his way forward and lit the candle. "See?"

"I'm sorry," Sydney said. "I meant light the candle without relying on any of the magic that you've spent years stealing from the Unseen World and collecting for yourself."

"Like this?" Lara said. She reached into her pocket and pulled out a small glass jar, silver-bound and humming with magic.

"That cabinet was locked—" Merlin bit off his own words, but the damage was done.

"House Merlin forfeits the challenge," Lara said clearly. "On the grounds that it was improperly made, by someone with no right to hold a House. As heir, I serve notice that I intend to petition for immediate removal of Miles Merlin, both from his position as Head of House and from the Unseen World."

"House Prospero accepts your forfeit," Ian said, and stepped off the dueling grounds, formally ending the challenge.

"I've had enough of this," Miles said.

"We're not quite finished here," Sydney said.

The gathering of shadows nearest to Sydney thickened, solidified. Resolved into the shape of a woman. Grace Valentine stepped out of them.

Miles stepped back.

"Oh, don't look surprised, Miles. That is what you sent me there to learn, isn't it? How to be a Shadow? Wrapping ourselves in them, becoming one with silence and darkness and secrets, that's one of the first spells we're taught.

"Although, I suppose you didn't actually send me there to learn." She raised her hands, and her scars shone silver. "All I was supposed to do was give up my magic and die. And not even for the Unseen World. Just for you. To pay a debt, you said."

Sydney stood at Grace's shoulder. "Though not the usual debt, not the one each House here has agreed to, not the one that they pay. A personal debt—one you owed to Shadows so that you could modify the spell your family had created. So you could keep that power for yourself. Even then, even after you stole Grace and locked her away in there, it wasn't enough. And now, not only is your power gone, but the spell is corrupted. Your actions caused the failures of magic."

Lara spoke up. "Which is why, as interim Head of the Unseen World, I formally renounce its ties to the House of Shadows. The link that we thought was to our benefit has nearly been our undoing." She followed her brother, the noise around them both a roar of whispers and disbelief.

"You can't possibly prove that," Miles blustered.

"I have become increasingly weary of people telling me what I can't do." Sydney raised her hands, fingers moving as if she were playing a game of cat's cradle, weaving and unweaving through the air. Not yarn, but magic—strands of magic that burned in the air. A spider's web, with Miles Merlin at its center, a center that was a gaping, hungry hole, a drowning place for power to disappear into, the opposite end of each strand connected to a magician in the room—to a member of the Unseen World who had agreed to the bargain with Shadows, whose House had paid the required sacrifice.

She dropped her hands, the magic disappearing with the motion.

"Eventually, what this means is that all of you will lose your magic. Each and every one of you who tied your magic to that of Shadows—to make it easier, to make it hurt less, to make it whatever it is you told yourself you were doing so you could sleep at night. Each of you will have your magic fail and fail and fail again.

"Or you could break from it, and I do mean break. I will undo the spells for you on the condition that Shadows—and anything like it—never happens again. Your choice."

"That's not quite their only choice."

Grace went white with shock. "Shara."

"Sydney did tell me that I could do anything I wanted now

that I was free. This is what I want. What I've always wanted—power here, among you."

As pale as a corpse that had clawed its way out of its tomb, hair tangled and dress tattered, Shara held power in her hands as she stood in the center of the room and spoke to the crowd. "I can undo my brother's mess. Give everyone here back their power and the ease with which they used it. Give them even more, if they like—Shadows has always been held back in what it could be and do. Miles promised me a place in this world, and I am claiming it now."

"No," Sydney said. "You're not." She looked out over the crowd. Laurent met her eyes, and when she nodded, said: "Candidate House Beauchamps challenges the House of Shadows, the challenge to have immediate effect."

"Oh, good," Shara said. "I was so hoping."

This was different from fighting the House. This was different from fighting anyone.

Unlike her brother, Shara was a powerful magician. And for all that Sydney had made herself, it was Shara who had trained her. She hooked power into Sydney's magic, tied it to the spell Miles had used that had been anchored into the Angel of the Waters, that had pulled power from the sacrifices sent into Shadows. That was now pulling power from Sydney, and from the Unseen World itself. Shara let the spell do the work, a terrible black hole of magic, consuming everything in its path.

Sydney felt like she was being pulled apart from the inside as that terrible hunger clawed at her magic, swallowing it down.

There were screams from the watching magicians, gasps of pain and terror, as their magic pulled away from them, too. Everyone who had used the magic that came from Shadows was being drained—not only of the magic that Shadows had given, but of their own, the hunger in the spell finally loosed to consume everything.

There was a weight, a balance. Sydney could feel the scale, cold and merciless, could feel the weight on the opposite side as she had felt it that first time she had signed her name on the contract to Shadows. She was very good at sensing magic. And the balance was this: There would be magic, or there would not be.

There was a choice.

Magic rose like spring, like green beneath her skin.

Sydney spoke a word, and the word was a knife, and with that word she cut a piece of her own shadow. She wrapped the shadow into the blade, sharpening its edge, until it was as cutting as life. She cut into her own skin and bone, following the scars that were already there. The scent of spring, heavy and thick and humid and full of life, rose into the air. Magic, amplified.

And then she opened her hands and gave her magic back. Stopped fighting the spell, the hunger, the pain as it unmade her.

"What are you doing?" Shara spat. "It's too much."

Sydney spun, whip-fast, and stabbed Shara through the heart with the knife of shadows. "I know."

It was not the normal end of a challenge. There was a victor and there was a body, and yet there was still a chaos of magic unweaving itself in the center of the room. Shara's spell had not died with her.

"Oh no," Verenice said. "Oh, Sydney, what have you done?"

"What's happening?" Ian asked, tension in every line of his body, both hands curled in different spells. "Can you help her?"

"Maybe, but—"

"You are the only one in this room who might understand the magic Shara used—you were the only other one strong enough. Please," Ian said, "if you can stop this, do it."

"You don't know what you're asking."

"Please," he repeated.

Verenice nodded.

Magic, spring and green, sparked like fireflies from Sydney as she stood in the center of the room, being unmade. "The spell just needs enough magic, and then it will end. Use the knife."

Horror on Verenice's face. "Sydney, no."

"Verenice, you said you would help. You would see Shadows ended. I need you to do this for me."

Fast, fast enough that the motions left no time for thought,

Verenice pulled the knife from Shara's unmoving chest. She then gathered Sydney's shadow, bundling it in her hand like fine cloth. She looked at Sydney one more time, and when Sydney nodded, she cut.

Sydney screamed like a broken heart as her shadow was severed from her body.

Verenice let go as soon as she finished the cut, and the terrible unweaving continued, each fragment of Sydney's shadow being consumed. It flew in sparks, green like fireflies, green like spring, green like hope, and then it disappeared.

And then the spell stopped. The shadow gone, the scales balanced, the debt paid. The assembled magicians felt their hands warm as their connection to magic returned.

All of them except for Sydney.

"Thank you," she told Verenice.

Verenice, weeping, looked away.

"There's a will," Sydney said to Grace. "The House is yours."

And in the middle of their shock, she walked from the room, leaving magic behind.

CHAPTER TWENTY-SIX

Sydney stood on the balcony of her apartment, looking down at a city that glittered and shone so brightly that some people called it magic. High enough above it all to be alone, in the night, in the dark, in air that smelled almost like spring.

Nothing hurt. No backlash from the magic, no pain in the ragged ends of her shadow. There was simply nothing there, not even numbness. Not even a shadow.

She dug her fingernails into her palms until her hands bled, needing the pain to focus.

Things had worked almost, almost as she had planned. Shadows was gone. Magic remained in the world. There had simply been a sacrifice.

Sydney did not look behind her, where the lights of the city were not casting a shadow. She did not reach to feel the green crackle of power running through her veins. But her bleeding hands moved through shape after shape, spell after spell. Not hope. Not precisely.

She had known Shara would come back. Where else would

she have gone, with her rage and ambition, but to the place she'd always thought should be hers? Sydney had just thought her spells would die when she did—Shadows and its avatar, both gone at once.

Maybe the spell had been too corrupt by then or the magic too bound into the Unseen World itself, into all the other magicians. Maybe Shara truly had outplayed her. Maybe she had just been unlucky.

Maybes didn't matter—she was what she was, now.

And the magic of the city, those bright and glittering lights, was all the magic that was left.

Sydney went inside and crawled under all of her blankets. She didn't sleep.

CHAPTER TWENTY-SEVEN

The message arrived in a variety of ways. Email. Via text. Type-written formalities on plain, business-weight white. Handwritten letters in bordeaux ink, sealed with wax. In each instance, the words were the same.

Fortune's Wheel had ceased its Turning. The world had been remade.

House Prospero—as led by Grace Valentine—would now head the Unseen World.

Laurent had been made, as he had hoped, Head of a new House. Very little else of the Turning had turned out how he'd expected it. He poured himself a whiskey and toasted its end.

Lara Merlin had been confirmed as Head of House Merlin. Miles had not been seen since the night of what proved to be the Turning's final challenge.

The House of Shadows was no longer in existence. The Angel of the Waters once again held only the magic inherent in art.

There had been no further failures of magic.

Fortune's Wheel did turn. Some had risen, and some had

fallen. It was a new beginning, and all would be different until it was time for the world to be remade again.

"I see," Miranda said, lips tight and thin, knuckles white as they pressed against her skin. "You said you were good at sensing these things—is it completely gone? Not coming back?"

She sat on the couch in her hotel room, tea growing cold in her hands.

Verenice pushed away the memory of Sydney's shadow in one hand and a knife in the other and explained to Miranda. "I told you that our binding to Shadows wasn't over when we left—that we paid a debt."

Miranda nodded.

"That debt was paid in small pieces of our shadows." She gestured to hers, moving so the torn and ragged ends were easier to see. "It's very akin to the way magic collects in the bones of the hand. Symbolic, but a symbol powerful enough to be made real.

"When the spell went wrong, Sydney asked me to cut her entire shadow off, to give back all the magic in it at once, in order to keep magic in the world."

"How could one person possibly contain that much?" Miranda asked.

"You'll remember the Four Seasons duel, early in the

Turning, where there was a failure of magic," Verenice said.

"Yes. I was there. It was an excess of spring, as if the spell was flooding the room with magic. Terrifying." She shuddered once with the memory.

"When Sydney stopped the spell, she channeled the magic that had been contained in it. She's been holding it ever since. That excess was enough."

"But the cut—the removal of her magic like that. It's survivable?"

"Yes. People live without magic all the time." Most of them didn't die of it. Most of them.

"I am aware of that," Miranda said. "I've lost mine as well."

Verenice didn't tell her that it wasn't the same, not at all. Miranda would believe what she needed to.

"But what I don't understand is why she would possibly give up her magic in that fashion. She made very clear that she hated magic, hated Shadows, hated the entire Unseen World. Why not just let the spell continue, let everyone lose their magic and be mundane?"

Verenice leaned over, gently took the cup and saucer from Miranda's shaking hands. "She hated Shadows, yes. Hated what magic had become in the hands of the Unseen World. But hate magic? No, that wasn't it. Not at all. She loved magic, and she saw it leaving, and so she did what she had been made to do—she became a sacrifice."

She watched Miranda break then, her eyes close, her face slide into lines of mourning.

"If you see her, if you think it will help her to hear it, please tell her that I'm proud of her," Miranda said.

"If those conditions are ever met," Verenice said carefully, "I will."

"Anything for me today, Henry?" Sydney asked as she walked back into her building.

"There's a gentleman over there, waiting, miss."

Ian stood by the elevators. "Verenice gave me your address. Do you mind if I come up?"

"Sure. Fine." She shrugged. "Thanks, Henry."

The silence in the elevator was thick enough to suffocate.

"I'm not sure why you're here," she said as she unlocked the door.

"You know, I've never been in your apartment. It's nice," Ian said.

"I didn't want people to know where I lived. Doesn't matter now." She started making coffee, bumped a mug off the counter with her elbow. Her hand flicked out, and she spoke a series of words that ended with the shattering of the mug and a loud, "Oh, fuck this!"

She slammed the other mug to the floor.

"Sydney?" Ian asked.

"Just get away from me. Just go." She slumped down to the floor, sitting among the wreckage.

"You're bleeding," he said. "Your hand."

She laughed, sharp and harsh, and tilted her head back to rest against the cupboard. "I don't even have Band-Aids. I never needed them. I had magic."

"I can—"

"Leave it. A little blood won't kill me." She opened her eyes and looked at him. "I hate being like this."

"I'd be surprised if you didn't," he said.

"Do you know what the worst part is?" she asked. "The worst part is I can still light a candle. Like some fucking mundane who knows just enough to be dangerous. It gives me a bloody nose, and yet every morning when I wake up, it's the first thing I do. And then the second thing I do is try to cast something else. Anything else. I can't, of course, but I try.

"I can't not try." Her voice was suffused with loss.

Ian moved his hand just enough that he was barely touching hers. "I know."

"I feel like I'm not me anymore. And don't you dare give me some bullshit platitude about how I still am and how nothing important about me has changed, or I swear, magic or not, I will figure out a way to throw you off my balcony."

"Mine's better. The balcony."

Sydney looked at him. Laughed. It sounded almost like an

actual laugh this time, not bitterness given voice. "Why do you think I'm always on yours?"

Then, quieter. "Magic was who I was. I felt it in my blood and my bones, Ian. It was me, and now it's gone, and I don't know who the fuck I am anymore."

"You'll figure it out," he said. "Who you are now. And I'd really like to stick around and see who that is, if you'll let me."

She blew out a breath and leaned her head onto his shoulder. He wasn't a solution, not at all, but he was an ease in the loneliness. A moment of warmth. For right now, that could be enough. "Do you want to stay and watch me light a candle tomorrow morning?"

"Yes," he said. "I do."

CHAPTER TWENTY-EIGHT

The elevator doors to Laurent's apartment slid open. Sydney hesitated for a moment, then stepped into his offered hug, held on. "It's really good to see you."

"How've you been?" he asked. "I got some of those macarons you like—flower flavors for you and chocolate for me—so we can eat while we catch up."

"It's really, really good to see you." She smiled and sat down at the long table, facing the windows, looking out over a city that still looked magical. "And I'd rather hear how you are—how's being an official Head of House?"

"Fairly normal right now, though I think that's mostly because everything is weird for everybody. People are still figuring out how to cope, what with no Shadows and everything else that changed. I'm spending a lot of time teaching people how to use magic, which is not a thing I ever thought I'd be doing."

"I bet you're good at it," she said.

"I learned from the best."

She shrugged the compliment off. It was still too hard to

think about the person she had been when she'd had magic and not see the person she was now as less. "And when things calm down and are normal? What are the plans for then?"

"I'm opening the doors," he said. "No more of this stuff about people not being strong enough for Houses, no more outsiders, none of it. If they have magic and they want to be in the Unseen World, they are welcome in my House.

"Sydney, if you want—"

"I don't," she said. "Thank you—truly—but I really don't. The Unseen World isn't my place. I don't think it ever was, and it certainly isn't now."

"The offer stands."

She nodded, polite, not wanting to hurt him by saying she would never take it.

"I had Madison scout you, you know," she said.

"What?"

"Before the Turning started. Shara had a whole plan for how things would go, and I had one of my own, which diverged from hers at a few key points."

"Okay, that part doesn't surprise me. Actually, if you only had one plan, maybe it does."

Sydney laughed. "All right, yes, there was more than one plan. But in all of them, I had to be named a champion, and so I gave Madison some characteristics that I was hoping for in the House or candidate that I would represent and asked her to find people for me. I'd hoped that she'd find someone who would be impressed enough with my magic to stay out of my way."

"Hence that first illusion," Laurent said.

"Hence." One side of her mouth quirked up. "But as it turns out, she couldn't have found anyone better. You didn't stay out of my way. You helped me. So thank you."

"I think that's my line," he said. "My doors are always open, Sydney. I'm glad you walked through them."

And they sat together for the rest of the evening, catching up on all the pieces of life that made a friendship and watching the sun set over the city and all its wonders, both seen and unseen.

Sydney walked through Central Park with Madison. They paused at the Angel of the Waters. Sydney tossed a penny in.

"For luck?" Madison asked.

"You never know," Sydney said. The statue had been mended, not by magic, but by the city, all traces of its connection to the Unseen World gone. It still wasn't an object of beauty for her. It probably never would be. But she could stand to look at it now. Small things.

"Is it true the only reason Prospero wound up at the top was because you forfeited to Ian?"

"Funny how that worked out, isn't it?" Sydney said. "Grace

will do an excellent job. And there's no chance anything like Shadows will happen on her watch."

The air was warm and green, lush with thick grass and flowering trees. Joggers ran past, a small flock of children with balloons tied to their wrists shrieked in delight as a gust of wind made the balloons wiggle and dance. The ball for a pickup soccer game scooted just in front of Madison's feet. Spring had arrived early, and everyone was indulging.

Madison nudged the soccer ball pack to the waiting players. "If it weren't for the part where you lost your magic, I'd think you planned all of this."

"If it weren't for that part, yes."

"Is it still . . . ?"

"Always," Sydney said. "I think the answer to that is forever now, and I can say that word and it almost doesn't hurt. I can still light a candle. Still do, every day, still try to find some scrap of magic left inside me that will let me do more, because apparently I am exactly that sort of person. Oh—you'll love this—Lara offered me the stolen magic that Miles had tucked away."

"Seriously?"

"Not directly, at least—she made Ian ask. And I think she genuinely thought it was a kind offer. I laughed so hard before I could answer that I think he was worried I'd finally cracked, but yeah." It had been an easy thing to say no to—all it would have done was extend her time in the Unseen World, let her cast a spell here and there, been a clock running down to remind her of what she wasn't. It wouldn't have been real magic—it wouldn't have been hers. And the place it had come from, the taint of it . . . She'd told Ian to break the flasks.

"Have you decided what you're doing next?" Madison asked. "You could always go to law school."

"What was it that you said when I told you I'd give you Prospero if I could? Oh, right: Bite your tongue."

Madison laughed.

"But maybe school of some sort. The money I earned working for Laurent—it was a lot. I don't need to worry, and I have time to try things out." There might be a pleasure in learning something arcane and complex, a challenge that could make her forget the way her hands ached for magic they no longer held, that would make her stop checking, looking for pieces of shadow that clung anywhere to her, hoping there might somehow be something left.

"And the freedom to do it."

"And the freedom to do it. Which is weird. But good. Good weird."

"Much like you, my friend," Madison said. "Drinks?"

"Drinks."

There had been a plan, of course. One imagined in the darkness, in the Shadows. It had ended any number of different ways, most of them eventually painful—there were always consequences to magic. Shadows knew that better than most, and even without magic, there was a part of her that would always be a Shadow.

But for all her plans, for all the possible outcomes she saw, Sydney had not imagined the ending that had happened. Had she been offered the choice, the loss of her magic might not have been a consequence she would have agreed to bear.

She had been at peace with the idea of dying, if her end meant the end of Shadows. That had been the weight she was willing to place on the other side of the scales, if it had been called for. She was not yet at peace with a world where the only magic she had was the small flicker of a candle.

As she walked through the green, spring light with her best friend, Sydney bent her hand into the shapes of spells.

ACKNOWLEDGMENTS

I owe a huge debt of gratitude to Megan Kurashige, whose feedback on an early draft not only helped me see the shape of the story that I needed to tell, but also kept me from deleting my draft in despair.

I am also so grateful to friends who offered support and encouragement as I was writing this book: Maria Dahvana Headley, Cat Valente, Theodora Goss, Gwenda Bond, Neil Gaiman, Roshani Chokshi, Sarah McCarry, Monica Byrne, Martin Cahill, Christie Yant, Dot Paxton, Keri Blatt, Becky Krug, Jen Miller, and Nicole Saharsky.

This book would be only a pile of words without my fabulous agent, Brianne Johnson, and my terrific editor, Joe Monti. Thank you both. Thank you also to everyone at Saga for your help and hard work, and in particular to Lizzy Bromley, Saga's art director, and Vault 49 for my amazing cover. I'm so lucky to be working with all of you.

And of course, all my love and gratitude to my family.